BLUE SHADOWS

S.R. CARSON

BLUE SHADOWS

ISBN-13: 978-1-959677-67-3 (Paperback)
ISBN-13: 978-1-959677-66-6 (eBook)
ISBN-13: 978-1-959677-68-0 (Hardcover)

Published by Defiance Press & Publishing, LLC

Bulk orders of this book may be obtained by contacting Defiance Press & Publishing, LLC. www.defiancepress.com.

Public Relations Dept. – Defiance Press & Publishing, LLC
281-581-9300
pr@defiancepress.com

Defiance Press & Publishing, LLC
281-581-9300
info@defiancepress.com

PROLOGUE

No, Daddy, don't say anything!" The young boy knew his father would never renounce his faith, no matter what, but the words blurted out anyway.

Unfortunately, the ten-year-old child's panicked entreaty would not be heeded by his missionary father. After his father handed the bearded men the ransom envelope, he ensured his fate with his devout words: "Repent of your sins and be baptized all of you in the name of Jesus Christ our Savior!"

Having paid the ransom, he thought he'd secured his kidnapped son's freedom from the Jihadis; he thought he'd avoided any violence and his missionary team would be allowed back into the field to work with the medical missionaries at the community center in the mountains east of Kabul. He prayed silently that they would show mercy on their benevolent mission. But to his horror, he saw the kidnappers push his wife to her knees directly in front of him and then place a black hood over her blonde head.

"No! Please no!" cried the missionary. "In the name of God and all that is sacred, please spare her and take me! She's an innocent school teacher, here to help your children learn."

The translator said something to the bearded man with the knife, and then, it was decided there would be no mercy. Instead, the wealthy Swedish businessman-turned-missionary watched helplessly while they cut off his wife's head directly in front of him. Then, it was his turn to fall on his knees, receive the hood, and suffer the same fate as his wife.

The killers saved his son. They had grandiose plans for the young Swedish boy who wailed and fell to the ground after witnessing his parents' gruesome death, screaming, "Where are you, my God? Destroy these devils!" The kidnappers laughed, then watched as the young boy ran as fast as he could down the dusty, unpaved road until he fell exhausted, and one of the lower-ranked warriors came after him, beat him, and took him back to the compound, now a prized possession.

"Death to the infidels!" The kidnappers shouted in unison.

The young missionary child was now theirs.

CHAPTER 1

Wyatt Barton, MD, loved being in the OR, cutting to cure. Especially now, because there were no explosions booming outside, and he no longer needed to bring his M-4 into the operating suite. But the calm shattered quickly when that damn recurrent nightmare decided it was time to play like a loud movie in his mind, in the middle of the operating suite, clearly uninvited. This time, the nightmare was triggered by the smoke from the Bovie electrocautery tool that efficiently cut and burned through human tissue, but it wasn't always burning flesh that caused the visions to resurface. Sometimes other events would decide to trigger them—a code blue announcement on the public address system, a lunch tray clattering on the floor of a busy hospital cafeteria, or even a loud door slam. No matter when the dark nightmare decided to play, Wyatt knew it would probably occur at the absolute worst time possible—at least that's what they told him would happen. But what he dreaded the most, was that if it decided to present in a way to attract the most attention, the dark scenes in his mind would gladly punish him with a brief tremor and facial flushing, accented by glazed eyes filled with a distant rage of fire, bringing him back to that day ten years ago and seven thousand miles away.

After exercising a deep cleansing breath, Wyatt closed his eyes for a millisecond, allowing his mind to return to the OR, concentrating on Mr.

Jensen's bowel resection. His eyes ventured away briefly and met the curious gaze of the scrub nurse who was scanning him, and he realized that she probably witnessed something strange. He felt the surging flush on his forehead that was only partially hidden by the pale blue surgeon's cap, and he realized immediately what she had seen.

"You okay, Doc?" she asked.

"Couldn't be better, Carrie. Just like eating cheese on a Ritz, lying on the beach, waves licking my parched pinkies."

Wyatt imagined she smiled after that quip, because he saw the middle of her surgical mask suck in and out quickly several times, and there was a glimmer in her eye but no sound. He experienced the flashbacks more often now, and his ability to hide them grew more effective with each event, he thought. And yet, he knew he couldn't show any weakness to the medical staff because they looked up to him and it could be embarrassing. Surgery and saving lives in the OR turned out to be his calling, or at least the calling that he wanted to protect as his final career. He had mastered the technique of hiding these dark scenes within his soul so that no one would be aware they existed.

Using a diagnostic laparoscope, Wyatt found the abscess cavity contained in Mr. Jensen's mesocolon. Since he couldn't enter it with a laparoscope, he opened the abdomen, mobilized the lateral sigmoid colon, and divided the colon with a stapler. He ligated the mesenteric vessels with zero silk ligatures, resected the segment of the colon involved with the abscess, and then completed the primary anastomosis.

Suddenly, a young OR tech tripped on some suction tubing on the floor and almost knocked the corrugated ventilator tubing off the patient's breathing tube. The anesthesiologist at the head of the operating table quickly secured the breathing tube, then tore into the tech like a hungry wolf. "If you can't be careful and do your job without messing up the operation, then get the hell out of my OR!"

Her face looked like it was injected in both cheeks with red dye. It was clear that she bit her lip, because the surgical mask ended up in her mouth, caught between clenched teeth. She then quietly said, "I'm sorry, Dr. Turner."

Dr. Turner, the anesthesiologist, was a bulky 6'7" oak tree, five inches taller than Wyatt and fifty pounds heavier. He completely ignored the embarrassed tech's apology.

Wyatt stopped closing the abdomen and stared at the oak tree with blue eyes that made cold steel shiver. "First of all, it is not your OR, Dr. Turner. It is the hospital's OR. Accept her apology now, Jim, or it's you who will be sorry."

Dr. Jim Turner remained stony silent while monitoring the ECG rhythm and pulse oximetry connected to the patient. The only sound in the OR was the in-and-out whooshing sound of the ventilator breathing for Mr. Jensen. No one dared to take a breath until Wyatt decided to break the silence and thus allow adequate breathing for the staff again. Wyatt looked up at Turner, this time with a slightly louder voice. "The tech simply tripped; she didn't harm anything. Now maybe you didn't hear me the first time, Jim, but I'm asking you right now to accept her apology or you may find your face on the unforgiving concrete of the physician's parking lot, begging for an apology to me." The breathing in the room stopped again for a few seconds.

Dr. Turner hesitated for a few moments, looked up briefly to the ceiling, and back down to the patient, then said, "Yes, sir, I will." Jim decided to accept her sincere apology, then said to the tech, "I appreciate your excellent work." Wyatt expected the oak tree's icy glare, and after he received it, he smiled and went back to closing the abdomen as if nothing had happened.

So much for physician collegiality, and Wyatt knew, as the new surgeon at the hospital, all eyes studied him closely and likely this event would cause him to be summoned to the chief medical officer's office, or the principal's office, as the doctors said, but he couldn't have cared less. It was the principle of the damn thing.

Wyatt Barton, M.D., had limited tolerance for bullies or people without integrity, even stately oak trees. He thought the OR tech would've been in her right to say to Dr. Turner something like, "Sorry Dr. Turner, but I was filled with admiration as you did such a great job of passing gas that I temporarily lost my coordination. Thank you for correcting my blunder, your highness."

Wyatt knew that wouldn't happen in the medical hierarchy, but he always believed that they must respect all members of the team, no matter what their rank. He made sure that he protected those who couldn't protect themselves from soulless people who preyed upon them. Occasionally, even stately oak trees in a forest fire needed protection as well, regardless of their character, and he would be there when called to save a single tree in the forest, no questions asked, no matter the size of that tree.

CHAPTER 2

After thirty seconds of heavy bag hitting, Wyatt sprinted down the road for a half mile out and half a mile back, usually at about a seven-an-a-half-minutes-per-mile pace, depending on what his creaky knees would allow. Then, he did one minute of fist strikes on the grounded heavy bag, another one-mile sprint, then one minute of carrying a heavy bag. Although he was a former Ranger, he learned this nasty anaerobic workout from his Navy Seal colleagues, and it was effective in keeping him relatively fit, along with some weight workouts in between, but his banged-up knees were now the main factor slowing him down.

It was Monday, 5:30 a.m., and Wyatt was now in the steamy shower, having already consumed a pint glass of fruit–vegetable smoothie, three hard-boiled eggs, and toast with peach jelly and an avocado. He put on informal black slacks, a light-blue and white pinstriped long-sleeved shirt that liked to cling to his toned chest and arms, and a light-blue sport coat. His final ritual, deeply ingrained, was to place standard razor blades in the bottom hem of his pants, a stainless-steel zebra pen and a micro-tech knife in his pocket, and a Panerai submersible watch on his wrist. There was always a razor blade taped on the underside of his car's shoulder harness as well. He had a concealed Sig P239 pistol on his body at all times, and this wasn't a problem for hospital security because he never had to go through their metal detectors as a surgeon with credentials. And finally, a wine cork, from Kim's favorite Bordeaux, lived in his pocket, and he took it out and sniffed the rich oaky smell sometimes when he needed some calmness from stress. This ritual had become ingrained in his DNA years ago, and since this training had saved his life before, even though he was a civilian and his rituals might not be applicable anymore, they became automatic, almost like breathing. Although he had a nice new job now that didn't feature bullets seeking to pierce soft flesh and explode, he still followed his mantra: *trust no one, unless it's clear they'll take a bullet for you.* But he missed his Kim, and he remembered she told him that he needed to pray daily—not just in times of stress to ask for God's help. He didn't go to church much and didn't talk about his religious beliefs very often, but she wanted him to become closer to God somehow, and she knew he believed, in his private heart. She always told him, "My prayers are always with you, my love, Wyatt."

Driving to Mercy Hospital, he looked to the west and never tired of the majestic view of snow-capped America's Mountain. She was always there for him, no matter what elements weakly tried to deface her. She laughed at the swirling blizzards, gale-force winds, and brutal lightning storms that forced humans to run for safety. So, he stared at her, every morning, devouring the view of her splendid majesty. When he looked at her beauty, he thought about Kim, and his hands quivered slightly on the steering wheel while his soul searched with a breathless hunger for the truth and her inspiration. He found himself remembering what Kim told him, and it brought him to say a prayer out loud while he drove:

Thank you, Lord, for giving me another day. Please guide my hands to accomplish good things and my brain to do the right thing in your eyes. And I will try hard not to suck. Amen.

And then, as was often the case, he thought of how life was empty without her. Her image, like all of the dream intrusions, begged for immediate attention. The difference between her image and the others was that her bouncy blond hair and heart-fluttering smile imbedded within him a loving memory that he never wanted to suppress. She went out that fateful night to the soup kitchen to serve, and the stray gangbangers sprayed some bullets, one of which took her life. If only he had been there, he could have taken the bullet for her or at least sensed the danger to avoid it and protect her. They had only been married six months before those animals took his lovely Kim away from him for no reason, and they would have been married ten years and six months if he had been there to protect his love. He always celebrated their anniversary, every May, no matter what the weather, on top of the peak, giving her a toast of her favorite wine, looking down below and realizing that nothing mattered in life but love.

CHAPTER 3

reasy hamburgers piled up and cascaded off to the sides of the heated serving containers, slippery sausages swam in the adjacent stainless-steel container with onions, chili, and of course thick, corrugated fries, all waiting for hungry physicians at lunch. Wyatt stared in amazement at the ravenous beasts in white coats and scrubs helping themselves to the free slop in the hog trough previously known as the doctor's lounge, though the nurse practitioners' lounge seemed more apropos since they seem to always get there first—even before the luscious food arrived. He also found it interesting how eighty-ish retired physicians would come to this doctor's lunch mess every noon, actually arriving early at 11:15, to simply cop a free meal and perhaps socialize a little with young physicians he didn't know. Wyatt hoped if he every retired, that he would never be found there.

He stared, bewildered at the cholesterol fest the hospital provided its doctors, then grabbed the only alternative available—some roast beef, tomatoes, and mustard, then made himself a sandwich and sat down with some of the colleagues he'd met since he started at Mercy Hospital a few months ago. One of them, Dr. Nick Franklin, was his surgical proctor. He'd evaluated Wyatt's surgical skills and medical knowledge before signing him off.

"Hell's bells, guys!" said Wyatt. "The cardiologists must've needed the heart Cath business so they ordered this artery clogger from the dietary department."

"You're ungrateful, Wyatt," said Franklin. "It could've been shit on a shingle, you know, SOS, your old favorite. We've got a bottle of Crestor handy for the cholesterol watchers after dessert."

"What is SOS?" asked Nick's fourth-year medical student, feeling a little aggressive.

"Shit on a shingle is creamed chipped beef on toast. Military lunch and dinner for heroes for God knows how long," replied Nick.

The student nearly turned blue with disgust, then immediately stared at his cell phone, which unfortunately wasn't ringing. Nick now turned his full attention back to Wyatt, and his expression changed.

"Nice job in the OR the other day Wyatt. Smooth case."

"Just another day at the orifice," said Wyatt.

Nick guffawed, and his pendulous belly continued to jiggle in resonance with his baritone chuckle for a few seconds after his voice trailed off. "But what happened at the end of the case Wyatt? Jim Turner has passed more gas in the OR than Exxon, and he knows a lot of important people. Why did you have to bust his chops like that?"

The medical student decided it was time to put his cell phone away and get up and do some scut work to avoid the impending eruption. The only problem was they no longer allowed young medical students to do dirty scut work—things like placing IVs and drawing blood to take to the lab—because it was now considered menial and beneath their station. So, he stared at a computer in another room, reviewed charts, and looked up labs.

"I guess it was a little aggressive, but I couldn't help it."

"You sure could've just swallowed your pride and kept your mouth shut. You should know that. I've got two more months before I have to sign you off to the surgical committee, which will forward the evaluation to the Medical Executive Committee. Make this easy for me and keep your nose clean, okay, Wyatt?"

As always, the small jagged scar bisecting Wyatt's left eyebrow turned a deep scarlet color while his face remained emotionless. His buddies told him they always knew when that happened it was a sign to back off.

"So, he complained, did he?"

"Yep."

"Imagine my chagrin. Got to do what's right I guess."

"What?"

"You know hearing aids are a great modern invention, Nick. You can get a great discount at Wally World. They're barely noticeable nowadays. You can even wear pajamas and flip-flops when you go buy them."

"Funny, Wyatt." Nick shook his head. "You don't get it, Wyatt. You need to play nice here, or they won't let you play at all. Do you understand?"

"Yes, beaucoup dinky dau."

"What on earth does that mean Wyatt?"

"Actually, it's beaucoup *dien cai dau*—Vietnamese–French slang for a crazy situation or plenty crazy in the head. Our Special Ops guys in Vietnam coined the phrase, and it's been passed down through the ranks over the years to describe certain difficult situations. It's not referring to you Nick, but this situation with Turner we're discussing."

Nick just stared at Wyatt, not knowing what to say after that.

Wyatt looked thoughtful, his right hand massaging his dimpled chin. "My favorite clinical instructor in medical school, Rolly McGrath, may not have been the university's golden boy, but he taught me a wise guiding principle: 'Do what's right, Wyatt.'"

"Nice. But students need specifics when they're learning, not philosophical bullshit."

"Right. But he taught me how to think, and let me learn the specifics myself because he knew I would. You see, Nick, I have a hard enough time sleeping as it is from the bad memories, but without the principle of doing what's right, I'll *never* sleep. That's why I'll sleep well tonight. I took Rolly's 'do what's right' motto and expanded on it a little. Instead, I say, 'Do what's right or I'll make sure you do.' Have a good day, Nick, and thanks for the counseling session. Hopefully, there's no charge."

Wyatt got up from the lunch table and went to his next case.

***

It was starry and black when he headed home, and he remembered her giggle again and the way she moaned when he kissed her full lips. The warmth of her image invaded him completely as if she were sitting next to him in the car, holding his free hand. He looked to the passenger seat, reached for her, and she wasn't there. Or was she? He thought he could smell her perfume—Paloma Picasso. He pulled to the side of the road to concentrate for a few minutes and let his rapid-fire heart rate cool down, then reached for the wine cork in his pocket and took in a nice soothing whiff. Unfortunately, the incessant honking behind him jarred him back to the reality of the danger of the black road and he drove on with Kim always in his heart.

CHAPTER 4

She ran in the morning because it was the only time available for her to run and also work, and she nearly always got her run in, no matter how cold or snowy it was in the Denver winter. It was also less busy out on the trails and roads at that time, meaning fewer catcalls from men admiring her long, toned legs. Of course, she seemed to always attract that kind of attention, ever since her years of ballet, which had done wonders for her legs as well. But there was no career future in ballet. Nor with an English literature degree. Who in her right mind wanted to teach English lit for the rest of her life while teaching ballet classes in the evening to little girls with spindly legs dragged in by their helicopter mothers?

In the car on the way to her office, her cell phone rang.

"Hello, Gentri? Mr. Rogers is here. How long will you be?"

"Patty, please tell him that I'll be about fifteen minutes late. Something came up."

"But, Gentri, you never—"

"Just tell him, he'll get over it. There are plenty of *Sports Illustrated* magazines in the waiting room. In fact, he may get lucky and find the swimsuit edition, unless someone stole it and ripped out the best bikini pictures already."

Gentri Lawrence, real estate broker, GRS, GRI, SFR, attempted to be on time, but the run today felt too good: her feet had seemed to barely touch the ground, so she lost track of time. And of course, she had to find shoes to match her outfit and raven hair. She loved heels, a necessity, unless she was back home on the sandy gulf beaches, running, or perhaps playing tennis. Sometimes, she temporarily wore them to bed on special erotic occasions, when the opportunity presented itself, although that was too many years ago, unfortunately. This was a work day, so she chose some more conservative shoes with a square back. She took the back way into her office, quickly reviewed the day's calendar and list of showings, and then rang Patty to bring Mr. Rogers back.

She looked quickly into her hand mirror from the purse, relieved she had her red lipstick on, but knew her hair was a mess. Who cared? She wanted to get on with it and sell some prime real estate.

Patty led Rogers into Gentri's expansive office suite, adorned with massive broad-leafed fig plants on both sides of her cherry wood desk, guarding her desk as if the desk were an outpost in the forest. The side walls displayed her diplomas intermingled with art work, and the window on the right of the desk boasted the majestic Denver skyline.

Gentri stood up to greet her client, her hand outstretched to receive his shake and she noticed that he briefly glanced down at her legs—not so subtly—and she knew she had him already. Typical.

"So, tell me, Mr. Rogers, What—"

"You can call me Tom."

"Right. So, Tom, what price are you looking to list your house for?"

"You sure get to the point quick. I like that."

She continued, unphased by his quip. "I reviewed the market for your range, and I have a pretty good idea what will sell it, and you may not like my answer."

His bright smile engaged, and that glaring dimple kind of puckered, both reminding her of her ex-husband, especially when his eyes resumed their not-so-subtle roving.

"It was appraised for two million replacement and 1.8 million market," said Tom. "I'd like to price it at 1.8."

She almost responded with 'honey' or 'y'all' or maybe even a 'bless your heart,' but she had learned how to avoid the Southern dialect in Denver. After all, the mountain air tended to suck the drawl out of a Southern girl. But she remained a woman from the South in her heart. "I understand, Tom, but I know the market, and you need to price it significantly lower, about 1.5 to 1.6 max.

"What?"

She wondered if she'd said it loud enough, but Mama always told her she was the loudest, and therefore she concluded he was either deaf or shocked. "Yes, 1.5 to 1.6. Otherwise, it stays on the market a long time, and there aren't many buyers in that range."

"Okay, you're the expert. How will you market it?"

She handed him her marketing packet including all the properties sold in that range in the past five years, as well as information about how many properties she had sold and her awards. "I have connections. I'll use professional photographers and drone photos to present a nice portfolio on websites such as Zillow and Trulia, as well as color ads in *The Sunday Denver Post*, pictorials, and flyers available for review at your sign."

"What's your commission?"

"Six and a half percent."

He thought about it for a while, shuffled his feet, then said, "Six percent."

She looked him in the eyes and smiled. "I can't do that, Tom. My commission of six and a half percent gives you my best attention and allows me to go the extra mile for you. That's why successful people who want to sell their houses quickly and efficiently for the best price come to me." He had no chance with her, and she knew he was out of his league completely.

Tom relented and signed the contract she already prepared at 6.5 percent. They shook hands, and before he left, he gave her his card after pointedly flipping it to the other side to not so subtly show her that he had written his personal cell phone number on it.

"I'll keep in touch, Tom, and send you updates and feedback when it's been shown. It will be a pleasure to list and sell your house. Thank you for your confidence in me."

"Of course, now even if there are no updates, we can have lunch some time."

She smiled, said nothing, and walked him to the door. Typical man. She noticed the sudden happiness on the front of his pants when he walked out, and it was nice to see he was impressed with her physical assets, but then she knew where most of his blood flow was at that moment, and it wasn't in his brain. She wondered, *Are there any good men out there who can think about anything but sex?* She missed hot, passionate sex, whatever that was, but then sex was sex. A true connection love was what she truly needed.

***

After the day was finished, she went home, poured a glass of merlot, and resumed writing her first romance novel:

She loved to read. In fact, she preferred reading to watching mindless TV or going to movies. She read about the real estate market and financials, of course, but also novels, including mysteries and thrillers, not just romance. What surprised people the most, though, was that she loved history, especially biographies about Lincoln and the Civil war as well as World War II history. One of her most prized books was Churchill's diary, Triumph and Tragedy, *published in 1953. But what really pisses her off is that she has trouble reading on the beach, because her bikini tended to attract men who thought with their penis, and she could only read a few pages on the beach before a man would invariably come up and interrupt her.*

"Whatcha reading, babe? Something hot and sexy, I presume."

Are there any real men left? *she wondered.*

CHAPTER 5

Full trauma, resuscitation bay one!

The voice page went off and Wyatt jumped out of his on-call bed, still in full scrubs, one sock on and one foot bare, threw on his running shoes, began to look for his M-4 rifle, then uttered to himself, *Fuck Wyatt, you're in a damn civilian hospital and no one is going to shoot at you.*

Second to arrive at the trauma bay after the ED doc, Wyatt started analyzing the situation when his surgical PA Walton hurried to join him with two ED nurses, the critical care charge nurse, an x-ray technician, and a respiratory therapist—the usual trauma team.

The patient—a sixty-five-year-old former opera singer had fallen down her stairs to the basement at home, and there was extensive bruising to her left chest. The medics arrived, gently breathing for her with the ambu-bag and bag valve mask, and she appeared to Wyatt to not be in much distress, except for complaints of chest pain.

While the nursing staff attached ECG leads, pulse oximetry probes, and an automatic blood pressure cuff, all connected to the main monitor at the head of the gurney, Wyatt performed a quick trauma physical exam. He found there were no breath sounds on the left, and there was asymmetry to the chest movement on respiration. Heart sounds were normal, but she seemed to be working hard to get air in with a squeaky voice. The abdomen felt soft, and there was no obvious trauma to the extremities. He performed a quick ultrasound and there was evidence of presumed blood and air in the pleural space between the lung itself and the chest wall. He diagnosed a traumatic hemopneumothorax, and the portable chest x-ray confirmed his suspicions.

The respiratory therapist grabbed his attention. "Dr. Barton, we've got to get her on a one hundred percent non-rebreather mask now. Barely able to keep the pulse oximetry at eighty-eight percent. She's getting harder to ventilate too."

He looked up at the monitor and verified the data. Her husband was standing outside the resuscitation room, hearing all the actions and words of the team, biting his fingernails. Wyatt had no time to talk to him but did learn from the staff that he told them the patient was on blood thinners for leg clots and the anesthesiologist had had difficulty intubating her airway in the past during surgeries.

"Dr. Barton, we're having trouble ventilating her!" said the respiratory therapist.

He observed the therapist struggling to ventilate the patient's chest, using increasing pressure on the ambu-bag. Her pulse oximetry oxygen values dropped quickly into the low eighties, so he immediately prepped the left chest for a chest tube and at the same time commanded: "Call anesthesia stat. This may be a difficult airway—possible tracheal stenosis or obstruction of the airway."

The respiratory therapist continued to attempt to ventilate the patient with a bag valve mask while Wyatt immediately made an incision on the left chest, spread the ribs with his fingers, found no adhesions, and placed the chest tube into the left chest cavity with an immediate rush of blood and air, causing bubbling of the water in the collection chamber below. Up at the head of the bed, the anesthesiologist was unable to place the tube into her larynx, past her vocal cords through her mouth. He tried again with a smaller tube, but the narrowed anatomy thwarted his attempt, and he looked at Wyatt, hoping for help, his face flushed crimson.

Wyatt quickly went to the head of the bed, almost pushing the anesthesiologist aside in his quest to save the woman and place the airway as quickly as possible, realizing that if he couldn't get the tube in quickly, she would die or he would need to do an emergency tracheotomy.

"Her saturations are dropping into the seventies, Dr. Barton!"

Wyatt didn't look up at the vital signs on the monitor. He tried to accomplish the intubation with a smaller tube, and again, her airway wouldn't accommodate the smaller tube. He thought there had to be mechanical scarring or an obstruction in the windpipe just below the vocal cords. At the same time, the size of her neck blew up from air dissecting up through the chest, to the size of a grapefruit, and he could no longer see the outline of her larynx. He knew she was bleeding from the blood thinners with air dissecting from the ruptured lung air sacs into her neck making anatomical markings impossible to see.

With a calm voice but with the confidence welded into his psyche from his training, Wyatt quickly glanced at the anesthesiologist, now observing from the side, and said, "I'm going to do an emergency cricothyroid puncture. Any objections?"

"None"

"Get me a cricothyroid kit stat," said Wyatt. The team rushed him the equipment. He could feel no anatomy whatsoever on the blown-up neck due to the internal bleeding and dissecting air, but one thing was clear: She was dying. Wyatt remained stoic, methodical, but all the while was saying a silent prayer, asking God to guide his hands, knowing that what he would do would be next to impossible; then, after a small incision on the area of the neck he hoped would surround the hidden larynx, he placed a catheter into her cricothyroid membrane, not by feel but simple experience and guessing, despite the blood obscuring his vision. Hearing the precious gush of air, he gingerly threaded the guidewire in while his PA handed him the equipment.

"Her pulse oximetry is sixty and she's losing her heart rate."

Wyatt heard but continued, not looking up or saying a thing, deftly placing the tracheal tube into the windpipe, connecting the end of it to the ventilator bag, and suddenly, her oxygen levels and pulse oximetry values accelerated upward toward normal.

"Pulse ox in the eighties and going up steady, Dr. Barton."

The anxiety level in the room immediately plummeted, and the staff sighed with relief. But Wyatt wasn't finished. Figuring the right chest was also in jeopardy from a tension pneumothorax—air leaking into the pleural space from the pressure of the ventilator—he quickly asked for a second chest tube and placed it into the right chest cavity, and again, a large air rush occurred, although there was no blood on this side.

"Pulse oximetry now ninety-five percent, Dr. Barton." The respiratory therapist now smiled at him, relieved, now speaking in a much softer voice. "We got her back, Doc."

The softball lurching around in his stomach suddenly disappeared, but he hoped he didn't show anything to his staff to suggest fear. The staff could sense this and his confidence, he knew, would trickle down to them as well. He prided himself on calm determination in the face of life-and-death struggles.

He sutured the emergency cricothyroid breathing tube to the patient's neck, knowing that later, once stabilized, he would call ENT to examine the tracheal anatomy in more detail and convert the tube to a standard tracheostomy. But he had a good airway now, and that was all that mattered. Then, the damn thing hit again, that nightmare movie that wouldn't go away, but always seemed to sneak into his brain at the worse times.

"Hit the floor, Jimmy, and keep your head down, I'm going to take out that guy on the fifty cal." Then, he ducked, his head tucked low, almost beneath the gurney as if he was avoiding gunfire.

"What did you say Dr. Barton?" said Walton. "Are you okay?"

Wyatt stared at him after he caught himself ducking, stood upright, and said nothing, his face now a little pale, then walked away, taking off his bloody gloves and gown as he went to talk to the patient's husband, holding his left arm to hide the faint trembling that always came with the nightmares.

The staff still had masks on, but their eyes connected and stared at each other, avoiding conversation. They knew Dr. Barton saved this woman's life in nearly impossible circumstances, but something was wrong. He was a talented surgeon—pleasant and always professional—but what nastiness was bothering him?

Wyatt changed out of his sweaty, blood-stained scrubs into clean ones, lay down on his on-call bed, and closed his eyes.

Lord, please keep those shit scenes from coming back. Beaucoup dinky dau.

CHAPTER 6

Wyatt Barton, MD, remained on probation, his surgical cases proc-
tored and reviewed because he was a new surgeon on staff. Dr.
Barton was called into the principal's office, and he knew he must
show up and display the company face they wanted him to show. Sure, he
was new to civilian life, but he was an experienced military surgeon. He
loved surgery and how he was able to help make a difference in people's
lives, but he also needed this position for his career and future, so he
needed to suck it up and take whatever mud pies the guy tried to fire at
him.

"Thanks for coming, Wyatt, and it's nice to meet you," said Paul Rogers, MD, chief medical officer at Mercy General Hospital. Rogers was a
retired plastic surgeon, and now enjoyed the plush chair life, pushing papers and making sure his children—that is, the physicians on staff—were
behaving properly and following the rules, written and unwritten, while
bowing to the culture of the hallowed institution. Drinking the Kool-Aid,
as they called it. He wore a perfectly pressed suit with a black bow tie,
and he sported a ponytail with an otherwise bald head that was destined
to draw your attention to the pony tail as if he had been partially scalped.

"No problem,' said Wyatt. He arrived in scrubs and Nike running shoes.

"So, you probably know why I've called you in, right, Wyatt?"

"Nope." His eyes told a different story, though. He was just curious enough to hear the explanation Rogers was going to provide. He figured it would prove to be heavily weighted to the other side of the fence that Wyatt chose not to be on.

Rogers nervously played with his shiny gold cross pen, then went directly to the business at hand. "Jim Turner from anesthesia filed a complaint against you, apparently due to some event in the OR. Do you remember that specific event?

"Yeah, Nick Franklin met me at the lunch room and told me he was going to complain. The guy chose not to speak to me face-to-face, though. I was hoping—"

"Be that as it may, we need to discuss professional collegiality among our physician staff, and that directly involves your behavior."

"Imagine my chagrin."

"Pardon?"

Wyatt didn't respond, just smiled and looked at Rogers without blinking. He could stare down a horned owl on amphetamines if he wanted to. After a leaded silence, Rogers continued. "Turner said you were nasty to him during the case and you embarrassed him brutally in front of the OR staff."

"Brutal? Funny, I didn't think we were in high school cheerleading camp where we discussed our hurt feelings. I've seen brutal before, Paul, and that little episode didn't come close to the definition that I am aware of."

"Wyatt, c'mon. Work with me on this. Did you embarrass him in the OR in front of the staff?"

"He embarrassed himself."

Rogers tried unsuccessfully to plaster down his protruding ponytail that was almost sticking upright out of the back of his head, then cleared his throat with his best-practiced authoritarian voice. "His statement said that you threatened him by telling him you would make him apologize in the parking lot with his face or something, while you two were still in front of the OR staff. Wyatt, we just don't tolerate that type of language here from our physicians—and certainly not in front of the staff. Do you understand?"

"Well, I do understand, but that's not quite what I said. I said that if he didn't apologize to the innocent technician he would find his face on the unforgiving concrete of the physician's parking lot, begging for an apology to me, or something like that."

"Oh, okay. Thanks for clearing that up," said Rogers. "You have a smooth way with words."

"Do you tolerate tall but weak oak trees intimidating well-meaning sapling technicians?" said Wyatt.

"Oak tree?"

"I'm sure you understand the metaphor. Turner's a towering giant but insecure as a guy watching his best friend dance with his girl at the prom. Someone needs to defend those who are unable to defend themselves or when they find themselves in an intimidating situation that doesn't allow them to respond without repercussions that may cause them to lose their jobs. So, that's what I do. If not, I don't sleep."

"So, I take it you will apologize to Turner."

"That won't be necessary."

"Yes, it will, Wyatt. You need to mend bridges. He eventually apologized to the technician because of you, I am told. But Turner is a well-respected physician in this community, and you need to do this, okay?"

Wyatt grinned. "Does he like orchids or daffodils? Don't you think you need to send him to anger management class or human relations training after the nice flowers I pick out?"

"No. But maybe I'll send you both to class. Do you both some good."

"Tell me," Wyatt said. "What do you see in me—anger or confidence?"

Rogers broke a faint smile. "Confidence."

"Anger or emotion causes mistakes and bad things will happen that may be irreversible. A man must control his emotions and not let them control him. Confidence exists through the strength of conviction and mastery of your inner self."

"Okay, damn it. Will you give him a simple damn apology at least? And after you do, I don't want to have to call you back in here again."

Wyatt rubbed his dimpled chin briefly, then stood up, looked down at Rogers, who remained seated, and said, "You can be sure that I will endeavor to do the right thing at all times."

CHAPTER 7

rik Jorgensen insisted he would drive his Ducati Superleggera the one hundred miles from Ontario airport to his company's testing facility at an abandoned airfield near Rogers Dry Lake, California. The Department of the Air Force maintained close airborne and ground security around their famous Edwards Air Force Base—a flight test center and home to the NASA-Dryden Flight Research Center—but the base allowed Jorgensen some limited airspace to operate in the area, within fifty miles of the base and at controlled altitudes, depending on tower communications from Edwards during the day.

Since he was a government contractor in the aerospace industry, the government allowed him to lease some land near Rogers Dry Lake to serve as a testing ground for his most advanced UAV technology and weapons systems. Although it was a private defense firm, Rondell Aerospace would occasionally allow military brass to watch some of its aircraft demonstrations before they were sold to the Air Force or other branches of the military.

The engineers who usually made the trip with him drove to the testing facility in a company van, but Erik, the boss, loved speed and figured the Ducati motorcycle could get him the hundred miles in less than an hour, since there wasn't much traffic on the way in the desert. His Ducati could hit 180 miles per hour, but he figured he would probably average around 100.

After taking a day to prepare the aircraft and equipment, and talk to the tower control at Edwards, his newest small UAVs were ready for testing. He specifically wanted to test the flight characteristics of multiple drones armed with laser-guided missiles. They were small and agile, protected by the newest defensive anti-drone technology. The engineers and UAV operators flew multiple drones, simultaneously, from simulated battle zones, including rooftops, and the drones successfully avoided crashes despite being launched within six feet of each other, using VTOL vertical take-off capabilities. Edwards allowed Rondell limited days for actual live missile drills in the desert, on the days when the Edwards Jets were either not in the air or taking off to the south or east. Tank simulations and simulations of buildings were easily blown up by the UAVs, without a single miss. After a week of testing, Erik called his men together to congratulate them on the successful testing of his newest UAV technology, the A-236 Striker.

"I'm proud of you guys," said Erik. We've worked hard on this project for four years now, and soon it will be ready for production and sale. It's a small but powerful UAV. Now, enjoy the beer and have a good time in this desert oasis, knowing you have accomplished a great achievement in aerospace and not only that, you're going to get some hefty bonus money."

"Long live Rondell Aeronautics," his men cheered, then drank themselves to oblivion the night before they had to leave to go back to Denver.

**

Cold beers are a mandatory refreshment on certain days—well, quite a few days—but especially after meeting with ponytailed chief medical officers who mindlessly enjoy guzzling the hospital administration Kool-Aid in the comfort of their offices. It was time to forget. Wyatt had found himself growing better at that over the last few years, but tonight, he was finally off duty and felt some quiet worship of an oversized brew would help immensely.

The problem was he didn't have a very good history in bars—especially those that contained stupid drunk patrons trying desperately to prove their manhood to the other customers. But the Kavernous Keg was far enough from the hospital to be safe from people he knew, he thought. He figured he could watch the Cubs vs. Rockies game on the widescreen TV in the center of the bar where the bartenders scurried about, and he hoped this time, it would be a peaceful night. He'd always been a Cubs fan, but now that he was in Colorado, he found himself slowly trying to become at least a partial Rockies fan. Coors field was nice, but it was no Wrigley field and would never compare to the friendly confines and the thick ivy in left field.

As always, he scanned the outside of the bar, the tops of buildings, the street, and the back alley before entering and then quickly scanned the four bulky bikers at the long bar in front, the exits, the location of the two bartenders, and the group of well-dressed but obviously misplaced ladies drinking exotic pink and blue drinks at a table along the back wall. They were far enough from the semicircular bar with big-screen TVs that they seemed to belong to a different world entirely. As far as the bikers in their leathers and chains, they were clearly not a threat. It took him only a few seconds to make the observations. Then, he selected a seat in the corner, behind the bikers but with a strategic view of the exits near the rear rest-rooms, and also a view that provided a scan of the entire bar while no one could sit behind him. Satisfied that the two grisly bikers in front of him on the far left of the bar were busy bantering with a couple of colorfully tattooed babes in tight leather chaps, he decided to allow himself to relax a little and hopefully they would ignore him. He quickly noticed he still had his blue scrub shirt on but was wearing jeans, and he cursed himself for not remembering to take the damn scrub shirt off. He noticed something different this time on the bikers' attire. He didn't like what he saw, but his thirst overcame his disgust temporarily.

One of the two bartenders walked over and took his order. "I'll have a Guinness—your largest draft."

The two bikers in front of him turned around and boldly stared at him and laughed, then flexed their sizable biceps for his view and played with their dagger tattoos that jiggled with muscle flexion and extension. Their bimbos saw this and giggled with excitement while playing with the chains and beads hanging over their well-displayed green-and-blue-tattooed breasts.

Both wide screens had a NASCAR race on, but Wyatt asked the bartender to switch the one directly in front of him to the Cubs game since there clearly were no other eyes looking at that TV screen. The biker closest to Wyatt watched him intently, and couldn't help but gaze at the quiet stranger gulping the refreshing darkness of the cold Guinness.

"What's wrong with you, boy?" said the biker. "You don't appreciate NASCAR? You damn un-American?"

Wyatt never allowed people to question his patriotism, but then, few people tried, and if they did try, they never tried again. He said nothing, staring at the game, but always keeping the bikers in his peripheral vision. The biker's nose and cheeks noticeably displayed a fiery-red hue that was clearly stoked by the beer.

"Y'all must've rolled into this fine establishment by mistake. The pussy bar is down the block. You can read books there and do crosswords and Soroku, or whatever they call it, if you want. I can give you directions, too, if you'd like to make a hasty exit," said the bulkiest biker.

Wyatt displayed for them a blank, uncaring look and continued to stare silently at the game. He looked at no one but saw everything. He deliberately slowed his breathing down, and mentally reduced his heart rate, just as he'd been trained to. They were massive and dumb and hairier than most humans. (Hair would always be a huge disadvantage in fights to the death.) Wyatt calmly drank his beer down halfway while keeping his peripheral vision in focus, then suddenly stopped, holding the mug in his left hand, savoring the beer and smiling as if it was a soothing lost friend. He was happy now with his new surgical position at Mercy General, and he loved helping save lives or at least making a difference for people the best he could. Finally, he had found a home, even now with Kim gone for so long.

The hairy biker mammoth closest to him walked over and pulled up a chair next to him on his left and one of his lower-ranked sidekicks followed behind and sat down next to his biker friend. Wyatt continued to look straight ahead at the game, seemingly oblivious to his surroundings, but whatever happened, he knew he wouldn't need his Sig Sauer. *Here we go again*, he thought. He was like a magnet to trouble, no matter how quiet he was. Shit magnet, they called it.

"What the hell's the matter with you, silent puke? You don't understand

English? Where I come from its rude to not talk when spoken to by a superior."

"Yep," said Wyatt. "That would certainly be the case if there actually were some superiors here to speak to me. And by the way, its Sudoku, not Suroku. I can write it down and spell it for you, but it's not worth my energy at the moment."

The hairy mammoth's flaring nose flushed like fire, and Wyatt figured the ropes of hair protruding down from this guy's generous nostrils would come in handy if he needed to tie him up to the toilet seat and then flush the handle multiple times after doing his business.

"Look what we got here, boys! A smartass male nurse!" The other bikers now all turned around at the bar and stared at the spectacle of a clean-cut man with a surgical scrub shirt on, drinking beer, with two bikers sitting next to him.

Wyatt's keen peripheral vision predicted the exact timing of the fist from the biker's right-handed punch attempt, spun around and caught the hairy mammoth's wrist in midair, and twisted it to almost the breaking point while simultaneously knocking the mammoth's chair from underneath him with a single leg sweep, leaving him squealing on the floor like a heaving sow giving birth to her litter.

"Let go, ass-wipe nurse!"

Wyatt twisted the man's arm just short of where he knew the bones would shatter, then for a millisecond, stopped and scanned the other patrons that required watching. When he saw them reluctantly coming toward their fallen comrade writhing on the floor, he stared them down with arctic steel eyes that had seen too much of the hell of war, and they stopped as if one more step would throw them over a cliff to their death.

"Next time I come here, I expect you little biker ladies to be wearing shiny American Flags on your leathers, proudly displayed on your attire for the world to see," Wyatt said. "I don't care where you put them, but they must be easily seen, and I will always look for them. Most of the biker guys I know are true patriots. If I don't see flags proudly displayed on your leathers next time, I'll rip your lips off individually, throw them in a pile and light them on fire with gasoline from your bikes while you watch, never able to speak your meaningless babble again. Now, I need you little boys to leave so I can finish my beer in peace. Is that understood?"

They shook their heads and walked out of the bar, bimbos bouncing behind. Wyatt lifted up his half-finished beer and said, "Have a nice day." And it was a helluva nice day. The Cubs were winning in the ninth inning.

Before he turned his attention more completely back to the game, he briefly glanced back more directly at the two ladies residing at the back table, smiled, and saluted them with his beer, realizing that he may have ruined their evening with his unfortunate encounter with the bikers. Then, he told the bartender to order them two more of their colorful drinks, whatever they were called. After their drinks arrived, he heard some giggles, looked back, and saw them with now easily-viewed crossed legs that had wondrously escaped from their short skirts, now in full display while their conservative pumps shook up and down, half off their feet, flopping invitingly in the air.

It had been too long for him, and there was something heavenly about the feel of a woman's tender lips while holding her soft feminine curves close to him, as if they were almost molded together. His Kim had had an almost kitten-like, helpless little meow that immediately flipped his power switch on as soon as he kissed her supple lips and neck.

"Excuse me, may we join you?"

The girls startled him from his reverie and proceeded to pull up chairs no matter what his answer, it seemed. He clearly had no self-defense for this determined feminine attack. The blonde wore a tight black skirt that hugged her luxurious hips, along with leg-announcing red shoes. Her hair was partly covering her right eye, and she had the brightest smile. She landed on his left, and the brunette with the red skirt and matching red pumps alighted on his right. Both had lean, tanned legs, just like he would have ordered in a pleasant dream.

"Sure, go ahead. My honor, ladies. My name's Wyatt."

The blonde said, "Connie" and the brunette said "Katy," and of course, they made it clear they were pleased to meet him.

"So, what brings you two fine ladies to this less-than-stellar bar?"

"We were going to ask you the same thing," said Connie. "But whatever the reason, it doesn't matter, because those bikers were trying to hit on us and they were disgusting, to say the least," said Katy. "What about you, Wyatt?"

"I was thirsty, I guess."

"So, we overheard the conversation you had with them. Are you really a nurse?" asked Connie.

"No, but without nurses, I'd be in trouble, and I guess all of us would be. Nurses are my angels, and they're amazing people with a noble profession."

"Right," said Katy. "So, you must be a doctor, right?"

"Could be, but don't tell anyone. I prefer to be known as a history teacher. Actually, general and trauma surgery."

The two hotties glanced at each other and smiled victorious smiles.

"What type of work do you ladies do?"

"We are actresses at the Denver Center for the Performing Arts. You know, singing and dancing in musicals, and I guess we were thirsty too after our last performance," said Katy. They both giggled in agreement, perhaps a little tipsy. Katy's left pump fell to the floor and Wyatt immediately picked it up, put it gently on her already pointed foot, then looked up and inhaled her perfume deep inside his hungry chest. He wanted to ravish her right there, starting with her legs.

Connie noticed the sparks flying between Wyatt and Katy and wouldn't be outdone. "We're having a pool party at the director's mansion in Cherry Creek a little later. Would you like to be our guest?" Katy looked at her and winked with a grin.

"Thanks, but I um, didn't bring my suit, and I've got an early case t—"

"Oh c'mon, Doc. Don't be a party pooper. We'll think of something. That is, unless you have a jealous girlfriend waiting at home, or worse, a wife."

Wyatt looked at his Panerai instinctively, then said, "Oh hell, why not!"

***

The other revelers seemed to enjoy socializing in their long gowns and suits in the house while Wyatt and his two new friends paid their respects with a few superficial introductions, then quickly slipped out to the private pool, surrounded by music playing through pool speakers, which were designed to look like boulders. The only lights in the pool area were underwater but the light from the full moon also reflected on the surface of the water . So much for suits, because all three of them tore off their clothes and jumped in, leaving a pile of skirts, shoes, panties, and a pair of boxer briefs, strewn over deck chairs. There was a lonely bra floating in the water that no one seemed to notice. The feminine giggling and splashing soon died down, taken over by quiet moaning and heavy breathing, and soft squeals of passion while the water from the pool slide tinkled down into the waiting pool that now was producing rhythmic, undulating waves. Wyatt's long drought finally ended in spectacular fashion under the moonlight, in a pool, with two young actresses while no one noticed but a wide-eyed horned owl in a nearby tree.

CHAPTER 8

Kurt Logan, the Secretary of the Air Force, enjoyed a former career as a fighter pilot, during the age when he thought pilots were special and talented, and therefore, irreplaceable. However, when UAV drone technology burst onto the scene and became commonplace in the military, he reluctantly forced himself to accept that unmanned vehicles were not only here to stay but were essentially indispensable. He made sure he appropriated the monies from the defense budget to the Air Force for the most effective UAV technology to fight present and future wars. He found that other allies or at least, pseudo-allies on paper, frequently called him to procure some of this technology for their own use and sometimes this was a difficult task to navigate for many reasons. One of the frequent callers was India, but Logan's counterpart in Saudi Arabia blew up his phone more than any other country's defense leaders, and he needed help handling them and their specific needs in a volatile part of the world. That's why he needed to talk to Erik Jorgensen, the head of Rondell Aerospace, and meet him face to face at the Pentagon.

"Nice to meet you Erik," said Logan.

"It's certainly my pleasure and honor, sir," replied Jorgensen.

When they shook hands, Logan almost winced at the strength of Erik's grip, and since he was five inches taller at 6'3", he had to look up somewhat to see the piercing, intelligent blue eyes and short blonde hair that reminded Logan of Dolph Lundgren, the tall Swedish actor who played Ivan Drago in Rocky IV. But this guy also had a PhD in aerospace engineering and was a rising star in the defense industry and could probably think Mr. Lundgren into a box without using a muscle.

Erik sat in front of Logan's expansive desk, which looked slightly smaller than a Nimitz-class aircraft carrier. The desk was cluttered with papers, and a model of the F-22 he flew sat in the corner, even though F-22s were Air Force and therefore didn't fly on flat tops, which this desk seemed to somehow emulate. Erik took a swig of cool water; then Logan did the same before getting down to business.

"Would you like some coffee or water, Mr. Jorgensen?"

"Sure, a bottle of water would be fantastic."

"The SecDef recommended you, and I think he's right. We need you to help us with the Saudis."

"Okay. Tell me what you need from me. Okay if I call you Kurt?"

"No problem, Erik. The Saudis are a difficult nut to crack. They're supposed to be our allies in the Middle East and a buffer to Iran and Syria, but at the same time, they have ties to some Muslim organizations that want to kill us. The fact is, they want to procure some more UAV technology from us, but they want the higher tech stuff now, and that's where Rondell Aerospace comes in."

"Right. Go on."

"Your company has the best technology, especially ECM technology, as well as weapon systems, for the cheapest price. We're impressed by how quickly you came on line and supplied us, faster and more efficiently than the other, more well-known firms. But we want to sell only a limited supply to the Saudis, without the greatest ECM technology or sensors you sell to us. No weapons systems at this time, just surveillance cameras and sensors. This will help both us and them."

"Makes sense. So, I don't see the problem. Just draw up a contract and we'll proceed with one of my scaled-down versions, the MX-4J. That should do the trick and we'll come in at the right price, on time."

"Well, the Saudis for some reason want to talk to the designer and executive in the company first for product details. They don't want to talk to me or General McCartney, who runs our UAV operation. So, since you're not only the designer but the owner of this private company, you would be perfect for accelerating the success of this program and making the Saudis happy. Oh, by the way, we also selected you because you're fluent in Arabic, and you apparently know the Middle East and something about the Sunni–Shia situation over there, so that should impress these guys in sand land. By the way, how did you gain that knowledge, Erik?"

Erik's sky-blue eyes stared directly at Kurt, never blinking. He smiled. "Besides my PhD in aeronautical engineering, I found that I had an interest in languages, and Arabic seemed a challenge to me, so I mastered it with a degree also in Middle Eastern Studies. My father did some work over in the Middle East years ago, so it seemed to make sense to me. Chinese was another option, but I was recruited to the workforce so quickly that I didn't have time to master that language too, unfortunately. Seems it comes in handy now in business circles, right?"

"You got that right. So, Erik, are you interested in packing your bags and heading to Riyadh, courtesy of the US taxpayers?"

"Just tell me when, and I'll be there."

***

It had been about thirty minutes since Erik Jorgensen had arrived at his office from his trip to the Pentagon, and although Sally knew he always requested several hours after a trip to concentrate on business in his office, she knew it would be okay to interrupt with this special new visitor. "Mr. Jorgenson, I have your son, Peter, here to see you."

"Let him in, Sally."

The security guard scanned Peter Jorgensen with the electronic wand as well as a physical pat-down, and after a successful retinal scan, his son was allowed into the boss's office. Peter was shorter than his father and darker-skinned, but the green eyes really set him apart. He had a dark beard and stocky, muscular features, and his T-shirt clearly displayed his massive arms, which he carefully sculpted in the gym. Peter was the perfect leader, as well as operator, a skilled and dedicated warrior. Father and son looked at each other silently, smiled, and embraced warmly. Then, Peter sat down in front of his father's desk, which displayed the emblem

"Rondell Aerospace" attached to the mahogany wood front.

The silence hovered like a low-lying cumulus cloud while they studied each other's expressions. At last, Erik spoke. "Are you and your men ready? Do you have the technology and weapons I helped secure for you to go to battle?"

"Strong and prepared—willing to die for the cause of good versus evil. Yes, all is in place and on time. I'll make you proud, my father.

Then, Peter silently walked to the door without looking back, and his father said, to his son, using his birth name, "Good luck, Saleem!"

"My father, our victory is assured."

CHAPTER 9

Wyatt usually avoided public gyms—the kind filled with tattooed muscleheads inhabiting the barbell grunting section, while the other side of the gym attracted a wide variety of people of various shapes and sizes plodding along on treadmills and tolerating stair climbers, not realizing that slow easy exercise wasn't going to burn fat the way they expected at all. But they were trying, and he respected that.

Knee injuries limited Wyatt's running, so lap swimming, boring as it was, gave his knees a necessary rest between his three-day-a-week high-intensity run-punch workouts with weight variations to break the workout monotony. But now with a nagging shoulder strain from his punch-run workouts, he found himself relegated to using the treadmill at the gym rather than the pool. He picked a treadmill on the right side of the line of machines in the back corner of the club, closest to the exits, as always. Repetitive training does brand the brain cells permanently. He would never change.

He started his warm-up while staring straight ahead at the never-ending soccer game on one of the TV screens attached to the ceiling on the front row. Soccer was a lot better than CNN, the mandatory news channel, it seems for public establishments. Then, this feminine form seemed to float up onto the treadmill machine in front of him, seemingly without touching the ground with her feet, did some hamstring and calf stretches, wiped down the handrails with antiseptic cloth, then finally started to run, not jog. Her long raven mane, held at the top by a bouncy ponytail clip, reached all the way down to the glorious end of her shirt, brushing gently back and forth on top of the garlic clove halves of her behind while swishing the air back and forth like a pendulum, in cadence with her stride, but several milliseconds out of phase. Those tights hugged her lean legs as if poured on like lucky melted chocolate on smooth ice cream, running out of material just below her pulsing heart-shaped calves. Wyatt was taught long ago not to stare at a woman, and he had well-trained peripheral vision, but he kept his eyes fixed straight ahead, not at the TV but on the bouncy raven-haired beauty gracefully leaping on the machine in front of him. There was no way for her to know where his eyes were fixed, and hell, for safety reasons he needed to keep his eyes straight ahead to maintain balance and not fall off and land in a heap of sweaty flesh.

She was running at a faster pace than Wyatt, and she inspired him to go faster as well, if his battered knees would allow it. His eyes counted the mesmerizing rhythm of her swishing pendulum and nonstop frog leg action, striding effortlessly in the quest to go nowhere. The sweat now dripped down his forehead, and he noticed she too was dripping—the wet line in the middle of her straight back sucked her pink shirt to her tanned skin.

She slowed down the pace of her machine, finally, for a warm-down, so of course, Wyatt decided it was time to do the same. She stopped, turned around, and took a quick glance at him. He smiled, and thankfully, she smiled back. He couldn't help it, he had to talk to her and take the chance before it was too late and she was speeding away in her car—probably a shiny BMW convertible. There was something about a stunning woman that sometimes paralyzed his actions, unlike any dangerous activity he faced when he was deployed with the Rangers. Back then, he was trained to act quickly with skill and confidence and to not let fear of failure cause paralysis of action. Kim was gone, still in his heart forever, but there had to be enough room now for an earthly goddess who could be touched and kissed.

He walked by and stopped briefly by her treadmill, the heated rubber smell from the fast-moving belt fumigating the air, and he watched briefly while she put her towel neatly in her bag.

"I would like to thank you," said Wyatt.

"Excuse me?" Her eyes froze him well before her full lips parted and showed him the smile that nearly blinded him.

"Well, you ran such a fast-paced workout, that since I was running on the machine behind you, you inspired me to work harder than I expected. So, I thank you for motivating me."

"Glad I could help, I'm Gentri." She held out her hand for him to shake. He did so carefully since it was so dainty.

"Wyatt. Nice to meet you." Wyatt felt immediate relief that she didn't reject him on the spot, but he figured he had a fighting chance since he noticed that she glanced at him when she stopped running. That was a good sign too. Neither seemed compelled to walk to their respective lockers, so they just stood there, sweating, but for some reason, Wyatt felt completely comfortable.

"I'm surprised I went for the treadmill today. I despise indoor running, you know, boring scenery, but then today, Gentri, you blew that out of the water."

"How so?" Her cheeks flushed it seemed, a little deeper than the post-workout hue he'd seen earlier. She knew what he meant but wanted to hear more details.

"I'll tell you over a strong drink of cold Gatorade on the rocks over there at the sweaty bar overlooking the heaving barbell hulks."

"Well, I do have an appointment in about an hour, so we won't have much time. You have given me an excellent offer, however, and you sure know how to impress a girl, so why not?"

At the gym juice bar, Wyatt treated her to a vegetable juice slushie, and he had a bottled water, with a glass full of ice to make it look classy.

"I loved your stride, Gentri. Smooth and athletic."

"So, you were staring at me?"

"Well, you were right in front of me, thankfully, and I had nowhere else to look."

"Hmm. A gym treadmill stalker?"

He soaked in her smooth, comforting Southern accent and hoped to hear some more. "Perhaps, but at least I wasn't grunting like the iron pumpers, right?"

"Good point. Although I must admit, I may not have heard your grunting over the treadmill noise and my ear buds."

Wyatt smiled and felt himself staring to blush a little. "So, Gentri, what do you do when you're not working out?"

"I do nothing but work out, sleep, and eat."

"Well, I believe the work-out part because of how you look but I don't believe the rest of it at all. I think you must dance too, on top of those other activities. You have dancer's legs as well as runner's legs."

"I am a running dancer, darling. No seriously, I'm a real estate broker here in Denver and a part-time novelist."

"Interesting. What genre of novels do you write?

"Romance, of course. That's what we ladies are best at writing about, you know. Men just can't touch that stuff. It's the number-one selling genre because so many women buy them. I want to write a whole series of them, publish them on Amazon for a dollar, and they'll sell like cold beer at a ball park in the desert sun. In fact, I'm working on one now, but I can't quite find the right leading man."

"That's a tough one, right? I mean he can't be all good looks—you know, the classic tall dark and handsome hero with bright teeth and an athletic body? He also has to have a brain because, you know, men can be dumb blonds too," said Wyatt.

"Dumber blonds, you mean. Men are good at destroying themselves, but the dumb ones can be a lot of fun when needed. I want a leading man who's a gentleman, maybe not as brutally handsome as some women imagine but decent-looking, accomplished at his job, a protector of women, full of faults, but not fatal ones ... and a man who's blessed or perhaps cursed with unpredictable intrigue of some sort. And of course, he's got to be great in bed because, after all, that's what my readers want to read about—sex and romance."

"Ha," said Wyatt. "That's not asking for much, it seems. But I wonder, are you referring to your book or real-life desires?"

"A good novelist certainly interjects experiences in her life in her books to make the reading exciting and plausible, but you won't be able to tell when reading, whether this applies to the novelist's life." Gentri looked at her watch, then said, "I've got to go to my appointment now, but it has been a pleasure meeting you, Wyatt. Maybe we can enjoy another slushie sometime."

"Sure," said Wyatt. "Or better yet, how about a drink with a little more kick to it—perhaps with a live band? I know of a great jazz venue down-town."

"I'd love it."

She gave him her number without much thought, and they went their separate ways.

Wyatt shook his head in wonder, thinking, *She's a divine symphony of feminine perfection.*

CHAPTER 10

Wyatt parked at the Old Chicago pizza place that they agreed on, in the back,near the garbage and grease enclosure, where the employees parked. He proceeded to methodically check out the perimeter, the exits, and the roof, and then he came inside to join his buddy Colonel Stanley for a few cold beers. Colonel Charles Stanley was a friend of his from his Special Ops days, when Stanley flew him and his team of Rangers on various covert missions. They were the first in to secure airfields, and Stanley now had been promoted to commander of Peterson Air Force Base, the 21st Space Wing, a prestigious job that he deserved. He flew over twenty different aircraft during his career, much of it with JSOC. His colleagues called him a 'pilot's pilot,' but Wyatt just trusted him as a friend he could depend on.

"Hey, Wyatt," said Stanley. "Are we secure, my friend?"

"Well, we may not be totally secure, but we seem to be in a decent position, Chuck."

"Ok Wyatt. I bought you a Guinness, like always. Since you're a little late, I couldn't help myself, so I took a few swigs of my Sam Adams already. Besides, I know you're a faster drinker than I am already."

"Good move, Chuck," replied Wyatt. "I would've done the same thing if I was in your shoes."

"Got to drink fast," said Stanley. "Never know when you've got to leave in a hurry, I say. I heard you're enjoying the civilian life now, operating on gall bladders and thrombosed hemorrhoids in the resort spa hospital, right?"

"Exactly. And I get a nice massage, compliments of my appreciative friends in the hospital administration, after each case."

Stanley laughed loudly, forcing the bartender to turn around and smile. "But tell me, Wyatt, are you happy?"

"It's been a bit of an adjustment, you know, from my previous life, but yes, it's what I want to do ... and *need* to do, actually. A little lonely and boring at times, I guess, but I'm trying to resolve that issue."

"Any luck with the ladies?"

"Not much, but I did meet someone promising today. Actually got a number."

"Excellent. I hope it's not a wrong number though. I know it's been several years now, but you do need to move on. You need someone. You know, the Eagles song, 'Desperado, you ain't getting no younger.' And then something like, 'You better let somebody love you before it's too late.'"

"Yeah, Henley and Frey did a good job on that one. Thanks for reminding me—again." Wyatt paused, looked briefly pensive, took a long swig of the Guinness, then changed the subject. "So, tell me, Chuck, when are you getting your first star?"

"I'm up for promotion this month actually. Thanks for asking. The star is going to commit me to the long term, but hell, it's my life and all I know how to do. I'm having fun at this job actually. I prefer to fly, but we do some good things here at Space Command. Space has become a busy place, filled with bad actors, and we need to work hard to be vigilant and not lose to the bad guys up there, because that's where they can cripple us the most, believe it or not."

"Yes, that makes sense, Chuck. Glad you're there to protect us."

"But you know, I love the challenge, Wyatt. In fact, we've now been tasked by General Norton of US Northern Command to work with the Air Force Academy's aeronautical engineering department to do drone–UAV research, and in fact, some of those cadets are excellent drone pilots.

They do some good work there, and we've developed a secret UAV threat elimination program here on base—one that I'm very proud of. I can't say much more about that program, though, as you know."

Wyatt nodded. "Of course. I wouldn't understand any of that technical stuff anyway. I was just a ground-pounder."

"Yeah, I remember. And you ground-pounders kept jumping out of my very nice airplanes when I made them fly nice and smooth," said Stanley.

"You know, Chuck," said Wyatt. "We need to stop talking shop and the good old days and maybe whack some Dunlops down long fairways someday. Problem is, you always kill me at golf."

"You can't even stay on the fairway," Stanley snorted. You have too much power but no finesse at all. So, *everyone* kills you in golf. You're like a gorilla out there in long pants and golf shoes."

"Yeah, but I'm pretty good at drinking beer in the club house. Anyway, I think you're on your way to four stars, my friend. The Air Force needs you as a top-ranking senior officer."

"Thanks, Wyatt. Oh, I meant to tell you Ron Cavanaugh went from the Agency to FBI counter-intelligence. Can you believe it?"

"Cavanaugh saved me and my men with his valuable information many times, Chuck, and he kept you out of trouble, as you know. He was dedicated and one of the best in his field, but you know, I want him happy. If he joined the feds, then, that means they have another good man to help them fight crime and domestic terrorism. Like you, he's one of the few men I trust and he believes in me, even when I act a little off."

"Good man," said Stanley. "But he's not an agent. He's the damn deputy director. Surprised you didn't know that, but then, you must be isolating yourself these days, Wyatt. Obviously, you're not communicating with anyone anymore from your previous life. Present company excluded."

They finished their beers and shook hands. "Thanks for meeting me," Wyatt said. "It's always a pleasure to talk to one of my previous colleagues."

"Likewise, Wyatt. Stay out of trouble, if that's possible, and please call me if you ever need me for anything. You know where to find me."

***

Colonel Tommie Palmer seemed to be born and bred to be a career military officer. He served as an operational commander of the First Special Forces Operational Detachment, and on one of his multiple Black Ops missions, he was shot in Afghanistan in the right leg and the right hand, causing him to lose his right pinkie finger. He walked with a slight limp; but it didn't affect his walk too much, except that his right foot did rotate inward slightly, so that he was no longer capable of being an operator. Now he was an excellent spook working a desk as deputy director of operations for the CIA. He felt strongly that the US was, unfortunately, losing wars, especially against terrorism, and Spec Ops was now of necessity playing a much greater role than regular units in order to show a smaller footprint for the politicians but also accomplish the jobs previously given to larger regular units. Since he was a former Delta Force officer, before he accepted the CIA position, he was able to enjoy a close relationship with his friends at JSOC to accomplish clandestine missions, providing HUMINT (human intelligence) and Sigint (electronic intelligence) for the operators on their secret missions. He had close operational relationships with commanders and officers of all three tiers of Special Ops units, including Delta Force (TF Green), The 75th Ranger Regiment (TF Red), DEVGRU, Seal Team 6 (TF Blue), The 160th Special Operations Aviation Regiment (SOAR)—also called Night Stalkers—TF Orange (Army of Northern Virginia), TF Silver (Air Force Covered Air Unit), and TF White (the 24th Special Tactics Squadron.)

Palmer loved his job, and when a National Directive came down under the direct control of the president, Palmer heard from the CIA director as well as the Director of National Intelligence prior to planning the mission with JSOC (Joint Special Operations Command). But he had some other loves as well. That included his wife, his two teenage sons, and another secret love that no one knew about—a love that turned into a consumptive addiction that he couldn't stop.

Tommie's civilian cell phone rang, and the caller ID came through as Cellini's pizza. He forced a deep breath, let it ring a couple more times, then answered.

"Yeah. I'm here."

"That ain't a very pleasant way to answer the phone, is it?"

Tommie said nothing, simply waiting.

"Your bill is way overdue, Mr. Tommie bigshot. Because of who you said you was, we covered the bets you laid down, but we ain't gonna do it no more. I told you before, if you want to play with us you need to understand the ups and downs of financial risk. Maybe you win sometimes, maybe you lose, but it seems you've been on the losing side for some time now. We are not very patient people, so you need to pay up."

"Right. Well, you know I've been busy lately, and I try to make the payments I can afford without my wife noticing anything. I need some more time, Giovanni."

"Time, you say? Seems like you've been using the T-word a little more than you should recently. You see, we're getting a little impatient here at the shop. We have overhead to pay, and the ladies need jewelry too. The bottom line is we want our $300,000 paid within two months, or things will get complicated for you, Tommie. Oh yes, and for your family as well. Do you understand me, Tommie?"

"Got it," said Palmer. "I'll have to—"

Giovanni hung up.

Tommie sat at the kitchen table, put his head in his hands, collected his thoughts, then walked to the refrigerator to get a beer, at which point his "red" phone buzzed and he picked it up quickly. His phone replacement key was changed daily and was a top-secret tier.

"This is Twenty-five."

"Twenty-four."

"Falcon needs to leave the nest to find some rats."

He knew this was a call to immediate action, and he grabbed his already prepared kit, and Task Force Silver picked him up to meet the director after a two-hour flight in covered air. The director never met him in Langley when a National Directive occurred, but this site was secure, bland, and unobtrusive.

"Palmer," said the director. "We've got solid intel that multiple high-value targets will present themselves soon. Top leaders of the FFWP. POTUS wants these people eliminated quietly and decisively."

"Each time I hear that acronym for Freedom Fighters for World Purification, I want to puke," said Palmer. "It really means Fuckers Frantically

Wanking their Puny Peters."

"That's too many Ps, Tommie, but I like it anyway. You're being too nice to these animals, and we both know that they need to be killed before they kill us and our families here. Anyway, we only have, perhaps, a ninety-six-hour window, best intel. JSOC wants TF Green to be the operators with the Night Stalkers and some black aircraft from the desert operation. Green will be commanded by Colonel Paul Johnson. Apparently, he served with you in some tricky areas some years ago."

"Good man. Damn good."

"We're going to need to complete a SOST (Special Operations Surgical Team). Johnson has assembled some top-notch people including two 18D medics, an anesthesiologist, two combat nurses, and two Spec Ops surgeons."

"Who are the surgeons?" asked Palmer.

"Why do you care?"

"They're going to be close to the action if not past the line, and we need our best," replied Palmer.

"You second-guessing Johnson already?"

"No. But let me ask you: Do you want the best at multiple positions—intel, support, surgery, and fighting?"

"Honestly, Palmer, I prefer the worst actually. What are you getting at?"

"We need to reactivate someone."

"Not happening. We're not reactivating anyone. We don't have time to hold hands here with some guy in a rolling walker. This is fast-moving shit."

"I recommend we reactivate 241 for this mission. He'll be perfect."

"Who in hell's name is 241?"

"He's kinda retired from the Agency. Self-imposed retirement I would say, unfortunately."

"Why do we need an agency guy on this mission? It's going to be a quick get-in-and-get-out, hopefully clean with no casualties because it's going to be a surgical strike."

"We need him because he has a Ranger background before the agency and because he knows Pashtun and Pashtunwali—the way of the Pashtuns. Also fluent in Arabic as a bonus."

"I don't think all that language skill is necessary. We don't need to mix with the natives and sing folk songs around a crackling campfire. We can leave that for the guys that are trained to do so—the Green Berets."

"Trust me on this. He's an ex-Ranger, a war hero—Silver Star and all that. Then, we sent him to medical school, and he became a trauma surgeon. Of course, we sucked him into the CIA fairly easily, and he kept his legend intact doing medical missions in hotspots overseas, gathering valuable intel."

"Interesting story, but I need to move on this. Tell me why Johnson needs this guy on his team. We don't need a guy with his head buzzing from PTSD compromising this mission, no matter how good he was at the time. Figure you guys vetted him extensively already, right?"

"Constantly watching him. And he says it's PTS. It's not a disorder unless you let it become one, he says. We've shadowed him, and he's doing fine, although he's having a little trouble adjusting to his civilian colleagues in the hospital at times, replied Palmer.

"And . . ."

"He's the best option. Good surgeon, top agent, and strong soldier."

"Will he kill?"

"Oh, by the way, Johnson knows him, he served—"

"Answer my question, Palmer."

"Doctors can't be operators, and you know that. You know, the Hippocratic Oath and shit like that."

"Answer my fucking question, Palmer."

"Yeah. He can fight like a junkyard dog. He'll kill if shit hits the fan, and he's shown he'll sacrifice his life for his men and the mission."

"What are his other assets?"

"He's alone. No baggage. No family. Wife killed a few years ago by a gangbanger. No kids. No real connections it seems."

"What are his weaknesses?"

"Music, if you can call it that."

"What?"

"He likes to sing, badly when listening to music on the flight in. His favorite is 'I wanna be an Airborne Ranger, live a life of sex and danger.'

Annoys the hell out of the operators, but they laugh it off. Takes the stress away for a few moments."

"What else?" asked the director.

"He's older. Forty-five to be exact. But he's in good shape."

"Okay, Palmer. I trust you. Now get out of my office, and let's press the button on this show. Reactivate 241. What's his name, by the way?"

"Barton. Wyatt Barton, M.D."

CHAPTER 11

D epending on traffic conditions on I-25 South, the trip from Highlands Ranch in Denver to Colorado Springs generally took about fifty minutes on a good day, but since this was Friday night, Wyatt gave himself extra time. *Never be late for a lady—especially not a first date.* Although he figured this was actually their second real date if you counted the juice bar at the gym. Either way, a woman had to be respected and treated well or another chance to be with her would vanish with the wind, and he didn't get many chances anymore, it seemed. And maybe Colonel Stanley was right. He wasn't getting any younger.

Wyatt chose the Broadmoor Hotel in Colorado Springs for their date. He had played golf a few times at the Mountain Course at the Broadmoor Golf Club with a doctor friend who was a member, and he'd stunk up the course bad enough that he wasn't invited back. Golf takes a lot of practice and he didn't have time to spend four hours twice a week or more to be good enough to impress his golf-brained Callaway-loving friends, and there wasn't enough action in golf unless you hit in the water and the alligators chased after you. Although there weren't any alligators in Colorado Springs, he was good at finding the water, sand, and woods. He preferred good solid exercise that broke a sweat and tore at the muscles with a pleasant but searing burn, although he figured if he bagged a few good holes out of eighteen then it would be an outing to remember.

Wyatt chose the restaurant at the hotel he'd never experienced—the famous Penrose Room at the AAA Five-Diamond Broadmoor Resort. He figured Gentri was the type of lady who would enjoy the elegant ambiance, live music, and dancing he'd heard about. She told him that she had a client in the Springs that evening and that she would meet him at the hotel, but even so, he was uncomfortable not picking a woman up and driving her on the date. Old fashioned, yes, but maybe that's what women did, or expected on dates now. He wanted to drive her, open the door for her, and escort her in, proudly, with some degree of chivalry at least, but then it had been so long since he'd had a real date since he lost his Kim.

He arrived forty-five minutes early. The maître d told him he had the table ready for him, but Wyatt said he would wait for his date to arrive; then, they would sit. Wyatt insisted on one of the cozy, gold U-shaped booths along the wall, closest to the door, with paintings by the Hungarian artist Bisttram adorning the wall behind them. As always, he insisted on a seat that was close to the exit. To maximize his time while waiting for Gentri's arrival, he walked around the restaurant, scanning the surroundings directly and with his subtle peripheral vision as well. He wore a black suit, white shirt, black shoes, and a red tie, and that certainly fit the dress code that he observed. The center of the Penrose Room boasted a 16-foot chandelier, like a shiny umbrella over the dance floor that extended out from the jazz ensemble musicians playing on an elevated stage. Smaller chandeliers graced the ceiling throughout the restaurant, and windows on each side provided panoramic views of the city to the east and the lake and mountains to the west. Behind the band was a large painted mural, artist unknown, showing two dancers—a woman in a Bordeaux dress and a man in a dark suit, dancing in front of a full moon. For a final scan, he smiled and asked the maître d to show him the balcony on the west-facing side of the restaurant, accessible only through the private chef's dining area in back. The balcony provided breathtaking views of the lake, surrounded by lighted trees and the brooding mountains of the Rampart Range and Cheyenne Mountain just to the south.

When he walked back through the main dining area to the lobby, he scanned the bar and saw a man in a dark corner but avoided eye contact, using peripheral vision as he was trained. The man wore a jacket without a tie, and the jacket was way too small—bulging at the seams from his muscles, and his neck looked like a tree trunk squeezing through a small opening in his shirt. Those guys usually wore baseball caps too, but that wasn't the dress code at the Penrose Room or bar. He'd seen shadow men who looked like this each time he returned from a mission, and each one was different yet the same in most ways. He knew shadow men would often follow operators after a mission, to make sure nothing was mistakenly compromised by the operator, but if this was, in fact, a shadow man, why was he here keeping tabs on someone who was out of the game? These guys were often retired or retiring Special Ops guys who wanted some quiet work before saying goodbye to the service completely. Couldn't blame them, but did they really think he wouldn't notice? He figured the least the guy could do was buy him a beer and shoot the shit harmlessly. After all, they were both on the same side—or at least he thought they were. Or maybe Wyatt was mistaken and a little too paranoid. No way he had a damn shadow man assigned to him now in his cushy civilian life. Just didn't make sense.

Beaucoup dinky dau.

She didn't really walk in. She glided. Her merciless hips moved to the rhythm of the bass player, and her stylish heels generously pointed the way to her lean, heart-shaped calves. She offered a more elegant but similarly enticing view compared to their treadmill encounter and Wyatt drank it in completely but his thirst remained unquenched. Yes, she was a divine symphony of feminine perfection.

"So great to see you, Gentri. You look amazing."

"Thank you, Wyatt, and likewise, my handsome sweetheart! So sorry I'm late. I had a client who wanted to talk and—"

"No problem, seems a lucky man must be patient for a quality lady."

He reached out and kissed her hand, then led her to their table, and he noticed everyone stopping their dinner, with forks frozen awkwardly in mid-air just to stare at the goddess—her long hair cascading back and forth during her walk, sometimes bouncing over one of her eyes, but she didn't fix it, letting the bounce assume its natural seductive freedom. She slid in first on one side of the luxurious booth, and he then joined on the other side, both sitting close enough to enjoy each other but not be on each other's lap. The waiter then carefully placed the gold napkin on her lap, and that napkin clearly had never been so lucky. Then, he did the same for Wyatt. A few minutes later, the second waiter came and brought the dozen long-stem roses in a vase that Wyatt bought earlier, and Wyatt handed them to her and said, "To a wonderful lady who brightens any room she's in."

"My my, Wyatt! Bless your heart!" She kissed him, not on the cheek, but softly and tenderly, both of them exploring the taste of each other and wanting more, until their lips naturally parted, each knowing there had to be more.

"You know, Wyatt, I'm not a woman who is Spartan with her words, but you have really impressed me. You're so sweet, and a true romantic gentleman. Yes, I've had roses before, but not in such a nice restaurant and, I must admit, I've never had my hand kissed before."

"I had no choice, Gentri. I figured you would enjoy the atmosphere here and you would fit in with the elegant ambiance that I heard about this place. Not only that, I knew you liked soft jazz, and so voila!"

She leaned in and kissed him again, then moved closer to him, her legs crossed daintily but expertly, while showing her shapely runner's legs, allowing Wyatt to imagine following the smooth terrain of the skin up above her mid-thigh hemline to quite a pleasant conclusion, simply by using that subtle vision. He smiled, knowing that his training served him well in multiple different ways, so tonight he was thankful for that. She had a small brown birthmark on the lower part of the left side of her neck, resembling a small feather, and a tiny mole on the outside of her right upper lip, almost imperceptible, but they became at once tiny imperfections that made her even more attractive to him, especially when her soft lips graciously moved to create words.

"I hope a nice smooth Bordeaux is okay with you. I selected a Chateau Beausejour, Saint Emilion Grand Cru, 2001. The sommelier is bringing it now."

"No way! Bordeaux is the worst. It makes me dance nonstop, giggle, and blush all night. You'll be sorry, my darling Mr. Barton."

"That's not my definition of being sorry; that's for sure."

The couple sipped their wine and talked after making their dinner selections, while Wyatt watched her energetic right foot bounce up and down playfully, heel only half on. This time, to hell with peripheral vision; he used full head-on vision now.

"So, tell me, Wyatt. What exactly do you do for a living? I guessed that you pick up chicks at the gym with charming banter and take full advantage of them with really cold and intoxicating fruit smoothies, then give them wine and flowers, hoping to find a hot rich one to take care of you?"

"Exactly. That would be the perfect life for me, but I haven't found the right one yet. Perhaps my luck is changing, though."

"Seriously though, what do you do?"

"Guess."

She looked at him, intensely, then closed her eyes as if in deep thought and said, "You're a romantic gentleman, educated, probably with an advanced degree of some type, but mysterious as hell. That rules out most men, I think. Perhaps you're a day trader, a lawyer, or a doctor with a certain edge to him."

"Good guess. I'm a surgeon. I work at Mercy Hospital downtown."

"Oh my, honey."

"Why 'oh my?'"

"My ex-husband was … I mean *is* a pediatrician, but unfortunately, he loved himself a lot. Too much. I'm not saying all doctors—"

"Of course not. May I ask when the divorce was finalized?"

"Three years ago."

She looked down, swirled her glass a little, then changed the subject. Wyatt noticed her pumps stopped swinging for a moment when she briefly discussed her ex.

"Sorry, Wyatt, but I'm just curious. You hold yourself in a certain way. I don't know. Makes me think this wasn't always your career or something." Her pumps began swinging again, a little more aggressively.

"Is that what you mean by saying a 'doctor with an edge to him?'"

"Perhaps. You seem confident with yourself when you walk, and your blue eyes are just so intense at times. I've met quite a few doctors socially in my previous life, but I don't know. You seem different, and it fascinates me."

Wyatt smiled, then watched the man enter the room, perhaps after visiting the men's room, and sat down at a small table in a protected dark corner, near the exit, making it very difficult for people to see him—even Wyatt. He ordered a beer, which Wyatt felt was slightly out of place in this Five-Diamond restaurant. But, was this a shadow man or just some lonely guy who liked to listen to jazz and drink beer in a dark corner of a fancy restaurant?

"Don't forget, Gentri, I remembered that your hobby is writing romance novels and I can't help but think your mind is creating a nice story here. Perhaps you need a real-life male romantic character to insert deeply into your story."

"Honey, I have that covered already. Most women have that image ingrained in their minds. However, I can always delete those words and rewrite them at any time, depending on my mood. I do a lot of rewriting, by the way. But, now that I have the floor, you need to finally tell me what else you did in your life. I know there is a lot more and you can tell me because, well, a girl must know these things."

Wyatt carefully poured her a second glass of the Chateau Beausejour, then smiled and said, "I served in the Army."

"That's it? You just served? That's all? How long did you—"

The waiter brought their food, all of it presented with silver-domed lids, and each course was timed perfectly for their pace of eating, all three courses pleasingly interrupted by interesting appetizers planned to accent the next course. The dinner and its presentation took over their table, and conversation became less important than the happiness in their palates. Wyatt wasn't ready to describe his entire life at this point, and he was happy she dropped her innocent line of questioning.

After dessert, she tried again. "So, how long did you serve, Wyatt?

"Twenty years. Saw the world the Army way, but now I'm retired."

Wyatt got up abruptly, glanced briefly at the shadow man's table, saw that it was empty, then said, "It's time to dance, my pretty flower." He alternated quick glances at her legs, then ankles, then her full lips while she swirled the smooth wine deftly inside her delicate mouth.

"Yes, that would be lovely."

He took her hand and led her to the dance floor in front of the jazz quartet on the elevated stage while the musicians played various classics by Dave Brubeck, Count Basie, Joe Sample, Ramsey Lewis, Diana Kraal, and others. They danced while the others stared at the couple gliding across the floor with the moon behind them—his left hand in her right, his right hand gently in the small of her back. Wyatt felt the rhythm of the music, and hers as well when he touched her thin waist gently, taking in the scent of her Boucheron. After several dances, she grew quiet, and he took her hand, leading her out the back way through the chef's private dining area he'd checked out earlier—out the back door to the balcony on the west side of the restaurant. They stood against the railing, enjoying the view of the lake, with the reflection of the sparkling lights adorning the trees on the shore, and the barely visible outline of Cheyenne Mountain, shadowing the darkness of the starry sky.

"Wyatt, this is such an amazing view here, and I must say—"

He put both hands on her delicate waist, pulled her close to him, looked into her eyes, absorbing her Boucheron once again, then kissed her as he had kissed only one woman before, while caressing her cascading hair, blowing in the gentle wind. There were no words between them, just a connection and desire. Suddenly, Wyatt's red phone buzzed, breaking the romantic silence.

"Hospital?"

"Yeah, gotta take it. Sorry."

"I thought you weren't on call?"

It kept buzzing, and both tried to ignore it. "I'm not, but sometimes my colleagues call me for advice at crazy hours."

"That's for sure."

"Would you excuse me, Gentri? I need to take this call."

"I'm not going anywhere, sweetheart."

Wyatt walked back inside to the empty private chef's area and took the call.

"Yeah."

"Twenty-nine."

"Go, Twenty-nine," said Wyatt

"Code Black, 2100."

Wyatt clicked off, quickly went to Gentri, picked her up, kissed her passionately one more time then said, "I must go and I don't know when I'll be back."

"What? Emergency?"

"Yep."

He took her hand, escorted her to her car, kissed her again, with some extra lingering, then said, "Be safe, sweet Gentri. I promise I'll come back to take you here again someday. Don't worry. We'll be back. I promise."

CHAPTER 12

They brought him to the secure briefing room—the place he never wanted or expected to see again. He felt the chills when he remembered last time and what happened but took a deep breath and tossed those thoughts into the polar coldness of his temporary brain lockdown vault. But Palmer was there, and he loved him as a colleague and friend, so he figured he at least had that going for him. Those nightmares that invaded his daytime psyche were better controlled now, and he knew he could handle what he was about to hear. After all, what could be worse than before?

Wyatt sat down next to Palmer in the barren room with two steel chairs facing each other opposite the plastic-topped table with collapsible metal legs for easy transport. On the far table sat five large pizza boxes labeled "Cellini's Pizza," and the amazing smell invaded the entire chamber. The building had no windows, and plain-clothed security guards were stationed around it.

"Wyatt, glad you could come. We missed you."

"Who wouldn't, Tommie? Oh, and it seems there are only three of you guys, but you must love pizza since there are five boxes there. Never had Cellini's before, but looks like you guys are huge fans."

Palmer displayed a half grin, not displaying any teeth, then erased it just as easily as it came, continuing without comment. "Intel found some high-value targets we've been looking for—key players in the FFWP. We've got about a ninety-six-hour window for a black SOF operation.

"So, they call themselves the FFWP now? What the hell does that acronym mean?"

"It now means Foundation for World Purification. Others say Fighters for World—"

"You mean, same old shit: killing us 'infidels' and establishing their world caliphate no matter what the cost?" said Wyatt. "Too bad the peaceful and law-abiding followers of Islam can't control these violent extremists. So instead, we must."

Palmer continued unphased. "Our president doesn't like to commit human resources unless there's minimal chance of civilian casualties, minimal ground troops, and maximal political gain for him. It's been quiet for a while, but they seem to be trying to make a comeback of sorts since they're not getting as much attention as the Chinese, it seems. But our intel indicates that, strange as it seems, the Chinese Communist Party and the FFWP may have become odd bed fellows, and we think the Chinese may be funding at least some of the new FFWP operations, while the Chinese infiltrate us from within the backbone of our society and gain the most attention as a smokescreen. This intelligence isn't fully verified though. As you know, we defeated these terrorists before when they tried to dominate the world with their violence and terror, and we destroyed their caliphate under previous leadership. But our new POTUS seems to think that these dicks will go away forever if we kill a few of their leaders—pick 'em off but avoid an all-out siege. So, he calls the best Black Ops and is willing to sacrifice us instead when these hotspots pop up."

"Yes, of course, my friend. We serve willingly at the request of the Commander in Chief," said Wyatt. "However, I think you must've forgotten that I retired and don't do this kind of stuff anymore. I'm a law-abiding, church-going civilian surgeon now. Life is good. I get to save lives while receiving a paycheck, not to mention vacations and occasional respect, all of which occur without anyone shooting at me with an AK-47. Don't get me wrong, Tommie, it's always nice to see you, but I've got to go now. You know, things to do, lives to save, pretty girls to kiss, and … other soft, fluffy things like that that I've missed over the years."

Palmer glanced at the burly guard at the door, who smirked and then looked away. "We need you, Wyatt. We need you to lead the SOST (Special Ops Surgical Team). Your team will be damn close to the operators within helicopter reach. We need a trauma surgeon and staff who can fight as well as treat casualties at a level-two casualty collecting point, then medevac ASAP if needed to a level-three facility. It will be a small staff, though, as you're aware: two surgeons, one anesthesiologist, two critical care RNs, and two 18D combat medics with security support by the loggies."

"You really love the taste of that agency Kool-Aid, don't you, Tommie?"

"What?"

"Got a nice promotion, huh?"

"Yeah, deputy director of operations."

"How are the wife and kids?" said Wyatt. "She still let you go to Vegas or Reno and bet on whatever you can get your hands on? My guess is she doesn't know anything about it, does she?"

"Family's okay. Kids are starting college next year but none of your business on that gambling stuff. That's my problem, and I've got it under control, Wyatt, but thanks for asking about the family and bringing up that other stuff. Now you need to—"

"I'll have to say no thanks to this job, Tommie. Thanks for asking as well. The reality is I have a job now, and I can't just up and leave without notice, because the hospital and patients depend on me."

"It's only going to be two weeks out of your luxurious civilian life, Wyatt—probably less. Who knows? But do you think we haven't thought of your position and how to smooth this out without making waves? The agency has already brought in one of our surgeons who will take your place. We've credentialed him with the Mercy Hospital system and taken care of the finances—and we've created a cover story for you. Nothing for you to worry about, Wyatt, in that regard. We have the hospital covered in your absence, starting day one. They know you're in the Army Reserves and that you've been called away on an emergency humanitarian medical mission overseas. We've already got our public relations office meeting with the Mercy Hospital administration tomorrow, and we'll have your replacement surgeon there as well. They probably won't even miss you—or maybe they'll have a little less drama without you there. Oh, and by the way we've been watching you out there."

"You think I wouldn't notice? If you made it any more obvious, you'd think I was performing in front of a live audience at Carnegie Hall. Where'd you get those guys anyway? Retired operators don't need that kind of work, I hope," said Wyatt.

"Whatever. You know we've been through a lot together when I was a Black Ops commander and you were an operator, but I know the truth: You always liked to fight rather than be a spook. You're like a little brother to me, but I know you're struggling to acclimate to life as a civilian surgeon, aren't you? You think I don't know about the flashbacks and your problems at the hospital? If you think the civilian administrators are watching you, then so are we, but remember, we have your back, Wyatt. We want what's best for one of our own, our brother, and if they come down on you for some reason for your performance, we can make those problems go away fairly easily."

"Looks like you're the one trying to send me away."

"C'mon, brother. One last mission. Your country needs you."

Wyatt remained silent while he thought about his options. The last sentence struck him, and he was trying his best to form his final response correctly. "You know I love my country and you're like a brother to me, Tommie. You also know I trust no one unless I know they'll fight with me and die with me in a fight with the enemy. But I figure you probably personally picked me and recommended me to your higher-ups to take the old man against his better wishes."

"Yep. I had no choice. You're the best for this."

"That's why I like you, Tommie, and yes, I'm going, and I'll do anything my country asks me to do if I still have the skill."

"I know."

"Anybody going I might know?"

"No. Some swoopy dudes and SOAR."

"Speaking of SOAR," said Wyatt. "Back in the day, you may not know this, but they checked me out in the MH-6 little bird, and I kept her flying and didn't crash, but they never let me shoot anything out of those rocket pods."

"Thank God," said Palmer.

"Imagine my chagrin."

Wyatt walked out and grabbed a piece of Cellini's pizza from the box on the table for the road.

CHAPTER 13

t was finally decided by both parties that the meeting should be held under the highest security at the Ministry of State Security, People's Liberation Army (PLA), in Beijing. The original site was going to be in Syria, per the request of the now-mobile caliphate. However, this was felt to be too dangerous due to the presence of US Special Operations forces gathering intelligence in the area.

The caliphate had been essentially destroyed during successful US military operations in Syria and Iraq. After the previous leader of the caliphate was killed by US special operations, the new caliph adopted even more secrecy and became constantly mobile, remaining in one place no longer than forty-eight hours at a time. Recent surprising events, however, allowed a stronger resurgence in Afghanistan.

On the other side, the Chinese were able to make contact with the new caliph through local intermediaries and after nearly a year of careful planning, this highly unusual meeting took place between the apparent new caliph, Abul Hasan al-Nasseri, and the CCP's Minister of State Security, Wei Zheng.

The Ministry of State Security successfully removed any chance that the two men could be recognized or located in the underground bunkers of the ministry. After all, the ministry was super-secret, and little was known about it worldwide, although most international intelligence organizations assumed it was responsible for all intelligence gathering for the CCP and People's Liberation Army, including espionage, cyber warfare using the cyber militia and hacker militias, counter intelligence, the social media disinformation campaign, and propaganda war room, as well as command of space war technologies and planning. Clearly, this was a perfect place for such a once-in-a-century meeting.

After the security teams of both parties were in place inside and outside the electronics-impermeable underground planning room, the two men introduced themselves and sat down at the table facing each other—a glass of water before each of them, along with a notebook and pen. No electronics of any kind were allowed in.

Zheng was the first to speak. "Thank you for making the long journey to meet here. I know this was a difficult process. Hopefully, despite our historic and sometimes less-than-cordial relationship in the past, we can put this aside to accomplish the common good for both of our countries or organizations, as the case may be."

"You're welcome, Minster Zheng," said Abul. "We don't have much time as you know, so let's go ahead with the discussion and hopefully we can make some mutual progress that can be quickly implemented for the goal we both know must be accomplished.

"Let us now define our common goal, and that is the destruction of the United States. Although the US is a powerful country—financially, industrially, and militarily—both of us know its strength has eroded over the past thirty to forty years. Its chief concerns now are political correctness, the destruction of real or created racism, woke indoctrination, and the weakening of the political will to fight for its freedom. Thus, Americans may be unwittingly allowing themselves to be overcome by the dominance of the CCP. Do you agree with this brief assessment, Abul?"

"Agreed, but our approaches over the years have been quite different from yours, Minister Zheng. We have observed that the CCP and PLA have planned for years how to overcome America's technological superiority by stealing military and industrial secrets and billions in intellectual property rights from under their large Jewish noses and convincing them to establish economic ties with your huge country, thinking this is the proper way to bring your country into the world economy. Their businesses and financial institutions think that receiving huge economic benefits from your country is more important than maintaining the interests of their own country. This demonstrates their huge and naïve weakness, as we see it. So, they put their heads in the sand to be politically correct out of their fear of being labeled Xenophobic against your huge country, while all the while allowing you to defeat them as you planned, oftentimes from within their own country of sin. And at the same time, they've become smug and complacent after successfully destroying our sacred caliphate in Syria, assuming they have rid the world of our righteous war against the great Satan. They are very wrong to think we are gone. But our techniques are more violent because we believe violence is a better way to intimidate and destroy the nonbelievers. The Kafirs will and do succumb to the will of our righteous FFWP under threat of death and annihilation."

"Well," said Zheng. "We do agree on some things, but our techniques are much different, as you say, and I need to explain further, for your benefit. We believe that we don't have to kill them directly. You may or may not know that it has been very easy for us to hack their universities, financial institutions, and defense firms and pay their governmental employees off handsomely for the betrayal of secrets. That's how we've built the world's greatest navy, offensive and deep-space missiles, space force, and cyber security—all to kill them with the technology they developed themselves. That's also why we send 370,000 of our students to US universities every year. Everyone knows our students are much better than theirs, and that will solidify our future. Our students who study in the US steal secrets and hide behind Confucius Institutes on their clueless campuses, and we use our diplomatic core as much as we can to corrupt their weak politicians with money and oftentimes sexy girls who are top spies. Sometimes, our leadership laughs, because their weak silliness is doing our work for us, and we smile gratefully for this gift. But I wonder, since we have this common goal of their destruction, how can we work together, Abul?

"I'm not sure yet, how it is possible, from what I have heard from you, but please go on, and tell me more about your plans, if you can," replied Abul.

"Our goal is a long-term one, that started as a thirty-to-fifty-year plan on multiple fronts. You don't need more details from me."

"Well, Zheng, we think differently—not just about race but about the one true religion: Islam. Many races practice Islam. Many millions practice our religion peacefully and honorably, but they need us courageous zealots to convert the world. All you say is interesting, but although yours is an ancient culture, so is ours. You have cared over the last fifty years or so about world hegemony alone. But where is your God and who drives your soul? It seems all you care about is money, power, and world domination. Yes, you have Buddhists, Taoists, and Christians in your country, but it's the Muslims whom you persecute the most. We'll talk about the Uyghurs a little later."

"Your tongue is nasty, Abul. But I must ask, how do you judge us with our ways while you kill in the name of your God? What is so wrong with how we do things compared to your killing?"

"Your lust for power leads you, but your souls will be lost without the one true God on your side," said Abul.

"Don't lecture me, Abul. Your little secret terrorism movement kills in the name of your God. Does that give you the higher ground? Most of the followers of your religion are peaceful and don't agree with your violence at all," said Zheng.

Abul's face reddened. "I will *not* hear more of this filth. You need to stop wasting time with insults and tell me exactly what you want from me and the FFWP."

"We will provide electronic as well as ground intelligence using our vast network of spies and college students in the US. We will also provide support with indoctrination and propaganda for consumption by the naïve and gullible American people. Also included is technological support as well as the ability to hack into US governmental computers to assist you. But we'll remain clean, and our hands will not be soiled with American blood. *That* is what we need the FFWP to do since that's what you terrorist extremists are best at."

"Our cause is just, Xheng—this is true. And we will gladly spill blood to advance our cause. However, you must do something for us first, Xheng, in order to receive this gift from us."

"What can that be?"

"The first is that you must release all the Muslim Uyghurs from your prison slavery camps forever and you must stop persecuting people of the one true religion in your vast country. And finally, you must leave all operational control of our sleeper cell terrorist operations to the FFWP. You will simply provide support, mostly financially and technically, for our operations when we ask for it. Whatever else you do in your country is meaningless to us."

"This will not happen," said Xheng

"My dog," replied Abul, "produces excrement that smells better than your words."

With that statement, Abul rose up from his seat across from Xheng, summoned the guards, and asked to be removed from the bunker room. As he walked down the lengthy corridor with his security team, Xheng sent his man after Abul, stopping him about 100 meters away, and requested that he return for further discussion.

Abdul smiled at the Chinese guard when he met him, knowing that now, the FFWP would receive what was requested, and he slowly walked back into the room and found Xheng still seated, with a face that was as cold as raw granite.

"Is there something you forgot to tell me, Xheng?"

Xheng stared at him and said, "You will have all that you requested. But I must ask you, what is your plan, and who will be heading your operation in the US?"

"Thank you for your cooperation. Minister Xheng. We will be pleased to collaborate with you. Basically, what I can tell you is that our plan will be devastating to the Great Satan on multiple fronts and cannot be discussed here, but trust me: you will be impressed with the results."

"I will ask you again," said Xheng, "who is leading the US operation?"

"All you need to know is that we have highly trained, special contacts already embedded in the United States.

The two shook hands and the clandestine meeting was over.

CHAPTER 14

With his temporary replacement in place at Mercy Hospital, arranged by Palmer's agency support staff, Wyatt began his new military mission. Wyatt received only piecemeal information about the mission that the operators were tasked to accomplish, but after being whisked high into the Rocky Mountains to a brief practice–rehearsal area, he deduced they were likely heading to the devil's favorite hiding areas: the rugged mountains of the Hindu Kush, probably somewhere near the Pakistan-Afghanistan border. He'd been there before and it was a shitshow then. Obviously, since he spoke fluent Pashtun, he figured this played a role in his selection for the mission. There were plenty of other good trauma surgeons to choose from who could shoulder a weapon when needed, but he knew Palmer had to have pushed hard for his friend. However, Wyatt knew if Palmer needed him, there must be a damn good reason for it, and of course, he would go.

Wyatt quickly took charge of setting up the ATLS (Advanced Trauma Life Support) and operating tent, working with nurses, OR techs, 18D medics, and the other docs. They rehearsed simulated casualty scenarios while the SOAR Black Hawk MH-60s and MH-6 gunships practiced the mission with operators a few close miles away. He was thankful JSOC had agreed to give him a second surgeon—an orthopod—to complete the medical team. Wyatt emphasized speed and attention to detail in the setup, working with minimal staff and supplies while maximizing surgical stabilization with DCS (Damage Control Surgery)—control of bleeding while avoiding infection. He emphasized that time was a valuable but rare commodity when the team practiced the type of surgery that involved abbreviated surgical time. This required control of hemorrhage, ligation and shunting without definitive repairs. If a gunshot injury or blast injury perforated the bowel, that bowel segment would be repaired, not reconnected. Orthopedic injuries would be treated with external fixation through small incisions rather than plate and screw or intramedullary fixation. The team became keenly aware that for patients who needed it, they would be flown to a level-three combat facility for more advanced interventions, CT scans, MRIs, and advanced intensive care units, then to level-four care at Landstuhl Regional Medical Center in Germany if needed.

After only thirty-six hours in the rehearsal area, the teams boarded the MC–130s for the voyage to the theater to execute the mission. On the plane, the teams received a briefing and became fully aware that they were on their way to the Pakistan-Afghanistan border in the Northwest Frontier to support the operators who were tasked to kill high-value targets while capturing sensitive intelligence information.

They arrived in the staging area at the foothills of the steep mountain terrace, received their final briefing, then landed at the Forward Air Refueling Point (FARP) briefly, then boarded MH-60 Blackhawks to set up the Forward Staging Base that was within two hours of the Final Staging Area—SOST—via chopper. Drones constantly monitored the area, feeding continuous information to the Special Ops commander regarding the high-value targets while the operators were at a black location. After sixteen hours of preparation at the Forward Staging Base, the medical team left for the final staging area.

Perimeter security was in place at the compound, including razor wire, and the medical team immediately set up the operating tent with two operating tables. Wyatt always carried his Sig Sauer 9-mm sidearm and his M-4 rifle over his shoulder, although when operating, he would put his M-4 down but not far from easy reach. He hated being separated from his most lethal weapon. After less than an hour, they were ready for surgery, hoping for no casualties.

Major Blane was the orthopod, and Wyatt knew this wasn't his first Special Ops mission as a surgeon, but he took him under his wings anyway and talked to him to make sure he was as calm as possible under these tense circumstances.

"Blane, I know this isn't Johns Hopkins and the nearest Starbucks is 3000 miles away, but it's all we've got right now.

"Roger that, Chief."

"You have flapping butterflies down below in that gut?" asked Wyatt.

"Nah," said Blane. "But my heart is racing a bit—you know, the un-known."

"If you didn't have butterflies, then I would say you were a robot. Anyway, it's normal, but never show your fear or anxiety to those below you, okay? They look up to you, man."

"You get butterflies anymore Wyatt?"

"Not a chance. I get steely marbles."

Phil Carroll, the anesthesiologist, appeared calm and at ease while he cleaned his rifle. He looked at Wyatt and Blane. "Piece of cake, my friends, but plain with no frosting it seems."

Wyatt walked around making sure the nurses and medics were prepared and understood their roles—Julie and Karen, RNs; and the two 18Ds, Bryan and Kent. Then, he gave them a quick pep talk.

"America is a great country, built on many freedoms, and we're here in this nasty place to support our guys in case they're hurt killing these assholes who want to destroy us and our way of life. You people are my team and I'm damn proud of you. Let's do it!"

"Hooah!" they cheered in unison, and then a couple of minutes later, they heard the radio message that there were incoming wounded—an abdominal gunshot and a leg wound. Uneasiness invaded Wyatt's belly, the steely marbles expanded immediately to softballs, and the visions roared back. Maybe it was the familiar sounds of the Blackhawk rotors. He tried to tune them out, but then, he heard what he never wanted to hear again: Heavy weapons fire and explosions.

"Hit the deck and stay down, everyone!" said Wyatt.

He grabbed his M-4, loaded the magazine, and ran for the far tent opening while everyone remained down on the deck. But then, he noticed Blane standing on the other end, frozen, right before several rounds exploded his head, essentially decapitating him. His body hit the floor with a thud while blood sprayed the previously sterile operating suite. Wyatt took a deep breath, told everyone to stay down, and he ran out the door while grabbing a grenade belt, and night vision goggles. All the while, his M-4 remained fixed in the shooting position. Clearly, the mission was compromised, and the Forward Staging Base was under attack at the very moment incoming wounded operators were speeding their way. His Ranger training engaged with lightning speed with muscle memory intact. He scanned the perimeter and saw immediately that the perimeter was completely breached and the guards were already taken out. The other unit at the base was on fire and the fuel tanks exploded, illuminating the entire scene that was previously blanketed in pitch blackness. He knew there were no other teammates to help him. They were now alone, and the operators remained engaged with their mission with casualties on their way. He saw the enemy with 50-caliber weapons mounted on a truck outside the perimeter, then rolled to the ground and found cover behind some sandbags, proceeding to shoot and kill the two bearded operators of the 50-caliber gun and fire rounds into the chests of three others as they ran directly to the now-vulnerable operating tent. He then located two trucks speeding down to the compound in single file, and that was lucky for him because they'd be easier to take out if they were so close to each other, and he figured both contained Vehicular Borne Improvised Explosive Devices (VBIEDs). He threw his grenade, a direct hit on the first truck, exploding it in a fireball, then concentrated on the driver of the second vehicle who swerved away from the inferno, stalled the clutch, and the engine stuttered, then started up again while Wyatt briefly looked up and spied a drone overhead. *The drone is smaller than ours*, he thought, *yet fast and quiet.* what's more, he could see the IR strobe interrogating for passive receivers on clothing and helmets, guiding what must have been a rocket launcher.

Damn. That's how the bastards found us. Advanced drone technology. Where did they get this?

Wyatt ran directly to the briefly stalled truck, and was close enough to see the driver was a young white man, with wide green eyes and distinctively blond hair, and shot him in the forehead, spattering blood onto the windshield. The driverless truck kept advancing, probably because the man's foot was still pressed on the accelerator, stopping and starting, driving in circles, weaving around uncontrollably. While running after the uncontrolled truck, Wyatt transmitted a radio message on his right shoulder transmitter: "We've been compromised! Abort!" He then jumped into the runaway truck headed for his comrades in the operating tent, yanked the wheel away from the dead bearded blond man's body, and turned the vehicle away from the operating tent and toward the trees, jumping out and rolling several times before the vehicle and it's VBIED detonated, well off to the side of the operating suite with a concussive explosion and fireball that left the suite intact.

Wyatt lay unconscious on the ground, bleeding from his chest and face while the medevac Blackhawks aborted, pulling away from the compromised FSB, per Wyatt's radio warning, and flying to the designated FARP to refuel before heading to the level-three facility with their wounded operators. The drone continued to circle the bloody and burning scene, IR strobes continuously interrogating what was left of the base, streaming video, and gathering data for the consumption of their controllers back at the enemy base.

Wyatt found himself at peace, and his pain vanished. He figured he was dead because he felt himself floating above his lifeless body. It was so beautiful—the celestial music, radiant flowers with vibrant colors he had never imagined (not just reds and blues and greens but colors that he had no words to describe)—while he gently floated above the compound and the earthly horror below. He saw nurse Julie on the floor with Bryan and Phil applying a tourniquet to her leg, and thankfully she was alive.

She screamed, "Go find Barton! He's out there alone! I'll be okay!"

He saw Karen and Kent working on his bloody body, doing CPR on his chest. He saw the panic in their eyes while working so hard on his lifeless body. The sweat dripped down from their own hard-working bodies during the CPR, onto his chest and his face, but he felt nothing. Karen said, "Don't leave us! Come back! Beacoup dinky dau, Wyatt."

He wanted to talk to them, to say it was okay, give them calm, but they couldn't hear him, not matter how hard he tried to communicate with them.

He smiled when he heard her say *beaucoup dinky dau*, the phrase only he used but Karen had now placed in her vocabulary. *Such amazing people*, he thought. He was now at peace, and he realized he was being pulled gently but swiftly into a dark cave-like structure or tube, being pushed at lightning speed toward a pinpoint of bright light, but the light wasn't blinding; it was showing unconditional love and acceptance despite its radiance. He saw his childhood friends who had passed, his lieutenant who was killed when he was a Ranger, and his deceased mother, still wearing her white wedding dress, smiling, and looking about twenty years old. He looked at her, and her smile was nothing but love. Her lips didn't move, but they seemed to be clearly communicating with telepathy.

"Wyatt, my son, you can't stay here. You must go back. You are not ready."

The beauty was overwhelming, filled with colors and figures of light that he believed were souls, singing to him without language, but immersing him in perfect peace, and the feeling was as if he was everywhere at the same time, and there was no time or place, and it seemed he had access to a pure knowledge he could never perceive in his earthly life. He communicated back to her without words, "But I don't want to go back, mom. There is so much peace and love with no pain."

"There is more that you must do, my son. The light of love will explain these things you must know."

With that, she vanished, and although he wanted to speak to her more, with this telepathy of souls he now understood, he knew she wouldn't come back to him. He now understood what the love of light was. It was Heaven, and he was being sent to meet God. Then, as if on cue from his mother, the light enveloped him completely—a bright but soft light that seemed to almost hold him like a tiny chick in a massive but gentle hand, the size of three railroad cars, but he couldn't see the arm that he thought should be connected to it. The light, he knew, must be God, and it seemed that he was communicating with Him through transmitted thoughts and telepathy. No spoken words were necessary, just communication between souls, without effort. Without warning, he then watched the movie God played for him, including all the scenes of his life, from birth until the moment he left his body. It was nonjudgmental, instead playing the good things he had done, the people he had helped—doing first aid on Bryan, his friend, when an ax he was using in Boy Scouts to chop wood found his leg; putting pressure on the wound, calming him, and calling for help. The patients he had saved and the families he'd consoled. He was waiting for the parts where he had failed God and sinned. That would be a bad movie, but he knew it was coming. Thankfully, though, it didn't.

Instead, the movie stopped playing, and he realized he was being taught that God was love and that he was on Earth to make a difference for other people and to give the love back unselfishly. He felt the message given to him from the light: *Nothing matters but love, Wyatt. Go into the world and do great things with your blessings. Protect those who need protection, and help those who need help. But you must not kill anymore, and if you obey these words, then you will receive a special gift from the light of love.*

Wyatt couldn't help himself and wondered what the gift was. Was it the gift of eternal love and life in Heaven? Or some other gift? With telepathy, he asked the light of love still holding him in his giant hand.

My son, you will know at the right time what your gift is, but you must show that you understand what is required of you.

And with that, Wyatt was released, tumbling back down and swirling into himself at a great speed, returning to his body, which was now in incredible pain.

CHAPTER 15

Wyatt found himself in his broken body once again, and the pain surged back like a roaring locomotive. His head felt as if it was slowly exploding, and he reached up and touched the bandages to make sure his head was still on, while an anvil was bearing down on his chest that had two chest tubes, sticking out, one on each side, draining blood from each chest cavity into two collection chambers on the floor by his bed. The critical care physician had ordered his sedation stopped, and the respiratory therapist had just removed the breathing tube from his trachea, which had been connected just minutes before to a ventilator machine that was giving him life-saving breaths.

He stared calmly at the angel wearing scrubs standing by his right side, holding his hand. "My name is Rhonda, and I'm your day shift nurse today and every day while you're here. You were in a coma for twelve hours, and you just woke up. We're so excited for you! You're going to be just fine."

He smiled at her and then said, "Yes, everything is okay, Rhonda, and remember, nothing matters but love."

Stunned by this powerful and spontaneous statement, uttered by a severely injured patient several minutes after sedation stopped and a breathing tube was removed from his trachea, Rhonda sat down for a minute to gather her thoughts while tears formed in her eyes. No patient ever talked like this under these circumstances. They were usually confused and unable to cogently speak or communicate for a while—sometimes hours or more, and that is why these words struck her deeply in her soul.

"Where are we, Rhonda?"

"You're in Landstuhl, Germany, at the Landstuhl Regional Medical Center."

"I'm late for my case, Rhonda. There are incoming wounded, and they need me, damn it. I must go!"

He started to get out of bed, then fell back down from the pain from the chest tubes pulling on the stitches holding them to his skin.

"No, you're not operating today, and all is taken care of. You were in a coma for twelve hours and suddenly you woke up! We just took out your breathing tube a few minutes ago and I'm surprised you're so awake."

Rhonda got up when Dr. Craig, chief of critical care, walked in.

"I see Rhonda is taking care of you quite well 241! I'm Dr. Craig, chief of critical care here at Landstuhl." He shook Wyatt's hand.

"Thanks, Doc, and you, Rhonda, as well, for taking care of me. But can someone please explain everything that happened to me? And what about my team?" said Wyatt. "Where is my team?"

"I see you're beginning to recall some events, and that's good news. I'm going to fill you in on everything, but before I do that, I would like to introduce you to Fifty-one, your chaperone.

In the corner of the room was a man with a trimmed black beard. He was wearing a baseball cap partially covering his eyes and an FDNY T-shirt that could essentially function as an upper body muscular anatomy textbook diagram that probably could be used to teach medical students upper body and chest anatomy, rather than the old Netter drawings. "Nice to meet you, sir," said Fifty-one.

"You're my new shadow man," said Wyatt. "I know why you're here. You're just doing your job, making sure I don't compromise the mission details, as always."

Fifty-one just nodded his head, providing no verbal response.

"Okay, well, time for me to chime in, gentleman," said Dr. Craig. "You were injured in the theater of operations and suffered bilateral pneumothoraces (lung punctures) with bleeding into the chest cavity, mostly on the right side, from penetrating bomb fragments. You were medevacked to the level-three combat support hospital on life support, where they placed chest tubes to drain the air and blood and, as you can see, they are still in place. We had to clean out the shrapnel wounds in your legs and knees, and you required some blood transfusions as well. And, I must mention that the medics did some CPR on you but not for long, only slightly less than two minutes, and thankfully they got you back quickly. And finally, you suffered a head injury when you—"

"That's enough, Dr. Craig. We can fill in the details later for him if and when needed, ourselves," said the shadow man in the corner of the room.

Wyatt looked at Fifty-one and studied him a little, knowing that he was doing his job, and then he had momentary images of a man similar to Fifty-one at the Broadmoor Hotel and a pretty woman by his side. Gentri. Yes, lovely Gentri. But he turned away quickly, due to the headache temporarily blurring his vision while he squinted to see who was talking.

Dr. Craig continued: "You suffered a concussive injury to the brain, and this is actually a mild traumatic brain injury. Thankfully the MRI showed no evidence of bleeding, and you didn't require a burr hole or craniotomy."

"Why does everyone have to yell so loud at me here?" asked Wyatt.

"We're not yelling sir," said Rhonda.

"My ears are ringing but mostly on the right, it seems. Must be another souvenir from this adventure, right Doctor Craig?"

"Right. You've got post-concussive syndrome and apparently tinnitus as well, which may certainly be permanent, unfortunately. The frequency of our voices is accentuated, now and you think we're loud when we're talking in soft voices. Down the road, if this continues to be a problem, we can get you hearing—"

"I won't need hearing aids, Doc. Let's not talk about that now."

"And one more thing," said Craig. "Captain Blane was killed. You need to know this. And nurse Julie was shot in the leg and eventually had to have it amputated, but she's doing just fine. We didn't know if you knew all this."

"I saw Blane get hit right when we were attacked, then yes, I saw that Julie would be all right, but I'm not surprised she lost her leg."

"No need to give any more information, 241," said the shadow man.

"And yes, I remember Julie. I was looking at her in the tent when they were working on her, and they were taking care of her. I was proud of them, how they stopped the bleeding and saved her," said Wyatt. "I want to tell Julie that I never left her, and they found me as she asked, and I was never alone. And Karen, I want to thank her for saying *beaucoup dinky dau*. I was proud to hear her words. You see, I never really left them."

Rhonda and Dr. Craig stared at each other, dumbfounded, unaware of any of the events that happened over there, or who was doing what at the time. They didn't care either, but how did this hero see and hear all of this if he was severely wounded and unconscious, receiving CPR? And who was he talking to? That information would never be given to them in their careers. They were there to treat the wounded man's injuries. But they knew he'd required CPR and was unconscious, so how could it be remotely possible for Wyatt to have observed anything happening in the tent if he was undergoing lifesaving CPR at the time and, in fact, lying in the dirt outside?

"I saw it all," said Wyatt. "I watched them do CPR on me, and they saved me. But I still want to get back to my procedures. They're waiting for me, and I need to make sure my team is safe."

"But Dr. Barton," said Rhonda. "How were you able to—"

The shadow man in the corner glared at Rhonda, and she took a step back from Wyatt's bed when she saw the man's eyes. "That's enough with the questions," he said. "He needs to rest now, and tomorrow will be a big day of rehabilitation."

Dr. Craig and Rhonda made eye contact and shook their heads. They knew there was no way he could have seen any of this from his position, and the head injury had clearly clouded his memory and also may have caused him to confabulate a little about the whole horrible situation he experienced. And yet, it seemed he knew the factual details perfectly.

After they left, Wyatt lay there in the ICU bed wide awake, looking at the clock, not knowing if it was 5 a.m. or 5 p.m. because it was dark when he looked out the window. He remembered the cold stare of the man in the truck, and they were green eyes, surprisingly, and his blond hair was certainly unusual for this enemy. He remembered Captain Blane and figured he was in sweet paradise now. The paradise that Wyatt himself tasted and enjoyed, ever so briefly, though his entrance was rejected this time. He was conflicted, though, about whether he wanted to stay here or go back to that wonderful place of love that was so peaceful and perfect.

The Special Ops debriefers filled him in on the other team members, and all survived, but only because of Wyatt's heroic actions. The mission was a success, and all operators survived, despite the compromise. He stayed at Landstuhl for another week, receiving physical therapy as well as neurocognitive rehab, which included memory training as well as logic tests and neuroplasticity puzzles.

He was flown back to the states with his rehab nearly complete. He'd saved the lives of two nurses, two medics, and an anesthesiologist while single-handedly killing the entire invading force that attacked the SOST. But they lost Blane, and as always Wyatt wondered how he could've prevented his death. He couldn't have. He told him to hit the deck, but he froze, and that was it. Thankfully, though, Julie survived. He knew he saw her clearly, even though he wasn't in the tent, but he had no explanation for how he obtained this knowledge.

He remembered what the loving light told him: *Nothing matters but love, Wyatt. Go into the world and do great things with your blessings. Protect those who need protection, and help those who need help. But you must not kill anymore, and if you obey these words, then you will receive a special gift from the light of love.*

CHAPTER 16

She remembered his instructions on the phone—four bedrooms, three-car garage, quiet area without much surrounding traffic, preferably in the Cherry Creek or Highlands Ranch Area, price range one to 1.5 million dollars, cash. And he said he was single. That voice, deep and commanding, infused with intelligence, was calming to her, but at the same time, it gave her a nervous yet tingly feeling.

Gentri still heard that voice playing over and over in her mind while she waited at the first house on her showing list, almost like a song she couldn't get off her mind no matter how she tried to suppress it. He arrived, as he said he would, right on time, parking right behind her on the street in front of the house in his black Jaguar. She got out and found her heart skipping a beat when he introduced himself.

"Hello, Gentri, I'm Erik Jorgensen. So nice of you to meet me today."

What a gentleman, she thought. And those blue eyes matched with a disarming smile neatly filled with sparkling ivories and a cute dimple caused her to want to run her index finger over the bump on his manly chin. *Stop it, Gentri. He's a client! What's wrong with you? Just because you have a thing for tall Nordic blonds who happen to be charming and successful gentlemen and you haven't had sex in an eternity doesn't mean now is the time to lose your freakin' Southern mind.*

"Gentri. Glad to meet you as well."

She held out her dainty hand, and he held it gently but respectfully, then kissed it. She didn't expect that. It jolted her memory immediately to Wyatt, and how he'd been the first one to kiss her hand. Now a *second* hand-kisser! What were the odds? She hoped that she wouldn't blush—and that her legs would stay sturdy underneath her. "I've got a list of five homes to show you today, if you like, depending on how many you want to see and your time availability."

"Lead me, Gentri, and I will gladly follow."

They walked through three homes of the five, reviewing the features, taxes, and nearby schools, although she knew he was single and apparently without children. Maybe he would start a family someday, He looked to be in his upper thirties or so. She couldn't ask, but he said it anyway, as if reading her curious mind.

"I'm forty-one, Gentri, and I don't need to know about schools at this time. I'm single, but if I ever do start a family, I'll send my kids to the best private schools available."

The third house was in Cherry Creek and seemed to be the most interesting to Erik. It was private on a quiet street with plenty of tree cover on all sides but not obtrusive or gaudy.

"I'll buy this one."

"Pardon me?" She certainly hadn't expected a sale offer so quickly after a brief walk-through.

"I said I'll pay cash for this one. You said they're asking 1.1 million. That sounds like a reasonable price. I'll need to close in one month if possible, and I figure you will make that possible. I hope that will be acceptable for you and the sellers."

"Acceptable? Are you kidding? Of course. Mr. Jorgensen I'll—"

"Call me Erik."

"Okay, Erik, I'll draw up the sales proposal and notify the listing agent today."

She smiled, and this time, she figured her cheeks were growing closer to the color of her red lipstick, but who cared?

He handed her his card. "My personal cell phone number is on the back there, and that's the one I want you to use. No need to call my office anymore. The quickest way is to contact me directly. And by the way, after we close, I want to share a glass of wine with you while we enjoy a theater production downtown some evening, okay?"

Gentri took a step back and attempted to catch her breath from the flurry of excitement and aggressive invitations.

"Well, I am flattered, Erik, but you know, I have a rule about dating clients."

"Of course, but rules are made to be broken, and as you know, after we close on this house, I'll no longer be your active client, so you'll be free to enjoy my personal company, without any ethical dilemma. You'll see—and enjoy."

He smiled at her again and waved as he drove away.

Gentri thought, *He sure is cocky and a little too aggressive ... but damn cute, though. What did he mean by "You'll see?"* She looked in the visor mirror in her car, noticed her red cheeks, and felt the goose bumps still populating the skin on her inner thighs. *Damn easy sale. Wish they were all like that. Business is good.*

* * *

Alexandra was already at the bar when Gentri arrived, and when the two ladies wearing sexy night heels and tight skirts joined each other, the men couldn't help but look. They always did. So did the women, although they were usually looks of envy, sometimes jealousy if they weren't confident in themselves when watching the roving eyes of their dates sitting next to them.

"How's your love life, Gentri?"

"No love life, but I've certainly met some interesting men."

"Please tell. I need some juicy stories tonight."

"Okay, well, I met a handsome man today, during a house showing, and he asked me for a date to a play and some wine. I mean, he was aggressive, although certainly a gentleman, and I don't know what to do."

"What do you mean?"

"He's quite attractive and charming, but I don't date clients."

"So, I'm sure he won't be a client forever—I mean it's not like a permanent doctor-patient relationship and you have a chronic disease with ongoing scheduled office visits, right? Although I must admit, I dated my allergist, and it was kind of awkward initially, but then, we no longer had a doctor-patient relationship, so we thought it was okay, and girl, it was more than just okay. Problem was, he was married, and I soon found out his dirty little secret."

Gentri nearly choked on her dirty martini. "Well, I'm healthy and the only thing chronic about me is the lack of a good man. And yes, you raise a good point. The same point he tried to make. But there's something else—"

"Let me guess," said Alex. You're thinking about that mysterious surgeon you told me about who kissed you into a wet frenzy at the Broadmoor, then vanished with a steamy poof?"

"Yep, exactly. It all happened so quickly with Wyatt, and it seemed perfectly natural, like it was meant to be. Then, suddenly, he's gone somewhere. I don't know."

"Has he called you?"

"Nope. But he did say he promised he would be back someday, and I assume that meant he would take me back to the Broadmoor."

"Someday? Are you kidding? Well, maybe he's not worth it, Gentri. You're a great catch, and you're better than that. You can have any man you want, and a good man would call you, give you attention, and fight to keep you, no matter what."

"Guess you're right. That's what bothers me. We connected so well, and the attraction seemed perfectly natural and unforced, and damn—now he's gone."

"Forget him, dear. Maybe you need to give this soon-to-be ex-client a chance."

"Maybe. I don't know. There's just something about Wyatt that intrigues me, and I felt there was something important or mysterious he wanted to share with me, but for some reason, just couldn't tell me. It doesn't sound like him to just suddenly leave and not come back, but then, I must admit we don't know each other very well at this point."

"Yeah, right. You need to strike while the fire is hot, or the poker is warm or whatever that saying is, you know. But I think this Wyatt guy is probably in bed with some hot nurse somewhere right now. No, Gentri, you need to forget him and continue to live your life and grab your romantic opportunities when you can, girl!"

"Okay, counselor! You're right, I can't wait forever, but I *am* going to call the hospital to see if I can find out anything about him."

When Gentri arrived home, she put on her bathrobe and slippers, plopped into her easy chair, and resumed work on her novel:

Missionaries have needs too, and she wondered if in that far-off place, he still remembered her scent and soft lips, the sound of her feminine moan that begged for just a little more before he left . . ."

CHAPTER 17

The wrath of God will destroy this cowardly infidel by ripping his arms out of their sockets, then burn him alive while he watches me fuck his woman and explode my glorious seed inside her trembling wet womb!" said Abdul. "Then, her bastard son will become a warrior for our just and worthy cause. He killed my son, our noble warrior who now is rewarded in Heaven with the seventy-two virgins."

"Abdul, we will find his murderer for you so you can avenge your son's death yourself," said Farid, Abul's chief of security. All our resources in this godless land, as well as the homeland caliphate, will be at your disposal, and of course, Chairman Yi has pledged some intelligence support if we need it during our search."

"Yes, you will concentrate your efforts on this cause, then bring him to me alive no matter what the cost in warriors or money. Tell me, I know my drone was streaming images in real-time, during the operation. Do we have a physical description or image of this godless devil?"

"The pictures are grainy, obscured by smoke and dust, so we haven't been able to obtain much detail yet. Our cameras on this drone are effective, and I'm sure we'll get his face identified."

"Farid, this drone, although small, had a gimbal stabilized 360-degree camera with a 16x optical-zoom lens, capable of a maximum 1500-mm focal length. It has a superzoom that can map every pimple on your ass from a mile away. It's not as good as other military drones such as the Predator, Reaper, and Global Hawk, but it was effective for the size and mission it was designed for. It carried ECM (electronic counter measures), which can counter most of their Anti-UAV defenses by disabling the radio beam shot at it from the ground. Too bad this drone we sent was unarmed because we could've destroyed him right there as well as many of his other soldiers, but the only drone we have that's armed, so far, is a laser-mounted stealth drone reserved for glorious future missions. Tell me what you know, Farid."

"Sahib, I don't mean to say the technology we used is ineffective at all." He was carefully choosing his words, hesitating, with a tiny tremble in his voice, careful not to inflame his master's rage that was known to boil to explosive levels in an instant.

"We could see that he had a scraggly beard, with no respectable length at all, and the drone triangulated a height of about six feet two inches, but we couldn't get a good look at his face because he was rolling around in the dirt, firing at our men and running in and out of camera view. Clearly, this asshole could shoot as accurately as a sniper, firing from the ground and when running. Seems he was superbly well-trained, Sahib."

"You idiot. Of *course* he was a well-trained soldier. We attacked where we did because it seemed to be a soft target, and we were tipped off to their location by our local spies. It wasn't an entire loss though, because now we have created fear in their weak hearts that we can strike again at any time, even with drones. We lost my son, our best fighter, and his team, as well as our best bomb makers. Unfortunately, the infidels found our training base for bomb technology, and that is gone now. Anyway, it seems to me that whatever his job was on that location, he had some other kind of special training, as you say. I aim to find out what that training was, and who he is—that is, if he's still alive at this point," said Abdul. "I just don't think support personnel can fight like crazed dogs. And this man is not standard issue, as they say."

"Yes, he's a deadly white fucker, Abdul." Farid kept his head lowered after the comment, waiting for the explosion from his leader.

Yet, Abdul remained emotionless and didn't respond directly. "What is your next step, Farid?"

"I'm going to make our engineers work on zooming in on the images and clearing up the graininess with a cloud subtraction technique so we can get a shot at his godless face. Then, we're going to try to hack into the military database, with the help of Yi and his Beijing hacker force, since it's been done before, and find out what we can about highly trained medical people—perhaps with Special Ops backgrounds," said Farid.

"They protect this information heavily and it won't be easy."

"True. The Chinese and Russians are able to hack some governmental and commercial agencies, so we can gather some assets to do it, for the right price. That will be the Chinese, because the Russians charge us too much and the Chinese have made it clear that they want to work with us, it seems, for a common goal. I don't want those chinks to know too much, though, because they're tricky and slippery. But the human factor we can exploit. Especially politicians. In fact, history has taught us that some American politicians can be bought like kids with candy, and so can others deep in their massive governmental structure. It's what the enemy now refers to as the 'deep state.' Anyway, the behavior of some American politicians depends on whether re-election is their primary goal or just cash in the hand, preferably wired to the Caymans," said Farid.

"The homeland will support us with money, plenty of oil, and extortion money stolen for our cause, but here's what you must do: Find him and bring the lowlife shit to me," said Abdul.

When Farid left, Abdul found himself alone with his thoughts, and this time, he was easily able to switch his mind's images from killing to sex. It was easy for him to make this transition because he found the two to be similar in his experience. He knew and believed killing those who stood in the way of their previous fight to establish the ill-fated caliphate was just, and women existed simply to provide soft bodies for pleasure and to receive his valued seed—*helplessly*, as he thought he killed their souls by conquering them sexually for the good of the caliphate. He usually took the most attractive Syrian, Iraqi, and Yazidi slaves or refugees from their Middle East onslaught—those who were brought to him to impregnate. Some were single with no children; others were married; it didn't matter to him. He would take their sons; kill their husbands if they didn't convert to the one true religion; and give the women food, shelter, and money when needed to keep them silent. His power made him smile with confident satisfaction.

Every now and then, no matter how he tried to blot it out, an image of love and beloved parents would enter his mind but that word, *love* had a different meaning to him now, and it needed to be rejected for the cause. He remembered his parents, said they were in love, and he sometimes wondered what it was like to love a woman and feel her love in return. Was it possible to feel this without treating her like a pleasure vessel and a toy, purely existing for his pleasure and to bear his offspring?

He quickly erased those weak thoughts of love, as always, and a wide grin spread across his face. He now desired some beautiful American-born women to lure into his bed as soon as possible. His genes needed to be spread quickly throughout the United States. He'd thus sow the seeds of *destruction* from within this country filled with naïve tolerance and puerile open-mindedness. This land would be easily penetrated and destroyed because of its' culture, and of course, a wide-open border that welcomes us in.

CHAPTER 18

Dr. Franklin's voice boomed. "Plane crash in Zaire? Are you kidding me?"

"No, I'm not kidding, and that would be a horrible scenario to kid about. Why the hell would I kid about that? He must be okay because the physician recruiters who were so kind as to provide his temporary replacement said he'd be back seeing patients within three weeks or so," said the Mercy Hospital CEO Carl Patterson.

"What do you mean by *they*? I never heard of this crash on the news, but then, I'm not sure there is any real news we can believe anymore."

"Not sure. I was contacted by some international medical mission organization. Forgot the official name actually. Compassion something, but the good part is this organization sent us a well-qualified locums replacement surgeon who'll remain with us until Wyatt comes back. In fact, I was amazed at how efficient and professional this organization has been. That replacement really saved us and kept us from being short-handed with a surgeon gone. These people are professionals—that's for sure," said Patterson.

Franklin grunted. "Great. Another locum. They're like a son-in-law that you don't really want in the family, staying for a brutal week or two during the holidays, but you know you've gotta keep your daughter happy."

"I'm not sure that goofy metaphor works, Franklin. But yes, locums physicians are expensive—not really invested in our institution, but you know, it is what it is. He has needs, and we have needs, and both sides are either happy or equally unhappy. But what's our other choice? Go without coverage for the surgical group until he's back? But that brings me to something I've been meaning to ask for a while. Do you want him back? I know I'm not close to the situation but I heard a few things about him having less than cordial interactions with some other physicians at the hospital," said Patterson.

"Hell yes, I do. He's a damn good surgeon—a little edgy at times socially, but I like him. He's gutsy but sharp. Not only that, I just signed off on his proctor review for surgery privileges, and I look forward to seeing him back. This place just hasn't been the same since he left."

"What do you mean?" said Patterson.

"Quiet. Brutally quiet, and it makes me nervous somehow. And it's been a little boring, I must say. There's just something about this guy ..."

***

"I'm sorry ma'am but we're not allowed to give out information about our doctors on staff besides their office number."

"But is he coming back?" asked Gentri. She was thankful it was a different operator today because she had already called multiple hospital operators over the last few weeks, several times per week. She didn't care if she was a pest, because she didn't know what else to do. Her next step would be to physically go to his office and ask his office staff, but each time she arrived in the office parking lot, she decided against it and left. She'd never been desperate in her life, and certainly, even if she was, she wouldn't let anyone witness that type of behavior.

"Ma'am, like I said, I can't provide any more information for you. I'm sorry. Have a good day."

She closed the call, then hurled her cell phone across the room. *How could he do this to me? Is he alive? Did he quit? Did he find another woman?* Then, her cell phone rang, proving the unbreakable protective case actually did work. She stared at the phone number, and it was unfamiliar, but she decided to answer it anyway because of Wyatt and there it was—that deep masculine voice.

"Hello, Gentri, have you thought about me?"

"Oh, hi, um, Erik, well I—"

"I thought about you many times, more than you can imagine. Listen, your office said you didn't have clients tomorrow night, so I bought tickets to a play at the Denver Center for the Performing Arts. We need to celebrate the closing on the house you helped me find. Dinner before, of course. I'll pick you up at six."

Gentri hesitated. "Well, I do have some loose ends to—"

"Yes, I know, short notice, but I really want to see you."

"Okay, you're right. I've got a perfect evening dress for the theater that's been sitting in my closet for two years—never been worn. So, I guess, why not?"

"Excellent. Time to bring it to life, sweet Gentri, and let it breathe and move to your rhythm."

She hung up, and the cell phone shook in her trembling hand. *What have I just done? But why not? He's handsome, interesting, and hell, I don't have any other prospects of this quality now, because the one I seem to care about has vanished completely.*

＊＊＊

Gentri wore an elegant long dress that clung to her feminine features. The neck line was low cut but not too daring, with a teasing skin-baring cut in back.

Erik wore a black sport coat with impeccably tailored grey slacks that fit his athletic body perfectly. The coat was unbuttoned in front with the first button of his shirt open, revealing a glimpse of chest that was quite used to performing large reps of push-ups. He displayed a wide and welcoming smile, obviously proud of the teeth his lips steadfastly refused to hide.

She enjoyed his show, as well as the theater performance.

At intermission, they tasted some wine at a small table in the lobby.

"So, your card says 'Jorgensen Engineering.' What kind of engineering do you do, Erik?"

He smiled for a while before he carefully allowed the words to come out. "Of course. Forgive me for not explaining, but we specialize in aeronautical engineering and aircraft design, with our main offices in Southern California, and now we're gearing up our design facility here in the Denver Tech Center. That's why I bought a house here, so I can be on-site during the start-up phase."

"Fascinating. I'd like to know more about what your business produces or designs, but then I don't know anything about space and high-tech stuff. I assume you have defense industry contracts?"

He quickly searched for a way to change the subject and found a way to transition. "Just boring stuff like aerodynamics, airframe structure, and computer modeling. What *is* fascinating is *you*, Gentri, and now it's my turn. So, Gentri, were you ever married? Any children?"

She answered, growing leery of his aggressive questioning on the first date, but then, maybe it wasn't unusual to have that curiosity. She wasn't sure she had any skills anymore in the dating department. Maybe it was the glass of wine now circulating warmth throughout her blood stream, but he was a man who was difficult to avoid staring at, so she decided to answer his questions carefully.

"Divorced, no children."

"Okay. Good. I've never been married," said Erik.

"What do you mean by *good*?"

"Sorry, yes that didn't come out right, but what I meant to convey was that it's good you are out of a bad relationship. I mean, I *assume* it was bad, and it's fortunate that you don't have any baggage to deal with—you know, with parental responsibilities or, you know, joint custody."

Handsome yes, but he was digging his handsome self into a deep ditch that could get muddy. Children are baggage? She'd always wanted children, but her ex-husband had completely different ideas and goals in life. She decided not to ask if Erik had children, even though he was never married. She sensed that he probably did.

He drove her home after the performance and walked her to her front door. She felt her heart flutter when he looked at her so longingly with those green eyes. She felt his masculine confidence surge, just the way he held himself when standing still. But despite his callous words about children, she felt a little tingle below when his left hand touched her waist and his right touched the small of her back, but his hand then began inching dangerously southward. He leaned forward, although somewhat slowly and surprisingly awkward, and although she felt some desire, she turned her head, and his parted lips now closed for a quick kiss on her right cheek. She just didn't feel the warmth she'd expected. She didn't feel ready for a mouth kiss with him and didn't know whether she would give him another chance.

He stepped back, shocked like a wounded soldier, then said with a half-smile, half – upper lip curl that she hadn't witnessed until that moment, "I had a nice evening with you, Gentri, and you're certainly a hot one, and I hope we'll soon be closer and share some intimate moments together."

She looked at him incredulously, then said goodnight politely with a brief smile, as she'd been taught in Birmingham, then locked the door behind her. What did he mean by 'intimate moments?' She assumed sex, but did he mean intimacy as in talking and sharing their lives? So, his body was easy to drink in and he was an accomplished man, but who talks like that about intimacy on the first date? He was just too aggressive for her taste, and it seemed artificial, as if he was a robot programmed for a mandatory sexual mission that had to be accomplished. And it sure seemed interesting that he was able to buy this Jorgensen company so easily, as a matter of fact.

A Southern girl needs to be charmed and romanced with at least an attempt at a warm connection before hopping into bed just to make your Yankee dick-brain satisfied.

CHAPTER 19

Centri's cell phone on her night stand rang, startling her out of sleep at 1:30 in the morning. She hesitated to answer, not recognizing the number, but for some reason, it felt right to answer this one. Most people don't call at that late hour, and if they did, it was generally due to an emergency of some type. She hoped it wasn't family, although she had both her sister's and father's numbers in her contacts. She also hoped it wasn't Erik calling with a newly created caller ID to fake her out. She picked it up, though, for some reason, without hesitation.

"Hello, beautiful."

"Wyatt!" She sat immediately upright in bed. "You're alive! What happened? Where are you?" She spewed the rapid-fire questions like word vomit before taking a second breath.

"Sorry, honey. I forgot what time zone we're in now, and it was rude to wake you up, but—"

"No, it's okay, darling. Talk to me."

Wyatt formed his words slowly, and the brief hesitations hung like thick fog over a busy airport runway, stopping the flow of traffic.

"I'm in Denver now. Glad to be home."

"Where were you? Why didn't you call? I had no contact from you since our last kiss at the Broadmoor almost three weeks ago."

"I know, honey. It was beyond my control, and we need to talk. I missed you, well, a lot."

"Talk? Really? We need to talk, he says. That's an understatement."

The fog on the other end rolled in again, and she felt the heaviness, so she decided to take it easy on him for a while until she got the answers she needed. She knew this man would never abandon a woman he cared for, but she needed to know what was going on in his head.

"When can we meet Wyatt?"

"I'll call you in the next few days. I yearn to feel your lips on mine. This is my new cell phone number. Put it in your contact list. We'll have a long talk and catch up. I have to get my sea legs, so to speak, and take care of a few things before we meet."

She could feel something was different about him—some subtle hoarseness and perhaps he was more reserved than she remembered, so she said, "I'll wait for your call, honey, and I'm glad you are back safe."

***

Palmer needed to talk to his agency colleague and friend one more time—a careful debriefing before he was comfortable releasing Wyatt back to his civilian hospital duties. Palmer made sure the agency's Operation Security Department expunged all record of Wyatt's involvement in the mission, erasing all information regarding his employment at the CIA and treatment at Landstuhl—scrubbing all details from the internet. But he was allowed to remain as Wyatt Barton, general surgeon at Mercy Hospital in Denver. The agency wanted him happy, healthy, productive, and above all quiet. His legend had to remain intact.

As always, the location he chose in Denver for the meeting was secured by his staff carefully and methodically well before the debriefing. No civilian phones were allowed, and no civilian technology could be present in the room either. That included TVs, phones, and music players. They scanned the walls for electronic eavesdropping as standard procedure. His team made sure they took care of all this before the car picked up Wyatt.

Wyatt entered the room, where he found Palmer in a comfortable chair, smiling and drinking an ice tea. With a slight limp, Wyatt approached Palmer, who immediately got up, and they shook hands. Then, the injured doctor took the other easy chair directly across from Palmer.

"May I get you an iced tea, Wyatt?" said Palmer

"Thanks, but no. I'm trying to cut back—it darkens my pearly whites. I prefer bourbon on the rocks, actually, but seems as though the organization has you drinking iced tea rather than their standard-issue Kool-Aid."

Within a minute, a broad-shouldered assistant brought Wyatt a full bottle of Maker's Mark and some ice with tongs for his glass.

"Well, what do you know? I finally get a real drink after all I've been through."

Palmer smiled at him warmly; then, they looked at each other, sizing each other up as if they'd just met, even though they had known each other for many years. They were studying each other's facial expressions and body language as they'd been trained to long ago. Wyatt observed that Palmer was tapping his index finger on the right chair arm and there was a brief tremor in his left hand when he raised his glass. He'd never noticed this before, and it was too obvious to ignore.

"Wyatt, we're all proud as hell of you. The mission was a success over-all, even though the SOST was compromised, and through your heroic actions, lives were saved. You may not remember all of the details, of course, due to your injuries, but we lost Captain Blane, and Julie was shot in the leg but she survived. Lost her leg, though, unfortunately."

"I know all of this. I need to talk to Blane's family and to Julie."

"Maybe in due time, Wyatt, but we can't allow it now. It's proto—"

"I'll do it. I don't care about your damn military protocols, Tommie. They were my people and I need to talk to the families."

"Of course, Wyatt. But it's already been done by our team. You are not needed for this."

"What? No offense, Tommie, but here is my learned opinion: Fuck your team. I was part of my team, although it looks like I'm now an ex-team member. None of this happened, and I don't exist, right? I'll do what I want and what I need to do, my friend."

Palmer glanced briefly at the guard at the door and the other burly as-sistant off to the side drinking coffee, and he briefly nodded his head.

"Wyatt, you were Black Ops, and that mission never existed. You're right. The families will survive, and Julie is okay. You didn't participate in anything, remember? No, we won't let you go. We need you back in that civilian operating room, and your agency legacy remains protected. And you need to know this: The Congressional Medal of Honor is given to military soldiers for uncommon valor and heroism. You were a Ranger years ago. But you may not know that this award has an equivalent in the CIA called the DIC or Distinguished Intelligence Cross. Have you heard of it?"

"Nope. Don't particularly care either."

"Of course not, Wyatt. But the DIC, unlike the Congressional Medal of Honor, isn't awarded by the president but by the agency in a private unpublished ceremony, because well, it was a clandestine operation and—"

"So?"

"You'll be notified of the time, and we'll fly you to Langley to receive this highest award from the CIA."

Wyatt said nothing, just stared straight ahead. He swirled the remaining Bourbon in his glass, then downed it. "Got to get back to work, Tommie. Problem is, I had a drink, so no operating today, so I'm going home to prepare for my first day back in the hospital tomorrow. This has been fun, but I can't afford to be taking more time off. They're probably calling me a slacker, and the truth is, I don't blame them."

Palmer knew his friend and was aware that he didn't expect a response about the DIC top award. "What do you remember about the action that day Wyatt?"

"I remember a few things, and some details are fairly clear. Others aren't, but it seems each day a few more images come into focus. I do remember killing those vermin in the trucks that were hell-bent on taking out my medical personnel. But the last guy was strange. Before he died, he stared at me with bright-green eyes, and he looked like some kind of damn Nordic Viking with blond hair. Didn't seem to fit, you know, with the type of enemy we were dealing with."

"Yeah, we're doing autopsies and CODIS DNA searches on him, cross-referencing with our international terrorist files as well."

"Tommie, there was a drone too, and it wasn't ours. I saw it monitoring us, and I'm sure there was a live feed to a controlling station somewhere. That shit's scary. They may have me ID'd, but even worse, they may have the ability to penetrate our operation and use that technology against us."

"Yes, that one slipped through and kicked our ass. First time those fuckers used drones to spy on us during one of our operations, real-time, although we have seen crude ones they have been using for a while. Thankfully, they didn't compromise the operators, just the SOST—a target they knew they could find and hit hard with devastating casualties. I have no idea how those trucks were able to penetrate the Marine guard units on the perimeter, but it happened. The problem that we need to figure out, my friend, is how the hell they knew and had a drone up in the area? Very few people knew about the operation, and I hope we don't have a mole. Highly unlikely with our team, but it must be considered. Could be, though, that this was a site they were watching anyway, due to the sensitive nature of their training camps. Maybe a safety precaution? And by the way, this is our problem to figure out, Wyatt, and we don't need you to become involved at all. That means zilch."

"Right. Don't worry, I'm just a basic civilian surgeon who's tired of this clandestine stuff. And by the way, you say the only casualties were just the silly medical personnel, huh Tommie?"

"C'mon now, Wyatt. They were all soldiers on the job. We grieve for Blane just as you do. You've been through a lot, Wyatt, and the bourbon might be dulling your senses. But you need to know that you're a selfless fucking hero to us. Too bad the American public will never know."

"I just did my job, Palmer. That's all. That's what my training was for. Nothing special."

"Bullshit."

Wyatt looked at the guard and surveyed the other "helpers" for Palmer in the room, then said, "So now, I'm sure I'll have shadow men watching me wherever I go, even taking a piss, right? Or kissing a girl?"

"Of course. You were in a top-secret operation, and we need to make sure you don't make any mistakes or talk and compromise the mission."

"Or what?"

"Or we'll give you the help you need—that's what. And by the way, you need to know that your cover story is that you were in an airplane crash landing in Africa—Zaire specifically—working as a medical missionary, and you were the only survivor but did have a head injury ... and the pneumothorax and hemothorax, requiring hospitalization and some rehab at an undisclosed location. In case anyone investigates, we've created some medical documents for verification of the story. Just don't show anyone your shrapnel wounds, though. Those are harder to explain. We kind of leaked this information to the hospital already, so you have a cover story in place, and our people have it all covered, including a locums guy who is part of our network who's been filling in during your absence. We've got it wrapped up pretty nicely."

Wyatt stood up and stared down at Palmer while he tried to suck nonchalantly on the ice cubes he found on the bottom of his iced tea glass. He thought about how Palmer would help him, and he looked at the guards acting like they weren't listening, then continued. "Yes, of course—help me when I need it. I've met these guys before, and I know what their job is. I've also gone swimming in the dark with alligators while the supposed life guards at the mud beach stood around and watched, even when I was sinking and the gators were snapping at my succulent ass! Like shit they'll help—and you know it."

"Looks like you're getting back to normal, Wyatt, my friend. Just like old times."

Palmer remained seated but uncrossed his legs, in preparation for any event, since Wyatt was now pacing the room, even walking behind Tommie's chair, making it hard for him to keep an eye on his hero friend, and that made him feel uncomfortable for some reason. Who knew? Maybe his head injury made him crazy, and he could attack his brother from behind, for no reason. That happened sometimes. He finally set his glass down on the table.

"It's the way it is, my friend. Nothing you can do about it, unfortunately. We've been through a lot together, and we're here to protect you, no matter what you think. You don't have a choice in the matter. Never forget: you're like a brother to me, Wyatt."

"I know, Tommie. You're ugly and mean, but you've always been a straight-up guy with me, and you've saved my ass before. I've saved your ass too. Remember when I decided to make you best man at my wedding, and sure enough, you could barely stand up because of all the champagne swirling around your buzzed head? Fact is, we got you home safe, just like you would do for me when I needed it."

"Yeah, I'm a lightweight with alcohol. Always have been."

"I want to tell you one more thing before you release me back into the civilian world with shadowy dudes wearing tight shirts following me at your brotherly request. Keep them away from my personal life, and let me finally live a reasonably normal life despite all this shit. I met a woman before I left, and she seems special, and I've finally been able to let go of Kim. I don't want you guys messing that up. Do you understand me or do I need to write this down for you, Tommie?"

"Scout's honor, we'll give you space."

Wyatt drove home in his Toyota Land Cruiser, having been informed that Palmer's team had already stocked his empty refrigerator and cleaned out the old moldy stuff, mowed the grass several times, and trimmed the bushes. *How nice*, he thought. *Wonder if they'll wipe my ass too.* Then, the thought occurred to him, that if he ever did have sex, would they tape that event so he didn't make a mistake in the heat of passion and compromise the mission? Yet, he knew Palmer was simply looking out for him, despite the inconvenience, and he trusted him.

During the drive home, the streets he knew suddenly turned unfamiliar as if he were in a foreign land, and he rubbed his eyes to clear them but still couldn't recognize landmarks—ones he should have known easily even in the dark. Then, he saw a bearded man grab a young teenage boy from behind, cut off his head, then place the severed, dripping head on top of a blue US postal mailbox, directly across the street from a Target store, with a luminous full moon hovering above the building, illuminating a sign that said, "Welcome to Target, Navy Pier."

He floored it, desperately trying to chase this evil man down to tackle him or run him over, but the images abruptly changed like a movie he'd seen a hundred times, and he was now suddenly driving down his familiar home street with a complete scene change. There was no bearded man. He pulled into his garage, closed the door, his breathing labored despite no exertion whatsoever. What the hell was that? Was it a dream? Part of PTSD? He'd never experienced anything like this before, but then, he knew he'd had a recent traumatic experience, coupled with a head injury, among other things. He walked out onto his front yard, looked up into the sky, and saw that it was a full moon. He shook his head and went back inside. Navy Pier was a thousand miles away in Chicago, not Denver. What was that about?

He propped himself up on three pillows on the couch, poured himself another bourbon, then fell asleep, thinking of Gentri's warm kiss, charming accent, and cute little giggle.

CHAPTER 20

Welcome back, Wyatt!" said Dr. Franklin. He shook Wyatt's hand for so long that he figured there must have been glue in Nick's stubby palm. "We missed you. We're sick of these fly-by-night locums guys who get spoiled in our fancy hotels, and I must admit it's been too quiet around here—no action or drama."

"Right. Well, that reminds me," said Wyatt. "How was my favorite oak tree behaving during my absence?"

"Not a peep. I think he's waiting to do your next case with you and you two can bond together once again just like old times. Anyway, got a call for a consult on the general medical floor from Rollins, one of the new internists, and I thought that might be a good way to get your feet soaked again."

Wyatt thought about saying, "Rangers lead the way," but thought better of it and said, "I'll get my best people on it, Nick."

"Excellent. Go get 'em. And by the way, we can talk about how you survived that plane crash in Africa over a beer sometime when you're ready to talk about it. Must've been hell. Truth is, I didn't know you were a medical missionary."

For some reason, Wyatt wasn't prepared for the plane crash question that Tommie had warned him about. "The crash, yes. Thanks for asking. I appreciate that, but I'm not ready to talk about it now."

The patient was a forty-five-year-old woman with right upper quadrant pain and tenderness, showing classic signs of acute cholecystitis, confirmed via ultrasound. It seemed like a straightforward case to Wyatt, and she had no other complicating medical problems except for well-controlled Type 2 Diabetes.

Wyatt was able to schedule OR time at 0800 for a laparoscopic cholecystectomy, possibly an open cholecystectomy, and sure enough, the anesthesiologist assigned to the case was Dr. Turner, the tree.

Since Wyatt had a few minutes before the case, he figured it was time to call Gentri. "Good morning, sexy!" he said.

He thought he could almost hear her smile widen on the other end of the receiver. "Morning, darling. No, I'm about five minutes away, enjoying the heavy morning traffic. Do you have any cases today?"

"Starting a gallbladder in a few minutes."

"I don't know anything about those, but my friend had one with a scope thing procedure and she said it was a fairly simple procedure. Maybe that's a good way for you to start back."

"Right. I hope so, but you never know. Listen, would you like to have dinner with me tonight?"

"I'd love to, Wyatt, but I promised my friend Julie I'd take her out after work for her birthday. Hope you'll understand. How about later? I'm sure we won't be long because she likes to tuck her kids into bed herself, instead of the babysitter doing it."

"Of course, that's fine. Come over when you're ready. I have a nice bottle of Bordeaux and Brie, so I can show you how faux French I am. *N'est-ce pas?*"

"Oui, honey. It's a date. I can't wait to see you!"

Wyatt started to softly whisper into the phone. "I'm breathing faster just thinking about your soft lips and rhythmic hips."

"Damn, honey. That's it. I'm coming over to the hospital for lunch because of that statement, but I can't guarantee how socially acceptable I'll be to people watching us. Meet me at noon in the cafeteria downstairs."

"I hope I'm finished by—"

"Be there. Don't make excuses, mister."

Wyatt entered the OR, and almost immediately, the towering oak tree shook his hand, and Wyatt thought his hand bones were crushed forever, and damn, right before the case. Should've offered him the left hand.

"Glad you're back, Wyatt! Sounds like you had a hell of an adventure there in Africa."

The tree's ebullience threw Wyatt off a little, but what the hell—he had no hard feelings, especially after all he'd been through overseas recently.

"Happy to be here—believe me—and how's the golf game?"

"Played Broadmoor the other day, and I couldn't putt worth a damn but had some great drives and never hit the forest."

Wyatt smiled and said nothing. Neither man discussed the past, and Wyatt saw the doctor's kindness with the OR techs and nurses—something that had been absent before—so something was going right, finally, in this messed-up world.

The case turned out to be a simple laparoscopic cholecystectomy without complications, and Wyatt was able to see a couple more consults prior to his semi-urgent lunch date, but he constantly glanced at his Panerai wristwatch so he could get to the busy cafeteria early, aware that other employees were staring at him sitting at a table in the general cafeteria in his scrubs and shoe covers, rather than in the private doctor's lounge.

Then, she made her entrance.

The distinctive clicking of her conservative heeled-shoes on the tile flooring forced quite a few heads to turn instinctively to search for the source of this tantalizing auditory stimulation, and Wyatt's eyes devoured the way her skirt aggressively hugged her shapely hips and those heart-shaped calves easily supported a perfect runway walk. They met and said nothing, just hugging each other as if they were completely oblivious to onlookers, and time no longer mattered. Then, they kissed—not with all the passion they both held inside, but it did cause a few "humphs" in the background, so then they stopped. The happy couple went through the cafeteria line, and Wyatt couldn't help grinning like a kid opening the main present—the magnificent one he had dreamed of—on Christmas morning. They sat down and tried to eat, in between staring contests and Wyatt was thankful he didn't get beeped.

"You know, I hate it when a woman with nice legs and a sexy skirt shows up when I'm trying my best to work. It's terribly distracting to us innocent men."

Gentri giggled. "Well, honey, if you're blameless, then I guess I'll continue to distract you until you can't take it anymore. Just wait until tonight, Mr. Innocent Surgeon!"

After lunch, while in her car, she had to jot down a few notes to add to her manuscript, but then, she knew these were words that she wouldn't forget to put down on paper:

Her missionary finally returned, and her heart rejoiced, but it wasn't at peace, because it raced when her eyes met his. What's more, his smile made her hop off her feet and into his arms before the long-awaited kiss enveloped her. She wasn't at peace, as she'd lost control—and yet, it felt so very right.

CHAPTER 21

pring in Denver proudly presented bright-blue skies and chilly evenings while the trees and plants bloomed, although this was later than in other parts of the country. By mid-April, the red buds of the crab apples and the crimson stains on the white dogwood blooms led the late-spring charge, and Wyatt's front window was immediately dominated by an expansive blooming crab apple tree, but this was almost outdone by the majestic Colorado blue spruce and sturdy scrub oak dominating the expansive panorama the back deck afforded.

When she arrived, the smell of the scented candles lit in various rooms wafted gently throughout the house, flickering a warm invitation, especially in the most important room, and smooth jazz played while the sensual Bordeaux decanted in the thin Denver air. Their kissing commenced uncontrollably even before her body passed through the plane of the threshold. They both stood motionless, kissing passionately with a hunger that was impossible to be satiated.

They finally stopped kissing, reluctantly took mandatory breaths, and Wyatt finally led her through the front entryway, then slowly out to the back deck to enjoy the wine, music, and scenery. The early-evening chill took hold while the sun reluctantly descended down over the white-shawled mountains, prompting Gentri to adjust her Parisian e`charpe to more completely cover the softness of her smooth neck. Wyatt poured her a glass of Chateau Franc Mayne, and they did the German Buderschaff hug—crossing arms, sipping the wine with crossed arms, then kissing with the wine still in their mouths.

Gentri smiled and took a generous sigh, causing her earrings to jiggle back and forth. "Wyatt, this was tough on me, sweetheart, wondering where you were and if you were safe. But I never forgot that you told me to wait, and that's what gave me some hope that I would see you again."

Remaining silent, he smiled and held her hand, knowing that he needed to let her release her emotion with words.

"I found out through the hospital grapevine that you were on a medical mission and you survived a plane crash somewhere in Africa. That must've been horrible for you, Wyatt! Please tell me everything I need to know. You know, you could've told me that you were going on a medical mission before you left. Would that have hurt you to share that with me? It makes me wonder—"

"You're right Gentri. It wasn't fair at all to you, and yes, I went on a mission, and perhaps someday I can explain some more."

"Why not now?"

His recurrent headaches exploded, just at the wrong time. Wyatt took a drink of wine, rubbed his forehead briefly, then, got up and walked a little to the railing of the deck, then quickly back to his lady, as if not to lose precious time.

"You okay, Wyatt? What's wrong?"

He said nothing in response, bent over, and whispered in her ear, "May I take off your scarf so my lucky lips can make love to your supple little neck?"

She sighed. "It's about time, honey."

He removed the scarf, kissed her behind her ear, then the neck, while his finger gently caressed her exposed and vulnerable collarbone. He listened carefully to the increased tempo of her breathing that he knew came from his feather-like touches. Then, she pulled him down and kissed him with lioness-like feminine hunger, and when she stopped for air, he whispered into her ear, "I want to make love to you completely and worship your body the way a Southern goddess deserves. Then, start all over . . ."

She offered her hand, and he took it and led her away back into the house, embarking on the long journey to the candlelit bedroom. After ten feet of walking, their journey was interrupted by a flurry of passionate kisses, and she exposed her neck to him again while he loosened her skirt skillfully, never letting his lips leave her skin while her skirt fell crumpled to the floor. She then awkwardly fumbled with his belt buckle, still with lips passionately attached to his, and he helped her a little with his pants button, and she peeled off his tight jeans, pulling them to the floor, while her curious fingers explored what they needed, lips still engaged above. Knowing they would never make it to the bedroom this way, Wyatt picked her up—one of her shoes off, the other dangling precariously—and Wyatt took his woman to his bed and laid her down gently. She stayed on her back, reached out her arms, and said, "Take me now, my man!"

He straddled her in push-up form, showing his tense abdominal muscles, slightly above her, kissing her lips and neck, and then took his time, despite her invitation, and devoured each course her feminine perfection had to offer, enjoying each morsel of her welcoming feast, prolonging the lovemaking while using all of his senses to conduct her heavenly feminine symphony patiently in undulating waves that peaked and crashed. Then, he returned again and again, letting her rest between the waves until finally, he let himself complete the sensual symphony with a paradise of exhaustion.

The next morning, Wyatt woke up first, at about five, made coffee, then went downstairs and banged out his multi-set push-ups, pull-ups, v-ups, and planks routine. After that, he went upstairs and started preparing breakfast before they both needed to go to work. Surprised that they were still throwing free copies of *The Denver Post* on his driveway despite the fact that he refused to subscribe to the rag, he brought in the latest issue and gave it to the now awake Gentri, who thanked him, then kissed him.

"I don't read newspapers, but I hope you enjoy it if you want, dear. It's free and not worth the subscription," said Wyatt.

"Yeah, sweetie, I do read the Denver rag, especially when I have my listings in the 'Home Advertised' section every Sunday."

He drank his coffee and watched her scan the newspaper quickly, entranced by her calm intelligence and gentle feminine charm.

"You're staring at me."

"Yes. I'm human, and if you're not careful, I'll do more than that, and you'll be late for work."

She smiled; then, her eyes caught an article that made her face immediately flush red.

"What is it?" said Wyatt.

"I can't believe this. Such nasty evil! I can't believe this can happen in America. Can't we stop this?"

She threw the paper to Wyatt as if it was on fire and just pointed to the article without explaining it, turning her head away, as though she didn't have the strength to describe it in her own words. He read to himself: *Chicago Illinois. Last night, a teenager was found decapitated with his body in front of a mailbox and the severed head sitting on top of the mailbox near the Target store in the Navy Pier neighborhood. A note was attached to the head, saying, "It's a full moon—a perfect time to kill infidels. More will come. We are the FFWP." Police are investigating the crime and are not available for comment on the acronym written in the letter.*

Wyatt dropped the paper and spilled his coffee on the floor, grimacing in pain, then got up and walked away.

"What's wrong, honey? I know it's disgusting and brutal. I had the same reaction. How could anyone do this?"

"The world is changing," said Wyatt.

"What do you mean?" His headache returned again, forcing him to sit down and hold his head in both hands, fingers running through his hair, as if this helped the pain somehow. His face now turned bright crimson.

Gentri rubbed his head softly, trying to soothe his obvious pain. "Don't take it so hard, Wyatt. Hopefully, they can find this evil criminal and stop him forever."

"He's not a criminal. He's a terrorist."

"How do you know?"

"I saw it, in detail, in my dream—or nightmare, the night it happened—Target. Navy Pier, head on the mailbox. The full moon and all."

She looked at him intensely, searching his face for understanding. "You're kidding?"

"Wish I was."

"I'm sure it's just a coincidence, Wyatt, and you've obviously been under a lot of stress after what you've been through in Africa, and those headaches. You need to get some help from a doctor who's not you."

"Guess you're right, Gentri. Too crazy to believe, I guess."

"Wyatt, will you promise to get some professional help for these headaches and finally get some rest?"

He said nothing and stared blankly out the window. Gentri could see his mind was taking him far away from her.

"Wyatt?"

"No problem, honey. I'll get my best people on it."

CHAPTER 22

The shadow men met with Palmer weekly to discuss various situations and issues with the operators they shadowed. Wyatt wasn't an operator anymore—not since his days with the Rangers, JSOC, and CIA—but his experiences remained closely protected for the sake of national security.

"Thanks for coming, guys. How's 241 holding up?" said Palmer.

"Seems to be adjusting as well as expected," said one of the shadow men

"Go on."

"He's back doing cases in the hospital now and trying to blend in as well as he can, despite his problems."

"Which problems of his many are you referring to?"

"Well, you know, he seems to be struggling with headaches ever since the blast injury, and now they're recurrent. Handles them okay, though, we think. Oh yeah, he's got a girlfriend too."

"Yeah, he told me about her. What does she do?"

"Successful real estate broker here in Denver. She's a looker too—a true Southern belle. No wonder he—"

"I don't care if she's a super model or not. Here's what I need to know: Is his head with the program?"

"His head's okay, best we can tell. It's early yet, but you know, he's a team player and a patriot."

"I know. Any risk for mission compromise here?"

"None that we can see at this time, sir."

"Excellent. He's my good friend, and we need to protect him at all costs. In fact, he's a fucking asset to this country, but no one knows it except us, and that's the way it needs to remain forever. Keep up the shit-hot surveillance work, guys."

Palmer took an emergency call on his red phone while the shadow men were still there.

"What? A bad guy drone here? You've got to be kidding me." He listened for a few more minutes, on the phone, silent with his face becoming increasingly pale. "They told me it wasn't possible, but now it seems we have a different reality. You're right, sir; we've got to hide this and clean it up right away. The general population mustn't be allowed to know about this or there will be panic." Palmer slammed the phone down in disbelief and horror.

"Well, guys, it seems a drone came out of nowhere, over the trees bordering a subdivision in Virginia, fired a laser, and blew up a truck sitting at a little league baseball diamond."

"I thought we had the rogue drone thing covered, sir, especially at military bases and secure areas. Even so, a small drone doesn't have the fire—"

"This wasn't a small one, and it had enough firepower to blow up a truck. Then, it vanished, and we have no radar tracking."

"Any casualties?"

"General McCord from JSOC and Commander Cornell, Chief of Naval Special Warfare. Both gone in the explosion. It was a fucking well-planned direct assassination with a drone on American soil! How the hell did we let this technology get into the hands of those assholes?"

They all looked at each other, frozen in the stark realization of what horror just happened on American soil.

***

Abdul called a security council meeting to discuss progress in FFWP missions and to go over immediate strategies. Present in the room were his chief of security, Farid, as well as his director of intelligence and the chief of IT.

"Gentleman, I'm happy to tell you that our first armed drone mission on US soil was a success, with the destruction of two high-value infidel targets. Well, one was clearly dead, but the other pig we don't know—couldn't get a good camera image on his body. Probably was incinerated. This, I'm sure, will strike fear into not only the soft general population but also their vaunted military, which was taken by surprise by my technology," said Abdul.

"Excellent, Sahib," said Farid. The others bowed down to Abdul in reverence, uttering *tahanina zaeimuna* (congratulations, our leader). They knew their leader was growing more powerful and successful, even with the cash-throwing Chinese, but the military-grade laser-guided missile was being held for a greater mission.

Abdul looked at his chief of IT, Saleem, and said, "Any progress on identifying the animal who did so much destruction to our mission?"

"We've examined the drone images with our matrix subtraction techniques, and we've been able to get a better look at him, but we—"

"What does his ugly face look like?"

"Well, he's got a scar bisecting his left eyebrow, and we can't be sure, but either green or blue eyes, and he's 1.88 meters tall, taking into account standard boot thickness."

"That's all you can get?"

"I am sorry, our leader, our zaeim."

"Not good enough. I need more. Anyone else here with info we can use?"

"Zaeim, I'm continuing to attack the Pentagon's database, specifically Special Ops medics or medical personnel. So far, no luck," said Farid. "I may have to get some help from some of my hacker friends in China. They're always ready to help us, without charge as long as their goals are pushed forward and aligned with our agenda."

"You know," said Abdul. "It's imperative that we find this animal, and I expect you people to make an identification as soon as possible so we can find him and eliminate this stinking pig before he causes us more damage. The bottom line is he must be brought to me alive so I can spit in his infidel face."

But, our fearless zaeim, he is but one man, and we must look at the larger picture, as they say, of all infidels in the US, right? Is it important to spend so many resources on just one man? After all, he's not Superman or Spider-Man as they say in the US comic books."

"You dog!" said Abdul. "He killed my son, our best fighter." He rose up and struck Farid in the mouth, drawing blood. "Our recent killing of a soft target in Chicago is one of the ways we've seen fit to inculcate terror into the minds of all Americans, and we must do more, so they'll change their culture and respect our cause and what we believe in. I think they call it here, 'political correctness' and 'religious freedom.' They beat us in our own land a few years ago and stopped us from achieving our glorious goal with the world caliphate, and the people in the West are now sitting in their comfortable chairs, unaware of or perhaps ignoring the fact that we can come back and destroy them, especially when they're weakened and occupied by other major political events that are weakening them economically. China is invaluable in this regard, even though ironically, they have cracked down on the Islamic faith in their huge country. But the most important thing to know is this: Naïve America thinks we are destroyed, and that is to our advantage, obviously, because they sleep now, seemingly satisfied after abandoning their friends and bases in Afghanistan so quickly."

"Yes, that is true, but what do you mean by political correctness, Sahib?" Farid dabbed the blood from his mouth.

"I mean, in the United States, it has been increasingly forbidden to select certain religious organizations or racial groups and investigate them with regard to any ties to terrorism. For example, it is forbidden in political circles to use the word *Muslim* with the word *terror*, and that is one of their grave mistakes. Yes, too many of our brothers are peace-loving individuals, but their view of the teachings is wrong, and we're leading our brothers away from the peaceful ways because peace will not destroy the Great Satan. We will lobby their weak politicians, and some of them are quite easy to pay off with laundered campaign contributions, bolstered bank accounts, and of course pretty women we hire with the help of spies from Beijing. They'll then go out of their way to enact laws or political pressure to protect our religious rights while we hide behind this curtain of protection and secretly destroy them from within. Their politicians, we have learned, only seem to care about how to get reelected, and feeling good and tingly inside about their self-serving and fake 'all-inclusive policy.' While we must be smart, we also must be practical in order to destroy the United States of America and break them from the bounds of their silly paper Constitution and their faith, because we understand that ours is the only true faith, and we will tolerate nothing else."

"Long live the FFWP!" they said in unison.

CHAPTER 23

Since Wyatt enjoyed outdoor activities and sports, he preferred to date athletic women who could participate with him on dates outdoors. Gentri certainly fit that requirement. He was relieved when she accepted his invitation to go for a moderate-grade three-mile hike in the mountains with a view that included several waterfalls and some majestic cliffs. He believed that he needed to try once more to somehow clear his mind and hopefully remove those visions and PTSD-related nightmares that now seemed to intrude into his wakefulness.

She came over to his house with sandwiches, fruit, a bottle of red wine, chilled water, and some plastic cups, then stuffed them all into Wyatt's backpack.

"Wine on a hike? How about water in case we become dehydrated," said Wyatt. "I prefer camelbacks."

"You bring the water, sweetheart; I'll bring the fun stuff. No arguments okay, my missionary?"

Wyatt grinned, shook his head playfully then added a few more items to his backpack, including a small survival kit, a hunting knife, and his 9-mm Glock. He always carried a concealed weapon wherever he went.

At the halfway point of the hike, Gentri picked an open spot with flat rocks to sit on for a picnic, overlooking a panoramic vista of forested canyons, including a view of the Denver skyline several thousand feet below and to the east. Wyatt opened the bottle and poured some wine. They toasted each other in the majestic beauty, beset by no other sound than the rustling leaves and the distant shrieking of eagles. They kissed gently, then with more passion, supplemented by the taste of wine seductively warmed from each other's mouths.

They gazed out at the view, and Gentri said, "Isn't this an amazing place, Wyatt?"

"Gorgeous."

"Are you ready to tell me about your mission now?"

Wyatt remained silent, his mind now suddenly transported into an image from far away: *He was watching a tall white man speaking in some unknown language, possibly parts of the Arabic he knew, to a group of men sporting business suits and wielding AK-47s, all chanting in unison, "Death to America; long live FFWP."* Wyatt continued to stare straight ahead, never moving or blinking, left dumbfounded by this unusual scene that had invaded his consciousness.

"Wyatt? Where are you? Are you even on this planet?"

"Pardon?"

"You've been doing a lot of staring out in space since you've come back. Are you sure you're okay?"

"Oh, yes, sorry. I'm just fine. Must've been the wine and the altitude, I guess."

"Darling, two sips of wine aren't going to hit your brain that quickly, unless, of course, it was accelerated by the tempting scent of a sultry Southern lady."

His smile was wider than she'd seen it since that night they made love for the first time. "Yeah, that's it. I was hypnotized by your beauty and—"

"Okay, now, tell me the truth. Where in this world was your brain traveling to?"

"Truthfully I don't know. Just a strange scene or daydream popped in. They're disturbing dreams, and they seem realistic and almost as if they are a sign of things that are happening either now, or perhaps in the future."

"You want to talk about it?"

"No, I have a better idea. Let's have some more wine and you tell me what you did while I was gone."

It was obvious to her that he didn't want to talk and wanted to change the subject, so she didn't push it. "Okay, let's see. I took a trip to some far-off exotic place, and lots of things happened, but I'm not going to tell you about it ... but I was thinking of you and waiting for you," said Gentri.

"Okay, I got it. You win. We're even now and it's time for more wine, even though we haven't reached the summit." Wyatt poured her another cup, they kissed again, then looked out silently again over the expansive canyon. After a couple of minutes, she said, "So Wyatt, are your headaches a result of a concussion you got from that crash?"

His mind insisted on playing an unwanted movie again: *The general and Special Ops leader were leaning against a Ford pickup parked just behind the middle-school baseball back stop, wearing jeans, T-shirts, and baseball caps. They turned, hearing a whirring noise near the treetops at the back of the baseball diamond, then looked up and saw the drone streaking toward them at tree level. They dove to the ground, but it was too late—the laser-guided missile fired and ignited the truck's fuel tank, and the explosion blew the truck onto its roof twenty feet away, leaving both bodies burning in the dirt.*

This is just absurd and impossible, thought Wyatt.

"Wyatt, wake up!" cried Gentri. She shook him out of his dead silence once again. "What's wrong now, Wyatt?"

He stared at her with blank eyes for about ten seconds, then began to speak. "I saw something awful happen. It seemed so real and detailed, but then, of course, it couldn't have been real."

"Wyatt, I think we've had too much to drink and you're not feeling well and maybe you're not fully recovered yet."

"You're right, Gentri. Let's head back down. No need to go to the summit now."

In the car, Gentri made her concerns quite clear. "Wyatt, are they nightmares from PTSD?"

"I don't know, honey. The PTSD events I had before were always recurrent nightmares of the same scene of actual battle that took place. They were real events that I experienced and repressed during the day. These scenes seem different. They're so detailed, as if I am watching the action take place step by step from some place above. I know it sounds nuts, but they seem like ... premonitions."

"Okay. Go on. What was the daydream or scene about?"

"It was just a bad dream, and I really don't want to talk about it, honey."

She studied his eyes intently and sighed before they drove away. When they arrived at his home, she got out of his car and said, "Wyatt, your head injury must be playing tricks on you. You need to get some professional help. You worry me because you're not the Wyatt I knew before you left. I know the real Wyatt is still inside you somewhere, aching to get out, but something keeps bopping his head when he tries to show his face for too long."

"I think you're right, honey. I'm not the same in some ways—new scars and wounds—but I still have the same heart. I'll figure it out. Don't worry. I'll get my best people on it."

CHAPTER 24

T he caller ID came through, reading, "Erik," and she hesitated, then picked up the phone hoping it would be for another real estate listing from him for one of his employees, perhaps.

"Hello, Gentri, it's Erik, but I'm sure you probably put that in your call contact list, long ago. You know you leave quite an impression on a guy."

"Hi, Erik. What do you mean?"

"Well, seems I can't stop thinking about you, so I finally summoned the courage to call."

"I don't know about courage, but aggressiveness—that you certainly do have," said Gentri.

"Love your feistiness. Listen, I need to ask you if you'll fly to Aspen with me in the corporate jet—first class all the way—for some wining and dining and beautiful scenery this weekend? You'll also love the sheer drop from the mountains directly to the runway. It's a tricky final approach for the pilots, but it'll take your breath away."

She knew he would ask something like this and had her answer prepared. "Thanks, Erik, but I'm much too busy this weekend. Please feel free to enjoy your trip with someone else."

"No one compares to you," said Erik. "Because of that fact, I cannot go with anyone else."

"Right, well, listen, I have a client and need to go."

His last comment prompted a wave of nausea that reminded her of previous suitors that found themselves lost in infatuation. When the nausea resolved, her thoughts turned to Wyatt and whether he would be able to get help with his headaches and nightmares. *Bless his heart*, she thought. Then, she remembered the natural connection that led to some steamy lovemaking and how it made her feel: finally content in life. She hoped the connection with Wyatt would continue to grow and his nightmares wouldn't overwhelm his beautiful mind.

***

The Blackhawk rotors drew near to the pickup point of what was left of his team—three men dead and one in Wyatt's arms, dying, barely conscious. Then, he heard the booming sound of the Vulcan cannon from the AC-130 Spectre, nicknamed "Puff the Magic Dragon," and the Gatling guns, which the enemy always feared. Then, Frank took his last breath in his arms. They'd come too late to save him.

He woke up soaked in sweat, his pillow wet, and the headaches roared back in. No narcotics. Ibuprofen was all he'd allow himself to take, hoping he wouldn't develop a gastric or duodenal ulcer from the non-steroidal pain medications. After four ibuprofen tablets and a brief walk around the house to check the surroundings, he came back inside and made sure his Glock remained under the bed and his 12-gauge was secure before he went to bed finally.

As usual, the dreams intruded once again, but this time, they were unfamiliar—brand new—not like the battle experiences he'd seemingly reenacted thousands of times. These were vivid, detailed scenes, almost like documentaries that told stories about completely unfamiliar situations—brutal, violent acts against innocents or colleagues. Would he have to live with this dark presence forever?

The new visions came again, and he saw a vision that showed Dr. Turner stealing fentanyl, an intravenous narcotic, from the Operating Suite, and taking it home for his habit, causing him to work part stoned. Then, the scene switched dramatically to a bombing of a Christian church rally in Charlottesville, Virginia, killing women and children as well as their men, all from a suicide bomber.

He no longer could differentiate if he was awake or asleep when the scenes invaded his consciousness or subconsciousness, and it wasn't clear if these were dreams or he was actually observing real events before they occurred, or even while they were occurring. Desperate for answers, he ordered a subscription to *The Denver Post*, curious to see if the events actually did happen, preferring this to internet news, which he often felt was fictionalized and over-politicized. At least *The Denver Post* got that first story right, about that evil Navy Pier incident in Chicago that he foresaw.

The next morning, he noticed a slight tremor while picking up the paper on his front porch. He felt a premonition that he wasn't going to like what he was about to read, and he hesitated before diving in. The tremors were new, and he stared at his hands in surprise, observing this unusual physiologic response, at least, for him. Sure enough, there was the damn headline he didn't want to see: Suicide Bomber Kills Five in Charlottesville; Possible Terrorist Attack.

Possible? he said to himself. *They need to call it like it is—a terrorist attack.* Then, he realized things had changed completely in his life after the mission. He had an epiphany. He now realized that he had a gift—a powerful yet horrible gift. It seemed too many of the visions that he experienced were found to be true events, documented in the news. Was it clairvoyance? On his cell phone, he looked up clairvoyance in the Merriam-Webster dictionary: "The power or faculty of discerning objects not present to the senses; the ability to perceive matters beyond the range of ordinary perception. Synonyms: second sight, ESP, sixth sense, and telepathy."

His tremor intensified when he acknowledged this new power and the responsibility he now shouldered when the visions came pre-event. Perhaps they were prophetic dreams, or he now had the skill of prescience: the ability to know something before it actually took place. But then, if this gift (or maybe curse) was real, then what should he do when the dreams or visions came? He had read about cases where some people who experienced near death and came back, had increased perceptions and sensitivities that they didn't possess before the event. Was he responsible to act on these visions and prevent all hell from breaking loose, and if so, how in God's name was he supposed to do that? He wondered, was this the mysterious gift that he was given when he saw the light after the mission? Then, he remembered what the light said to him with telepathy: "No more killing, Wyatt, and you will receive a gift." He now understood where the gift came from: the loving God of light who saved him and gave him another chance in this precious life.

He tried to hide the recurring tremor and the blank staring off into space when people were talking to him at the hospital, but it proved impossible. Wyatt knew it was a matter of time, and the hammer would surely strike him again. But now he understood what he had to do.

CHAPTER 25

After his near-death experience, Wyatt made a habit of saying a daily morning prayer. Then, he'd place a call to Gentri that always started with, "Good morning, beautiful," and only then would his morning case begin.

Today, it was a bowel resection for localized cancer, and after the uneventful surgery, he talked to the grateful family.

When he arrived in the surgeon's locker room, he observed that Dr. Turner's lock was off his locker and his "I golf, therefore I am" sticker had been scraped completely off of his empty locker. Wyatt knew then exactly what happened because he'd seen it before it happened in a vision. Turner must have been caught stealing fentanyl and the hospital had no choice but to fire him immediately. Wyatt left the locker room and walked down the shiny hospital corridor, numb with the knowledge of his newfound abilities.

"Dr. Barton?" The hospital administrative secretary had found him. But then, he wasn't trying to hide.

"Yes, good morning. How are you today?" said Wyatt

She showed him a half smile and said, "Dr. Rogers wants to see you in his office today if possible. Are you available at 11:30?"

"Sure, my next case is in an hour, so I should be available. May I ask what it's about?"

"He didn't say, but he did tell me thirty minutes should be sufficient."

Wyatt knew what was probably coming, and as always, prepared himself for the worst-case scenario, then learned to deal with the worst and make the best of it somehow. When he arrived at Roger's office, he nodded at the secretary, didn't break stride, and walked right into his office without sitting expectantly in the small waiting room. No time to waste anymore. If they say 11:30, they better be ready at 11:30.

"Wyatt, thanks for coming. Rogers did betray a little crackly sound in his voice, possibly taken aback by Wyatt's sudden entrance. "Can I get you some coffee or a bottle of water?"

"No thanks, Paul, I'm okay."

"Right well, maybe you're not as okay as you think you are, my friend."

No response at all from Wyatt after Roger's cold statement. They weren't friends, and Wyatt bristled when non-friends called him a friend. He just stared at Rogers, and eventually, the principal cleared his throat while trying to free his ponytail, which was caught under his sport coat collar in back. He was obviously stalling and searching for the right words to say to Wyatt, his problem doctor.

"Well, Wyatt, I'm going to get right to the point here. We've had complaints—well no, actually *concerns* raised about you since your return and—"

"Like?"

"To start with your tremor is obvious in the OR. Staff notices these things, believe me."

"Has it affected the surgical outcomes?" said Wyatt. "You know, some doctors fart when they stand too long during a case, but I've never been accused of that, to my knowledge. I always try to blame the anesthesiologist because they're the best at passing gas."

"C'mon now, Wyatt, this is serious. No, it hasn't affected your surgical outcomes at all. Your surgical care is excellent."

"So, what's the problem then? Fine tremors are illegal in our hallowed little OR?"

"Fact is it's the other things—both hands holding your head when you think people aren't watching, the blank stares in the middle of simple conversations. It's making people uncomfortable."

"You playing with your pony tail probably makes people uncomfortable too, but I'm sure you still do your job quite well, Paul. Doesn't bother me in the least bit at the moment."

"Okay, Wyatt, and there's an example of your bad attitude too. So, I've decided you came back to work too early after your accident, and therefore I've arranged a month's sabbatical for you, but before you come back after the sabbatical, you must be seen, evaluated, and treated by a behavioral psychologist and a neurologist. You can't return until they certify that you're ready. You're not being fired, but this is a direct warning that you clearly need some help, Wyatt."

Wyatt gently scratched his eyebrow scar, which had already turned red, as it often did when his pot was steaming before the bubbling boil. "Okay. Maybe you're right. I do need some help. Hell, we all do sometimes, I believe."

"Right. Glad you see it that way too. You can't be a hero all the—"

"See you in a month, Chief, when I'm certified with a diploma in hand from crazy school and my head has been properly examined."

***

Each time they kissed, he realized she was perfect for him, or at least as close it was going to get in his lifetime, but he wished he didn't have so many problems that loomed to threaten their happiness. So, Wyatt listened to her talk at the rustic little wine, coffee, and sandwich café next to the swift-flowing mountain stream—the lucky wind caressing her raven strands, flopping them into her eyes while she deftly put them back into place, though never immediately. She let the strands linger a little, as long as she could see through them. But he especially loved when she drank red wine, creating a wine mustache or actually a parenthesis-shaped red mark on the slight curve of her upper lip, always on the right side, and that made him desire her even more for some reason.

"C'mon, Wyatt. I know it's there. What side is it on, right or left?"

He smiled like a kid who knew where his grandpa kept his stack of *Playboy* magazines but wasn't going to divulge the secret. It was too sexy. "It's in the middle this time, honey."

"No, it's not Wyatt. Now tell me truthfully before I have to get out my mirror and fix it."

"Right side. Always and forever, right side."

She wiped above her right lip with her index finger.

"Okay, is it gone?"

"Oh, sorry, I meant left. So sorry." Wyatt grinned.

"Wyatt I'm going to have to smack you down!"

"You look fabulous, honey."

They laughed, and after his wine was finished, he suddenly turned serious, almost fumbling for words, constantly scanning the room.

"What's wrong Wyatt? Some hot chick you noticed and didn't want me to see your roving eyes?"

"You're the hot one, dear. You sizzle while the others are just, you know, lukewarm at best." After a brief pause, he pressed on: "Gentri, I need to tell you something that I finally figured out, and it may explain some of my weird behavior you've noticed."

"Do tell. I worry about you, sweetheart."

Well, I believe I'm a clairvoyant."

"A what?"

"Clairvoyant—someone who sees things or predicts events beyond the normal senses that everyone has, you know, ESP."

"Yes, I've heard about it. They say some police departments and the FBI use psychics to track down criminals or killers, by having these people touch objects or examine the scene of a crime so they can become closer to the criminal. Is that what you mean? You're a psychic?"

"I think so. I guess that's one way of putting it."

She bit her lip and stared at him, this time without brushing the hair away from her face at all. It stayed right in front of her face, and she didn't seem to care.

"Why didn't you tell me this earlier—like you know, when we met? It may have been a nice tidbit of information to know before our relationship grew."

"I guess I would've told you if I'd understood it or was aware of it, but I don't think I received this gift, or maybe curse, until after my accident and near-death experience. But, I wonder, does it make a difference between us?"

Gentri laughed in a somewhat higher pitch than usual. "Well, of course not, but I must admit it's a little unusual. I never met a real psychic in the flesh. I've only seen them on TV shows, I guess. And well, here you are and—"

"Remember the horrible beheading at Navy Pier in Chicago, the bombing in Virginia, and the recent removal of an anesthesiologist, all of which I saw and predicted the day before or simultaneously with the event."

"Yes, but I thought that was a manifestation of your PTSD."

"I thought that was the case as well … at *first*. But it's different. When I had my NDE, I saw the bright light beckoning me into the tunnel, and the light immersed me with love and his commanding, yet soothing voice said, 'Wyatt, no more killing, and you will receive a gift.'"

"Is this the 'He' I think it is?"

"I'm sure it was the Almighty, our creator, Gentri, and what's more, I feel you may be in danger now, possibly because of your contact with me and I must somehow protect you. I need you in my life, Gentri. The truth is you're very special to me, but I think it's best that I avoid seeing you for a while … but at the same time, I'll be protecting you from a distance, my dear. And one more thing before I let you react to this strange information about me. The hospital administrator put me on a sabbatical to get psychological testing and treatment as well as a neurology evaluation."

"Oh my God, Wyatt. I'm so confused by all of this happening all at once! I don't know what to believe anymore, or maybe I never did, I just—"

"I understand. You didn't deserve this, but I will never abandon you and will always protect you from a distance until I get my head figured out and keep you from the danger that I feel I'm dragging to your doorstep."

"Protect me from *what*? Will you tell me?"

"I'm not exactly sure yet, but you need to trust me, sweetheart."

She looked at him, her eyes searching deeply inside his, but she knew she would not—could not—get an answer from him at the moment.

He hugged and kissed her, without an answer that he could safely provide, then he drove her home.

Neither of them spoke another word along the way.

CHAPTER 26

The text was from Erik. *Hi love. I have tickets to a play with dinner before, of course. Don't disappoint me.*

Gentri thought, *Who the hell does he think he is? God's gift to women? He just won't take no for an answer and hopes that when my defenses are down, I'll say yes and he'll win his prize, or worse yet, he actually believes I want him, like all women should, but I'm playing hard to get.* She poured herself a glass of Pinot Noir, read some languishing emails that demanded responses, then took a deep breath and said out loud "I'm not afraid of this blue-eyed Scandinavian wolf."

She texted back. *Erik, thanks, but I need to work this weekend.* She avoided any words that suggested there would be another time.

He responded quickly. *You're a goddess, Gentri, and a goddess needs the best in life, so a man must be patient.*

She felt a dead-fish type of nausea once again and thought about writing, "I know the best when I see it, and it certainly isn't you." But instead, she thought better of it and simply deleted the entire text, finished her wine, and called her Wyatt.

"Hi, honey. Are you feeling better today?" said Gentri.

"Always better when you call. I'm feeling fine and always thinking of you. And I'm wondering why you haven't washed off your wine mustache yet. Is it because you're drinking alone, thinking of me?"

She was near the mirror and there it was, the wine parenthesis planted on her right upper lip. How did he know she had this on her face on the phone while not on face time? And for that matter, that she was drinking wine? She wiped it off and said, "Maybe it's on the left side this time, Mr. Know It All."

"Never on the left, honey. But I must say I appreciate your call so I could excuse myself from this psychotherapy group session I'm in now with the hospital-appointed shrink."

"Oh, I'm sorry, sweetheart. Are they making any 'headway' into your problem, Wyatt?"

"Hey, that almost brought me to a chuckle."

"Sorry. I couldn't help it. I had to say it."

"No problem. I'm sure I would've gone for that one too. Served up on a silver platter for you. Too early to say, honey. I guess they still think I'm crazy, and maybe they're right. I go to some interesting classes, though, or maybe it's better to call them ordeals, and I smile while trying not to smack my lips too hard. But I'm trying to get through this ordeal, and—who knows—maybe they can help me deal with some of these PTSD nightmares. Anyway, he's motioning me back to session now. So sorry, sweetie, but I've got to go get my head examined for all the other crazies to look deep inside."

She hung up and poured herself a larger glass of wine this time, initially swirling it in her mouth, then gulped it down with unusual gusto. She thought, *Why are my men so weird? Erik is handsome but an aggressive womanizer who's in love with himself. Wyatt is a good man—a good-looking, intelligent surgeon who unfortunately brought the war and the Africa crash back with him in the form of PTSD with nightmares and headaches, and now he claims he suddenly sees certain events before they happen. And now he believes I'm in danger simply because I'm dating him. What the hell could that danger be? Do people hate medical missionaries? And if so, do they want to kill them and destroy the people they love? That makes no sense. And how did he know I was drinking red wine the moment he called and had another damn wine mustache on my right upper lip without seeing me in person? I need a vacation badly.*

CHAPTER 27

The psychiatrist prescribed Minipress to Wyatt—an older anti-hypertensive that had proven effective in treating nightmares in patients with PTSD, although that wasn't the primary application for the drug. He gladly accepted the medication, knowing it wasn't an anti-psychotic or anti-depressant, because he would refuse those medications outright. Some of his buddies with this disorder were on combinations of Seroquel and antidepressants, and he refused to be a zombie without a libido, although it seemed he had already screwed up his relationship with his bed partner. He wanted to be prepared in case there was a call to action. He just didn't want to be dependent on crazy meds, because after all, he was a damn trauma surgeon, for God's sake.

Wyatt made sure he was always on time for group therapy, promptly at 9 a.m. Even though he thought therapy was generally a waste of time, he dutifully attended so he could keep his career. Why listen to other people's problems? He knew what this was—nightmares and headaches, but more importantly, he had visions that often came true, and he knew he must not ever discuss this ability, or skill, or whatever this gift was with his psychiatric team or the group, because he would be labeled a schizophrenic with visual hallucinations and then, the game would be over and the fat lady would finally bellow her melancholy song as his surgical career was flushed down the toilet in a gushing swirl.

The group therapy leader went around the gaggle of patients—five in total—asking each individual what thought intruded into their mind the most—and bothered them the most as well. One patient said, "God talks to me, telling me I'm not his son Jesus but I look like him with my long hair, so now I must act like him before he calls me back from my earthly mission." He played with his shoulder-length hair and smiled triumphantly.

The leader asked, "Does that bother you, Hank?"

"Well, yes. Mostly because I think he will soon ask me to be crucified, too, since Easter is coming. Seems I have so much to do with so little time remaining. I hope I don't have to be crucified because I'm averse to physical pain. I hope he'll call me back before Easter arrives."

Wyatt stared straight ahead, arms crossed, face emotionless, despite his overwhelming urge to sprint to one of the exits with his arms pumping hard.

"What about *you*, Wyatt?" The therapy leader purposely avoided saying "doctor" so as not to give Wyatt away to the other patients. "Do you have anything to share with the group? Don't be shy, Wyatt."

Wyatt paused, thought about it; ignored the previous disturbing clairvoyant images of beheadings, killings, and chaos; smirked, and said, "I sometimes dream that I go fly fishing in the mountain stream naked because my dog took my waders and pants away, but I can't catch any trout because they laugh at me and say, "Sir, you better be thankful we're not flying fish because we would fly circles around you, then steal your flies and spit them back at you, hoping someday you'll learn how to present the correct flies to us properly in the water. And by the way, most trout aren't scared by noise as much as they are of naked humans wading in our homes, uninvited. There's a mountain stream dress code, you know." Wyatt wasn't sure how he was able to come up with this silliness so quickly, but he tried not to laugh at his own concocted fish story. He proudly maintained a deadly serious face for all the group participants to see.

The whole group, including the therapist, remained emotionless after hearing Wyatt's fish story, and of course, no one laughed in group session. That would be a cardinal sin. After Wyatt's story, the session that day was no longer effective for any of the participants. All the patients wanted to talk about was trout fishing and the proper clothing for such activities. Thereafter, all the patients addressed Wyatt with reverence as the Trout Whisperer.

Wyatt made sure he worked out every morning, alternating between his hybrid Navy Seal heavy bag–sprint workout and a high-intensity routine with little interval rest, including push-ups, pull-ups, front and side planks, and "man-makers"—a combination of burpees with push-ups and dumbbell renegade rows before finishing with the burpee jump press. Not only did he want to maintain his fitness the best he could despite his chronic knee pain and creakiness, but he knew this was the best way to reduce the stress of his complex life. It seemed to keep the pesky demons in his head at least partially controlled. His PTSD therapy revolved mostly around Imagery Rehearsal Therapy. His psychiatrist taught him to recall the nightmare, write it down, then change the scene or storyline to a more pleasant or perhaps positive one, with a happy ending, then rehearse it during the day to displace the unwanted ending when the nightmare predictably recurred. The idea was to refute the premise of the original nightmare. He was also told not to drink any alcohol, but hell, he couldn't live without it, so after several days of individual IRT and brutal group therapy, he poured himself some bourbon on the rocks, kicked back on his comfy deck chair, and collected his thoughts.

Finally, after several weeks, the Minipress effectively reduced the frequency of the nightmares, and when they occurred, they no longer seemed to influence him as much. He felt he had a better handle on his mind now, and even the headaches—though still present—seemed much less intense.

On day fourteen of his psychiatric therapy, he woke up suddenly at 2 a.m., bolted upright, and realized who this blue-eyed Swedish guy was in his dreams—the one who spoke Arabic rather than Swedish, carried an AK-47, and chanted, "Death to America." The vision of this man now became clear as Pikes Peak on a sunny morning. This man looked similar to the blond terrorist fighter he'd shot between the eyes on the Black Ops mission, just before the truck blew up. He now had the feeling, through his gift, that this Swedish man may be the dead fighter's father, and he wasn't the good man people thought he was. Wyatt saw—felt—that he was a leader ... and a dangerous one. And what's more, he continued seeing disturbing images of Gentri associated with this beast somehow, and that danger burned deep within his soul—something he believed completely now, but unfortunately without any solid objective evidence. Gentri, his love, was in danger. Each time he thought about it, it felt like a softball rolling around in his gut, knocking into his insides and threatening to drive him insane.

***

"Wyatt, great to hear from you. Haven't heard from you in a long time. How the hell are you?!"

"Doing well, Kevin. Yeah, I think it was after we returned from Kandahar, and I pinned The Purple Heart on you."

"Right. And you pricked my skin when you put The Purple Heart on me. But I survived. We were a good team, Wyatt. Rangers lead the way! So, tell me, what can I do for you?"

"I heard you're working civilian security now," said Wyatt.

"Roger that."

"I need your service for a special female friend of mine who's in danger. I called you, Ranger to Ranger."

Wyatt carefully told him what he could about Gentri—in vague terms, because that was all he could do anyway without the man becoming skeptical or even worse, concerned about Wyatt's mental health, the way everyone else seemed to be.

"I need you to put some eyes on her. Watch her home and her activities because I think she's being marked as a target."

"By whom, Wyatt?"

"I can't say now, Kevin. But you and your boys will know it when you see it, I'm sure."

Wyatt counted Kevin's breathing—two long silent breaths that controlled the moment. "Okay, Wyatt, I'll do it, but only because it's you, buddy."

"Thanks, Kev. I appreciate it."

Keven Riley, ex-Army Ranger and now the owner of the Stratos Security Corporation was now contracted to Wyatt, secretly protecting Gentri.

Wyatt put the phone down, somewhat relieved, but that statement given to him by the loving light that day came back to him again: *Nothing matters but love, Wyatt. Go into the world and do great things with your blessings. Protect those who need protection, and help those who need help. But you must not kill anymore, and if you obey these words, then you will receive a special gift from the light of love.*

CHAPTER 28

After three weeks, they decided to release Wyatt from therapy, so he immediately called his girl for a much-needed date.

"Thanks for calling, sweetheart," said Gentri. "Did they fix what's inside that handsome head of yours?"

"Not sure if what remains is fixable, but believe it or not, there are people quite a bit more messed up than I am. Some of them believe they're very important people, but then, how are we to know the truth? Anyway, you'll be happy to know that they now call me the Trout Whisperer."

"What?"

"I'll try to explain later, dear. Just a little nickname I picked up from some interesting friends," said Wyatt. "I need to see you, Gentri. It's been way too long, so I bought us tickets to the Denver Center for the Performing Arts, Buell Theater, for dinner and a play Saturday. Hope you can go. Seats are in the back, not so close to the stage so we can make out without causing too much of a scene."

"Honey, I already picked out my dress multiple times during the eternity I was waiting for your call."

***

Dr. Rogers received the report from the mental health consultant and called Wyatt into his office.

"Dr. Pinkerton sent me a summary report on you, and I thought I would read his recommendations. Is that okay with you, Wyatt?" He avoided playing with his ponytail this time, which Wyatt took as a promising sign.

"Sure. I'm anxious to hear his thoughts about what's inside my head. Just wondered, though, why you're reading it to me rather than allowing me to read it myself."

"More effective this way, I think. This way I know you heard the words and you didn't skip any of the important parts with your own independent reading or lack of reading. Don't worry; you'll get a copy."

"Trustful soul aren't you, Paul?"

"Anyway, here it is: 'Dr. Barton has nightmares associated with Post Traumatic Stress Disorder directly linked to his previous military service but shows no other evidence of mental illness. With Minipress and Imagery Rehearsal Therapy, his nightmares are still present but more manageable, and we've found that his headaches are improved because of better sleep, although they will likely remain to a certain degree after his head injury. As far as the tremors, he was seen by our neurologist on staff, and these are benign essential tremors that don't seem to interfere with his hand use or effectiveness to work, and there is no evidence of clinical Parkinson's Disease. We recommend resumption of full employment as a surgeon with no limitations.

"Congratulations, Wyatt," said Rogers. "You're back on staff."

"So, I guess I've earned my diploma now—certified by the crazy house. But I wonder, how about the Good Housekeeping Seal of Approval?"

Rogers didn't crack a smile. "You're back to work tomorrow, Wyatt."

Wyatt walked away, happy to have his career back again, but his happiness found itself trapped in some dark clouds because he knew there must be a horrible terrorist organization that he could sense that was infiltrating the country he loved, and he realized he couldn't ignore it because it seemed he was the only one who could see the horror before it happened. Deep within his soul, he knew he must fight it. Would he have been able to prevent the beheading he saw and the church killings? It seemed unlikely—but not impossible.

The frustrating thing was that he didn't know how in the world to use his gift and yet intervene … somehow without attracting attention from his ever-present shadow men and, worse yet, disobeying the command from the light that demanded he not kill anymore. It all seemed impossible.

Perhaps he could neutralize the embedded terrorists individually before they killed more innocent civilians, but to do that without proof of the upcoming event would certainly be considered by the courts, murder in cold blood. But he now came to the stark realization that each of his new brutal visions of attacks on innocents had come true.

The other problem was that he wasn't an operator; he was a surgeon, and the shadow men would never allow him to engage the enemy, wherever that enemy was. But what if he slipped, made a mistake, and killed one of these terrorists here on US soil rather than on the battlefield? Was that such a bad thing to do? And how valuable was this newly received gift? He felt trapped with these visions and the inability to act on them with lethal force to prevent the death of innocent civilians, but at the same time, he didn't want to have direct knowledge of these horrible events without actively intervening somehow to prevent the loss of innocent lives here in America. He slept on it for a couple of days, and eventually, his conscience won, and he made a decision.

God has saved me and has given me one simple rule to keep this gift— so, I must honor it.

***

During the drive home from the play, on I-25 South, Wyatt felt the comfortable warmth of love for Gentri, and his overriding thought was to protect that love. But he wasn't sure how she would handle the degree of protection that he was going to provide for her.

"Gentri, I want you to know I hired one of my ex-Ranger buddies, a private security contractor, to provide you some protection until this thing is over."

"You did *what?*" said Gentri. "There you go talking about protecting me from some unknown danger again."

So much for her taking it well.

"You can't even tell me what the danger is, and what I should be looking for, right Wyatt?"

"I don't know. I just feel it. And the danger is because of your closeness to me because I know I'm the target. I feel a dark presence coming toward you Gentri, from somewhere. So, although I don't want to separate us, I mustn't be seen with you for a while, but I will always be thinking of you and protecting you from a distance. I love you, Gentri." That was the first time in many years those words had come from Wyatt's mouth, but they'd come out as easy as a rainbow after a brief summer rain shower.

He pulled up to her house slowly after driving twice around the neighborhood, scanning the area, and finally, she spoke.

"Damn you, Wyatt! It seems you're the best man, and then at the same time, you're kind of the worst man as well. I just don't know what to think about you and . . . well, this situation you're in anymore. I don't know if I'm blessed or cursed to have you in my life. Sorry to say that, but it's true. You're struggling with secrets deep inside your soul, Wyatt, and you won't share them with me . . and that will continue hurting us as a couple until you decide to tell me the truth. But even worse than that, I think it's a parasite deep inside you that will destroy you if you don't let it out and resolve your issues."

Her words surprised him, and he felt the punch to his belly that he knew he deserved from her. He never liked to lose, but he didn't think he could survive losing another relationship—not one that was finally allowing him to heal and grow. "I'm sorry, honey. I hope to be able to tell you everything someday, or a portion of it anyway, but at least you can't say I was boring."

"That's for damn sure, sweetheart," said Gentri.

"May I have a kiss, my Southern goddess and master of real estate and romance novelist with the fucked-up boyfriend?"

She leaned over and kissed him passionately, hugging him hard for a minute, and then she walked away from the car with her mascara smudged from the tears she wouldn't let him see.

CHAPTER 29

C ode Blue, Room 364, ICU. Code Blue, Room 364, ICU." The Mercy Hospital public address announcer continued to calmly repeat the request for emergency personnel to run to this room to assist a dying patient. After a long minute, she resumed her announcement this time broadcasting, "*Code Blue, Room 364 is secured. Code Blue, Room 364 is secured*"—meaning a physician had arrived to take over as the team leader for the staff during the resuscitation.

Wyatt asked to be on call, in-house the next day after his reinstatement on staff because he knew he needed to start work full force again to make it known that he was back as a member of the Mercy Surgical Team and was unimpaired. He heard the code announcement when he was in his call room, lying down, and he bolted out of bed, forcing his running shoes on. As he ran out of the call room, his scrub bottoms were untied at the waist, and his shorts were on partial display, but he tied the scrub drawstring while running. He was sure the cameras had this well-recorded, and he wondered if he would catch hell for that too, but who cared? The administration had butt cracks too.

When he reached Room 364, he was the second physician to arrive amidst the pandemonium, which included respiratory therapists doing CPR; nurses injecting epinephrine into the patient's veins, trying to get her heart restarted; and ICU pharmacists preparing the drugs for injection. Wyatt immediately yelled, so he could be heard clearly above the din, "Can anyone give me the story on this patient?"

The bedside ICU nurse attending the patient told him the patient was a forty-five-year-old female with triple-negative metastatic breast cancer that had spread to the brain, with pleural effusions in the chest cavity causing respiratory failure and the need for mechanical ventilation. Unfortunately, she wasn't responding to immune therapy with a PD-1 inhibitor. "This is her second code today, Dr. Barton, but the first one was brief bradycardia that responded to some atropine and about thirty seconds of CPR. She's been hypotensive all day, though, and is on a pressor agent to raise her pressure. But I want you to know she's a retired nurse here that we all love, and we just can't lose her!"

The internist who was already running the code commanded, "Time for a pulse check, after the second dose of epinephrine." The pulse checkers responded. "Faint pulse. We have a pressure of only fifty systolic."

This time, Wyatt chimed in and ordered, "Place her on an epinephrine infusion, and get me the ultrasound machine stat!" It was now obvious to everyone in the room that Wyatt was taking over and was on a mission to find out the reason for her arrest before she lost her pulse again—and potentially her life.

Wyatt placed the ultrasound probe below the patient's xiphoid, then quickly found what he'd expected on the far-left side of the chest—a large pericardial effusion, which was a collection of fluid, likely bloody in this case from the spread of cancer, in a sac surrounding the heart muscle, which was causing a collapse of the heart's right ventricle, in turn triggering shock and cardiac arrest.

"Get me a pericardiocentesis tray, size-eight sterile gloves, and some Chloraprep antiseptic stat," said Wyatt, firm but not overbearing. Then, he quickly prepped the skin and found the correct angle for needle entry into the pericardial sack, with the entry point at the fifth intercostal space, close to the sternal margin, which was where his ultrasound images displayed the optimal entry point. He followed the needle entry with ultrasound imagery into the pericardial space, withdrew free-flowing bloody fluid, and advanced the guidewire over the needle. Dilation of the tract followed his

successful placement of the pigtail catheter into the bloated pericardial effusion, and 700 ccs of bloody fluid were immediately drained. In a matter
of seconds, the patient's blood pressure jumped up to the 110 range, and
her pulse rebounded to normalcy. She was now out of shock, and her heart
began to happily beat with the vigor necessary to sustain life and blood
pressure, unimpeded by a constricting sack of cancerous fluid.

Per hospital policy, the patient's husband and teenage daughter were
allowed in the room during the resuscitation process, if they requested
it, and they witnessed the CPR and pericardiocentesis procedure on their
loved one. The internist looked at Wyatt, clearly relieved, and said quietly,
"Thanks, Wyatt. I'm glad you were here. Looks like you've saved this
lady. Do you need me to talk to the family?"

"No, I've got it from here. Thanks, Charlie. Have a good night."

Wyatt glanced around the room and saw the family hugging each other.
Then, he surveyed his colleagues' faces, which had been stripped of dread.

The patient's daughter, who was crying, walked over to Wyatt, hugged
him, and said, "Thanks for bringing my mom back. We thought we were
going to lose her much too early."

Wyatt smiled. "It's my job."

The patient's husband then took Wyatt to the far corner of the room
while the staff cleaned the blood from the patient's chest and removed the
used syringes and bloody dressings.

"Doctor Barton, what's next? Will her heart stop again? Will she have
brain damage from these cardiac arrests?"

Wyatt paused, looked at him, and said, "I don't usually discuss these
things in front of the patient. You never know if they hear our conversations, even when we think they're unconscious." In fact, Wyatt knew
from his own near-death experience that a person who has had a cardiac
arrest may not be able to use their senses, but in some cases, the soul has
been described as floating above the lifeless, dying body and it sees and
feels everything as if the soul is an independent and interested observer
of their own body's death. This knowledge he was careful *not* to share
with the patient's daughter and husband. He asked them to join him in the
conference room outside the ICU. Wyatt knew that although he saved this
retired nurse from immediate death by diagnosing the pericardial effusion

that was constricting the heart with cancer-filled fluid, she still had a poor prognosis overall due to the spread of her nasty cancer. He looked back into the room and smiled when he heard the nurses and respiratory therapist cheer, because the patient opened her eyes suddenly, looked around, and then squeezed their hands, on command.

The family beamed their joy and relief to Wyatt, and he couldn't help but feel a few tears forming in his eyes too. After all these years, and all the death he had seen, this one seemed to surprise him with the emotional effect it produced in him. He responded to their questions. "Well, I was lucky that I was able to drain the fluid around her heart, which, most certainly is malignant, and of course, we'll send it to the lab for testing. Thankfully, it looks as if she may not be neurologically compromised from the lack of cerebral blood flow during the arrest. Wonderful news, that's for sure. But, her cancer is unfortunately stage four and incurable."

"What should we do?" asked her husband. "I don't want to lose her."

"I understand completely. But the cancer is going to take her, unfortunately. Not today, but certainly down the road. Did you talk to your oncologist about the prognosis with immune therapy?"

"Well, no, not directly. We avoid that conversation. She said the PD-1 inhibitor was the best option for her cancer that recurred after surgery."

"I understand," said Wyatt. "But to answer your question, I think there is a strong possibility that she will fail again and have another cardiac or respiratory arrest requiring the same process you have witnessed today. We may not be able to save her next time, and it will become futile. This is a very tough decision, but my advice to you, sir, is that you make her a DNR, meaning no further CPR if her heart stops again and let her go in peace. We will let her wake up and remove her from the ventilator machine when she's ready, so you can talk with her during the last stages of her life rather than keeping her on a life support machine that's associated with pain and discomfort when her condition overall is untreatable."

The husband looked at his daughter, and they both nodded. "We agree, Dr. Barton. She wouldn't want this. Hopefully, she can discuss this with us once she's off the ventilator, but let's keep her comfortable and celebrate our remaining time with our Suzy-Q. Thank you for your expertise and taking the time to talk to us with honesty … and giving us a little more time with her after you saved her for us."

With that, Wyatt shook his hand, hugged the patient's daughter, and walked back to the on-call room, answering phone calls about other patients as he walked, feeling gratified that his first day on the job after graduation from the crazy house was beneficial at least to one struggling family.

CHAPTER 30

Secretary of State John Randolph Robinson lost his bid for president during the primary election. In fact, he was soundly defeated, having won only one state, California, his home state, which had been a steadfast fortress for his party for many years. But he knew he was, without question, the best of multiple candidates for the job, and although he may have been less experienced, the average American voter clearly wasn't intelligent enough to perceive this obvious fact. Robinson believed they weren't low-information voters but were, instead, no-brain voters who were easily persuaded by good looks and shallow promises. But there was always four years later, and the consolation prize was an office with significant power and influence he could use on world leaders and influential people in the US—especially wealthy donors, who would come in handy when he finally won the big election.

After the defeat, Secretary Robinson decided to form a foundation called Giving for World Peace. The basic idea was to advertise that the foundation funneled money into developing countries to improve their health and standard of living because obviously, people with better incomes and a higher standard of living would be less likely to seek America's destruction. He believed, as did others in his socially correct party, that giving them money would make them happier and love America while making him look like an altruistic and benevolent statesman who simply cared for others more than himself. Creative accounting and front organizations would make it easy for a large percentage of the money meant for the poor in parts of the world to be transferred into his company for his benefit and also to be used to allow donors to influence policy decisions quietly, under the table. Every year, the foundation organized a gala for fundraising, and this time, it occurred on a political donor's 60-foot private yacht, cruising across the Atlantic, carefully outside US territorial waters, not on US soil, which had certain legal and political advantages. The figurehead CEO of GWP was Monica Pruitt. She'd earned a PhD from Harvard in International Relations and essentially ran the day-to-day operation of the organization but always made sure the secretary was invited to meet with international businessmen and influential political figures of other states at biannual social functions and fundraisers.

At the semicircular bar dominating the upper deck of the ship, there was a tall, athletic gentleman with blond hair, drinking a cocktail and surrounded by well-dressed women boasting outrageously expensive heels for all male eyes to fixate on. Always the social gentleman, John made a point of meeting this tall Nordic man who had been so generous to his benevolent foundation. Air Force Secretary Logan had already briefed him on Rondell Enterprises and Erik's upcoming trip to Saudi Arabia, courtesy of US taxpayers.

"So nice to finally meet you, Erik," said the secretary

"Likewise, John. I appreciate what Monica's—I mean *your* organization—does for the poor in the world, and I'm happy to provide a gift for the organization, courtesy of my company. We're happy to donate to worthwhile charities around the world."

"When I saw the check with a five followed by six zeros, I was impressed by your generosity, and I'm going to make sure you have a say in much of our organization's plans, and ... well, you will now have an honored seat on the board of directors. So, tell me about your company, Rondell Aerospace, and how we can perhaps build a working relationship that makes all of us happy? I must say, Secretary Logan was impressed with you and has already invited you to help us out with the Saudis and their defense insecurities."

"Yes, Mr. Logan was quite generous to my company, but I assume he received the green light from you and the Pentagon beforehand. Anyway, we provide aerospace consulting and manufacturing of UAVs for the defense department. We're small but powerful. We don't like to advertise, nor do we need to, as you have already seen. We design secret aircraft for the department of defense, and we sell to the US only, although many countries want to do business with us. We're a patriotic firm, and we believe in US exceptionalism."

"I'll make sure to mention your company to the president. I'm sure he'd be interested in hearing some of your opinions about the defense industry when the opportunity is right. Clearly, we must do better protecting our country from those who would do us harm."

"Yes, thank you. I hate to ask this, but I suppose it's time to be direct now that we have established a relationship and a mutual agreement. When you talk to the president, could you do me a little favor, John?"

"Of course, Erik. You now have clearly earned a lot more of my ear."

"It would be nice if he were to ease the travel restrictions for Pakistan, Syria, Yemen, Somalia, Sudan, and Iran. It just doesn't seem right to me, and I think it's hurting the good people of Muslim faith who desire a better life and income, which only the benevolent United States can provide. Although Islamic terrorists do tend to fight us, the largest majority of people in these countries are peace-loving Muslims. But then, forgive me, John; I think you can't possibly do this for me and my bleeding heart. I know—"

"I'll do what I can for you about this situation," said the Secretary of State. He thought, *Jorgensen is quite impressive, and Logan was right in engaging him. He could be a great ally for my next presidential campaign as well, especially with the funding aspect but also with the Muslim community, it seems. But why is this guy so interested in Islamic policy here? Shouldn't he just concentrate on making weapons systems for us? Logan said he learned fluent Arabic in college and maybe that explains the cultural influence. However, perhaps he makes a good point. We have to not be so harsh on our Muslim citizens at least with our words and policies, allow open immigration, and treat them with respect. He's a shining star, and I'll definitely keep him on speed-dial.*

"Oh, and one more favor I need to ask of you, John."

"Sure thing. You definitely have both of my ears now."

"There's some increasing rhetoric around Washington about the Chinese and how they may somehow be our enemy now. I believe that is counter-productive thinking, and we need to realize they are a world power and a financial power that we must deal with in a positive and productive way, with full cooperation, and less saber-rattling and offensive speech. Would you be able to talk to the president and perhaps work something out in a more positive way with our Chinese partners?"

Secretary Robinson looked at him, somewhat taken aback about how this guy was pushing his weight around on the world stage and making these unusual requests of the president. Maybe Rondell was working out some business deals with the Chinese that he wasn't aware of. It was clear to Robinson, though, that Rondell Enterprises was now an excellent financial supporter of his campaign, and so this guy's requests should be considered, at least. "No problem, Erik. I'll see what I can do. No promises, you know," said Secretary Robinson.

"Of course. I understand, John."

They shook hands and walked away to mingle with the other VIPs on the yacht.

Later, back in his cabin, Erik turned on some smooth jazz, starting with Joe Sample and then some funky Down to the Bone. He then called the steward to bring a few bottles of Dom Perignon for the upcoming nocturnal fun. He smiled at the soaring progress he'd made at this yacht meeting, took off his shoes, put his stocking feet up on the leather divan, and ultimately decided to make an important call.

"I thought I told you not to call me. You know that. Probably not a good thing for you and *certainly* dangerous for *me*."

"Yes, I remember," said Erik. "But I also know your situation pretty well, and oftentimes, personal lives affect our professional lives. I want you to be happy and successful on both fronts, so I'm calling to help you. A man in your position needs to have a stable financial foundation. Don't you think? Otherwise, things get complicated quickly, and you become less effective in your work."

"I don't need your help on either front."

"Will five hundred large change your mind?" said Erik. "Offshore account of course."

There was a hefty pause on the other end of the line. Erik could hear the man on the other end take a deep breath. "I'll think about your offer, but don't call me. This is dangerous. And how did you get my number?"

"Try to ask me to do something more difficult, my friend. These issues don't challenge me," said Erik. "Oh, and as far as phone calls go, you'll be calling me. I'm sure of it. Just let me know the name and location of the ape who's sitting on your shoulders, and I can remove him for you and make him leave you alone."

After he hung up, Erik smiled, stood, and freshened up with a brief spray of Paco Rabanne. Then, he brushed his teeth and flossed, admired his bright smile in the mirror, and texted the brunette with long legs from the State Department he'd met at the bar. She told him she was an intern, and he could tell she was interested in and impressed by him. But then, of course she was. They almost always were. He texted: "Cabin ten is now available for your carnal pleasure."

CHAPTER 31

They followed him everywhere in the shadows, but Wyatt never let them know that he was aware of their presence. He knew why they were told to do it. He had been on a Black Ops mission—one of multiple missions over the years—and this one went had gone bad, something the American public wouldn't know about for years, if ever. The government hired them to make sure Wyatt didn't compromise information about his clandestine operations in some fashion, and to then take appropriate action if there was a compromise. Although he wasn't an operator anymore, he performed like one, and sadly, one person—who wasn't even an operator—had died to complete the mission.

Wyatt realized that although they were supposed to be on his side of the conflict, the shadow men had become a hindrance to him, at best, and that if he didn't act, more horror would befall innocent Americans. If only he hadn't agreed to participate in this last mission and come out of retirement, his life would be easier as a civilian surgeon, operating on overweight people with inflamed gallbladders and later in the evening, drinking martinis with a hot Southern belle and living the good life.

Wyatt completed two relatively uneventful cases that day—a simple bowel resection and, later, a radical debridement of necrotizing fasciitis in a septic ICU patient. When he was called to see the ICU patient, he found that the individual had been previously bitten by a brown recluse spider; then, about a week later, they'd come down with fever and had a swollen left leg that was red and very hard to the touch. Following a brief examination, Wyatt diagnosed the patient with an infection of deep soft tissues of the leg, after the spider bite, resulting in what was most likely the destruction of the muscle fascia and overlying subcutaneous fat tissue. Despite the appropriate antibiotics that the patient received, Wyatt knew the patient was at risk of worsened systemic toxicity, loss of the leg, or even death if he did not take him to the OR for immediate exploration and debridement of the affected tissue.

The case was successful in the OR, taking about an hour, and after recovery, the patient was brought back stable to the ICU. After Wyatt discussed the results of the case with the critical care attending and was confident that the patient was improving and stable in the ICU, he left the OR to take a break in the doctor's lounge where he joined Dr. Franklin for some coffee.

"Hey, Wyatt," said Dr. Franklin. "How was your case today?"

"It went well, thanks. How have you been? Stamping out disease and pestilence, I assume?"

"Mostly disease—not much pestilence. Listen, Wyatt. There's a hospital system-wide picnic out in the park today. Kind of a gift of appreciation from the administration to all the employees. It lasts for three hours, so people can get away and get coverage to attend. I think it would be good for you to go out and mingle—do a little socializing."

"No thanks. I think I'll just relax for a while and review some charts and read about my case for tomorrow."

"Suit yourself. I'm going for a little while. I hope you change your mind."

Wyatt just wanted to be alone and collect his thoughts, and a picnic was the last thing on his mind. After reviewing his charts for an hour, and his case for the next day, hunger hit him, and he went to the physician's lunch area. Yet, he found there was no food at all except potato chips and soft drinks, because the culinary workers were all out in the park nearby, preparing barbecue for the picnic. *Oh, what the hell*, he thought. *Maybe I'll just go for a few minutes, have a burger, shake a few hands, and head back to the hospital. No big deal.*

***

The hospital system barbecue picnic occupied a large chunk of the park near the tennis courts, adjacent to the hospital and west of the legal smoking area. The hospital had hired a large event company to erect multiple tents with picnic tables and folding chairs inside. The hospital organized this as a show of appreciation for up to three hundred staff every summer, complete with hot dogs and hamburgers and booths to test skills, kind of like at a county fair.

Most employees arrived in scrubs, and the female administrators arrived in their most conservative work pumps to serve the food, sinking the heels of their pumps into the wet sod while serving the common folk, just to show they were regular people too.

It was 1:30 p.m., and Wyatt had no more cases scheduled. He was simply to be available on day-call for the general surgery service until 5 p.m. He downed a cheeseburger so fast that the catsup had no time to drip, then just as quickly vanquished his baked beans and corn on the cob while simultaneously surveying the large city park filled with hundreds of people chattering away as live music drifted through the air. To the north, west, and south were city streets, and to the east was the hospital structure itself.

Wyatt finished his meal, greeted a few employees, then got up to leave and walk back to the hospital. As he walked, he suddenly felt a strange chill on this humid day. Despite all the laughter and fun, something didn't feel right.

He surveyed the area, and each side of the park was vulnerable to attack—a super soft target, with large numbers of unarmed people all in the center of a grassy park with a gravel access road cutting a path to the center of the park, next to the tents. His situational training never left him, and it seemed to be dominating his thoughts at this moment. The shadow men were there too, but he located only one of them, about thirty meters away, wearing a Colorado Rockies cap and dark sunglasses, his tight shirt barely holding his ripped upper body. He didn't bother Wyatt at all, but he did see a nondescript white van, sitting far on the other side of the southeast side of the park, near the small barricaded gravel access road leading to the inside of the grassy park.

This van *did* bother him. It just looked out of place and too isolated. Wyatt decided to walk to the porta-johns near the van and saw that the driver had a beard, was wearing sunglasses, and using small field binoculars to survey the park festivities.

Why, he thought, *would he want to look at the park festival with binoculars? Delivery men don't need to do that. They just come in, make their delivery and leave. Was he a dirty pervert looking for little girls?*

Then, it happened, clear and bright. He saw a brief vision of explosives, a van, and carnage. His Chicago Navy Pier vision was much more detailed, occurring after the fact, but this vision jolted him enough that he felt he needed to act on this one because maybe this was the real thing, about to happen, now in real-time, rather than after the fact. He couldn't be a passive—helpless—observer any longer.

Wyatt walked fast, so as not to draw attention with a run, then when out of sight, he sprinted to the doctor's parking lot, 150 meters east of the park. He didn't look back but knew the shadow men were following the best they could. He jumped in his car in the doctor's lot, flew out of the garage and as expected, the black suburban with shadow men was waiting for him at the only exit from the garage. *C'mon guys, I need a break now, not a wall.*

He obeyed the speed limit until off the hospital grounds, and then the chase began—a frenzy of weaving and zig-zagging in his Toyota Land Cruiser—and finally, he lost his constant pursuers. He figured the shadow men would go back to the hospital, knowing he was still on duty but instead he decided not to go back.

He parked his car in an alley behind a bar, several blocks from the park, took off his scrubs, found the emergency bolt bag he always kept on his back seat, put on some jeans and a T-shirt, a Chicago Cubs baseball cap, as well as a fake mustache. He exited his car and started walking back to the park in his new garb.

On the way, he hotwired a Toyota Camry—a car that all special operators knew was easy to start—and drove it off the side street to the area where he saw the suspicious man in the van. He knew he needed a car for pursuit, just in case. The man in the van was still there and thankfully not moving, so he parked three spaces behind it on the opposite side of the street.

After ten minutes of surveillance, he felt his pulse hammer heavily on his temples because he now realized his vision was, in fact, accurate—running real-time—and therefore may give him a chance to finally intervene in whatever event was going to occur. He used his breathing techniques to slow it down, just as he had been taught years ago in the military, especially at the shooting range. He got out of his Toyota, calmly walked slowly to the van's driver side, wobbly, like a hapless drunk, and made sure his hospital phone was turned off. Wyatt found the bearded man slouched down in his seat, his head flush with the steering wheel level, typing on a cell phone, using an awkward pecking action with his index finger. then, Wyatt suddenly leaped toward the driver's window, smashed the window with the rescue hammer on his keychain, and slugged the man hard enough to incapacitate but not kill him. Then, he opened the door, tied the man's hands and feet with prisoner ties, and gagged him. He got in, looked through the back of the van, and saw it was filled with gas cans and black boxes of explosives with connecting wires, so this clearly was going to be a suicide crash bombing into the crowded picnic. He checked to make sure the bearded demon was still breathing, then grabbed the man's cell phone, turned it off, and left it in the van, knowing it could potentially be traced by the FBI.

He looked in the glove compartment but found no registration papers, so he checked under the floor mats—no luck—and finally, the back pockets of the driver's-side and passenger-side doors. In the passenger's side door pocket, he found what looked like a crinkled invoice, with some ink stains from it being wet previously. It read: *Johnson's Automotive Painting and Body Shop. Your satisfaction is our number one priority.* From what he could make out, the invoice itemized the charges and fees for painting the van, then as the method of payment, it read: *loyal customer premium credit plan*, but no credit card number was provided. Under the customer name section, he found a signature that he couldn't make out.

He put the invoice in his pocket, figuring the FBI would do their job with fingerprints and DNA on everything in the van, while Wyatt would proceed on his own to figure this out. He didn't trust anyone anymore—unless, of course, they would take a bullet for him. The bearded man wore a necklace with a metal crescent moon and star in the middle, and a similar crescent moon and star was hanging from the rear-view mirror. The monster was awake now, and registering his wide-eyed fear, Wyatt promptly dislocated the man's right shoulder, just for good measure, took the keys, and left the car while calling 911: "There's a white Chevrolet Van, license number VUL 6324 filled with bomb material on the southeast corner of the Park, near Mercy Hospital on Pikes Peak Avenue. Please evacuate the area!" Then, he jumped in his stolen car and fled the scene, dumping the car on the same street he'd borrowed it, confident the owner would never ever realize it had been gone.

He got back into his Land Cruiser, which he'd left on a back street a half mile away from the hospital, and drove back to the physician's parking lot at Mercy Hospital. After removing the mustache, he turned his cell phone back on and found a message for a new consult on the medical service at the hospital, only five minutes old.

In a flash, he entered the hospital-side entrance with his badge, found some scrubs, and evaluated the consult in the medical ward. A shadow man found him outside the doctor's locker room.

"Wyatt, what the hell do you think you're doing? We're going to have to tighten your leash now, and you're not—"

"I don't care. Get out of my way, sir, before your face licks the dirty linoleum clean, including the wax build-up in the cracks."

The shadow man wisely stepped aside, and Wyatt walked down the hospital corridor alone while the shadow man immediately made a phone call.

***

A massive contingent of police cars and bomb containment trucks descended on the park, surrounding the van, and the park was efficiently evacuated due to Wyatt's 911 call. All that was left in the park were large empty tents and uneaten food and barbecue pits—still smoking. The police bomb squad investigated the van, first with bomb robots and video surveillance. Once it was determined that detonation was not going to occur, the driver was extricated, already bound and tied up. The news media had monitored the 911 call, and multiple TV trucks arrived with the police to film the event. They were pushed away by the police, to provide a perimeter, but several cameras were able to film the extrication of the bearded driver from a distance.

The video feed on the news focused on the park evacuation, the man's Islamic crescent necklace, and the empty van, in which a similar pendant was strung from the rear-view mirror, blowing back and forth as wind wafted through the broken window of the vehicle.

The police captain confirmed with his bomb squad that the scene was now safe. "Who the hell did this?" he asked his bomb squad.

"I'm sure the FBI will be all over this," the bomb squad leader replied, "They'll find out who this animal was and what his motivation may have been."

"That's not what I meant," the police captain told him. "Who the fuck was the hero who found this guy, disabled him so quickly, and then called it in? And where the hell is he?"

The bomb squad leader just looked at the captain, silent and dumbfounded.

Karen Thompson, one of several TV reporters on the scene reported on live TV: "I'm here on the scene of the bomb scare that caused the evacuation of the annual picnic at Mercy Hospital. Hundreds of hospital employees have been evacuated safely, and there are no injuries. As you see on our feed, the police have apprehended the man in the van and we don't have access to the contents of the van or what the individual's motivation was at this time. However, although we have no proof, there seems to be some evidence that he was of the Muslim faith, and it does suggest that this may have been an Islamic terrorist here on American soil. Karen Thompson, Channel 11 News, signing off."

CHAPTER 32

T hat huge soft target—the picnic gathering—should've been blown up, and we should be reading about our glorious success all over the media throughout the world! Such an idiot! How did he let this happen? So many infidels could've easily been destroyed because they're the softest targets possible! Now, instead, one of our idiot fighters is alive and in custody, probably being interrogated by the FBI as we speak. Tell me, Farid, how could this happen? And why did he not blow himself up before being taken captive like a helpless puppy?"

"It can't be explained, Sahib. I told him to examine the target first and make sure everything was perfect before driving into the crowd. I wanted him to maximize casualties, and that required a little patience. Unfortunately, that same patience got the best of him. Certainly, some infidel must've gotten lucky and found him somehow, then surprised him."

"Lucky?" Erik Jorgensen, a.k.a. Abdul, slapped Farid hard on the face with his open hand, leaving red finger marks. "You act like a sniffling little woman. Maybe I should give you a hijab to wear, huh? I reviewed the video from our drone overhead. The guy had a mustache, jeans, and a blue baseball cap, and I couldn't see his face. Walked like a damn drunk and the last visual was when he was walking near the van. He's the man who must've disabled him and called to evacuate the school successfully. But how did he know about our secret mission? Everyone we work with has signed loyalty agreements with FFWP, and we rarely use outside contractors for security reasons"

Farid said, "The owner of the van rental place that provides some of our company vehicles and excellent maintenance is loyal to the core. He prays with me, and I consider him my brother. Not only that, he is paid well on a monthly basis, and he was honored to let me take his teenage daughter's precious virginity and have her whenever I want. So, I'm not worried about him. He has too much to lose. That's why he had me personally inspect the bomber's van to make sure it was outfitted correctly to our specifications. I looked it over myself before he allowed us to drive it off to our shop for arming. Those bombs were engineered correctly to blow up the van completely with extensive shrapnel and a concussive blast that should've devastated that entire park area, once he detonated it at maximum effectiveness."

"Our fighter, who will now never be a martyr, waited too long before deciding to make his move, but how did this fucking infidel know? Don't you see how critical it is to find him? This was a simple, soft operation, and we failed, and with this guy, who's most likely part of a large operation, they will certainly try to stop us again. But how can they without intel? Maybe this was an inside job. If so, heads will roll courtesy of my bloody knife."

"As you said, Sahib, we have him on video and—"

"That video is worthless, and you know it. He was too smart. No face shot except for a mustache—likely fake—dark sunglasses, and a Cubs hat."

"The FBI, as far as we know, don't realize we exist," said Farid. "Or at least not until now. Your Rondell Aerospace is well respected in this country, and it's the perfect cover, especially due to your connections in Washington. But I wonder if he was acting alone. Why would their team send only one man if they knew anything about the hell that was about to be unleashed? Why wouldn't they call in a swarming team of Swat police, bomb squads, and multiple other agencies? And why didn't they evacuate the park beforehand if they knew all the details about your plan? It just doesn't make sense, Sahib."

"Good point," said Erik. They may not have known because nothing else makes sense. Maybe he's just a rogue guy who saw something fishy and walked by and went berserk. But he didn't kill our man. That's bizarre too. He took great lengths to keep our man alive so that he could be captured. Obviously, there was no way a drunk guy could be that efficient and calculated in this situation."

"Don't worry, if there is an organization, we'll find it and overcome it, Sahib."

"That you will or you will be disposed of too, my friend. If you can't plan our operations to succeed, no matter what the circumstances, or at least take some infidel lives with our soldiers so they can become righteous martyrs, then I'll have to start planning all the operational details myself while you no longer breathe! My job is to shake hands and smile, make friends with elite politicians, create our global cloak of power, and design drones for the government, but I can easily take over your job and do the operational details myself if you prove incapable."

"No, Sahib Alsumui, that will not be necessary. We will find him, or I will gladly martyr myself."

"Yes, you are right on both counts," said Erik. "Let there be no question that our mission will continue full force, despite this small hiccup."

CHAPTER 33

Mr. President, thank you for meeting us on such short notice. I know your schedule is quite—"

"You usually call me Jim. You're employing increased formality because you brought a friend from the agency, is my guess."

"Okay, Jim," said Carl Dorman, the Director of the CIA. "You got me. This is Tom Palmer. He works for me as assistant director in our counter-terrorism operations."

They shook hands, and Tommie, at 6'4", was a full six inches taller than the president. Tommie tried to look into his eyes to learn more about him face to face, but the president gave him only a cursory glance.

"Jim, we need a private meeting here—no offense to your staff," said the director. He was looking at the man in a comfortable chair off to the side of the president's desk.

"Not going to happen, Carl, and you should know better. For our protection, or mostly *my* protection, someone is always here as a witness." The president looked briefly at the White House Chief of Staff sitting quietly on a sofa with hands clasped comfortably, smiling at the president. "So, tell me, Carl, what was so important that you needed a private meeting separate from our daily briefings?"

"Tommie came from black SOF and was a Delta commander before joining us at the agency, so he comes with a helpful operational background."

The president looked at Tommie and smiled briefly. Tommie remained emotionless, then started right in. "Anyway, you heard about the thwarted bombing attempt at a Denver Hospital picnic, I am sure. It's in all the news media, and we're trying to—"

"You're damn right, Palmer, I heard and my ears are ringing from the demands for an investigation into how this asshole drunk guy somehow singled out the perp before expertly disabling him. Secretary Robinson just got off the phone with me, filling me in on this and that. One of our most respected defense contractors called him from Riyadh, where he was kindly serving us in a diplomatic fashion, describing the displeasure this news is already having on our few remaining Middle Eastern allies. The Muslim defense organizations are up in arms about this profiling incident and are calling it racially motivated and they want this profiling to stop against the peace-loving Muslim community. I had breakfast with some of their leaders this morning, and I promised them there would be no further harassment of their religion if, in fact, that's what this was."

Palmer spoke up. "With all due respect, sir, race had nothing to do with this, nor did it have anything to do with religious affiliation. We don't even know what religion he professes to follow, sir. Race and religion are two separate issues and aren't one and the same, despite popular opinion. Forgive me for my bluntness, but why should we care about a defense contractor in Riyadh and what he thinks? And for that matter, who is this contractor acting in a diplomatic role?

"Okay, Palmer," said the president, "you're asking for too much information that's beyond your pay grade. Clearly, we are in a culture now where we must take all measures to avoid any perception of racial profiling or religious profiling so we can accept all races and religions into this country. We don't have many friends in that region, and news like this gets blown all over the world now." The president looked at Dorman, surprised by the incredulous temerity of Palmer, but he *still* didn't seem to be getting through to him.

Palmer continued. "One of our former operators took him down, sir, resolving the situation and saving many innocent lives in that park. He is, in fact, a hero to our country, sir."

"Ah, so that's it. He's one of yours?"

"Well sir, he *was* one of ours, but now he's a civilian surgeon working in the Denver area," said Palmer.

"You've got to be kidding. A civilian did this shit?"

"Well sir, it wasn't shit, he actually—"

"Palmer, you listen to me. This sounds like one of your men going rogue, disabling a possible terrorist, sitting in a van. Yes, he's a hero; that's for sure. But then, I wonder, what was he thinking, and how was he able to find this guy, to begin with? The news media has this crescent moon and star insignia on his necklace—clearly a Muslim symbol—plastered all over the TV. Okay, maybe he *is* a Muslim, but it's not yet verified that he was an Islamic terrorist, now, right? Either way, I'm sure your men understand that we shouldn't make any assumptions that he was an Islamic terrorist until we have this thoroughly investigated. Maybe he was simply unhinged and psychotic. America protects all religions and freedom of religion her on our soil and America is an accepting, benevolent country. Not only that, but Muslims vote too."

"Sir, that van was filled with explosives," Palmer said. "There's only one reason it was there: to kill innocent civilians."

"You clearly haven't investigated this completely at this time," the president insisted. "Yes, as I said before, this guy, whoever he is, was a hero and saved lives. Although it seems, he's a rather bizarre hero. Do you have any information on the guy who was apprehended yet?" Palmer looked at Dorman to get approval to proceed, received a nod, then continued.

"No, sir, we don't have a confession from him and no information. We were going to interrogate him, but he was charged as a civilian with unlawful explosives in his car rather than attempted terrorism, so he was read his Miranda Rights and the local police department sent us away without interrogation since it was a criminal investigation. The ACLU is involved already as well, due to his arm being violently dislocated by this surgeon. Either way, it's unlikely we'll learn the truth or learn who he works for because we're not being allowed to interrogate him, unfortunately."

"As well it *should* be a criminal investigation, Mr. Palmer. These people aren't terrorists until proven otherwise. So, I assume you are absolutely sure this man of yours is the perpetrator?"

"Well, um, yes, I mean no. What do you mean by 'perpetrator,' Mr. President?" replied Palmer.

"The guy who disabled him without clear evidence of terrorism about to happen. You know, the damn vigilante. Our Dirty Harry."

"Yes, he was the guy who stopped the man and disabled his arm, then called 911 and started the evacuation alarm for the hospital picnic. But he isn't a perpetrator. He's a hero, as I said. An unorthodox and highly methodical hero."

"Okay. Thankfully, this all worked out safely, and the man is in custody—and I hope we can resolve this issue without any political ramifications. Now, tell me about this wild man, of yours. You said he was or is a surgeon? And one more thing: Aren't doctors supposed to be peace-loving flower-sniffers?"

"Ex-Army Ranger, received the Army Silver star while serving with the Rangers in Afghanistan and a few other places, then served with the CIA as a field operative for some years before we retired him, legacy or cover intact."

"Impressive. Why'd you retire him?"

"Well, actually I think it was a mutual agreement, sir."

"So, why did you let him go rogue? Don't you guys keep a close watch on dangerous guys like this?"

"He's a good man, sir. A patriot who served his country well. We actually have no idea why he did this or how he figured out this man was driving a van filled with explosives. It doesn't make sense to us at all. We were broadsided by this surgeon. But we'll figure it out, I assure you, Mr. President."

"Not only will you figure it out, Palmer, but you will stop it from happening again. This rogue doctor, although a hero, can theoretically do some more damage if he isn't controlled. Who knows? Maybe he'll do this again sometime, and it will have worse consequences, and he'll kill someone for no reason. We have courts of law and police who can protect us from criminals, using the rights written in our beloved Constitution. I suggest you will, as you say, 'disappear' this violent doctor if anything else happens, and if you fail to do that, then I'm sure will this will become quite embarrassing for your agency."

"Sir, that won't be necessary. We'll take care of this our way," said Carl, looking sternly at Palmer.

"Mr. President," Palmer said, "I know this man well. He's my friend with whom I served, and I would go to war with him anytime. I think he should be protected and certainly not punished. We need more men like him in this country." Palmer's fists started to clench behind his back, but his good sense made him stop the clenching before it became obvious to the observer sitting in the chair.

The president looked at Palmer and laughed. "You need to be careful what friends you keep, Mr. Palmer. He may have been a hero before, and you need to know I appreciate his service, but now he seems to be an uncontrolled vigilante menace, possibly against Muslim Americans."

Palmer remained silent, his face turning light crimson, effectively accenting the sudden appearance of a crooked vein bulging on his forehead.

Thankfully, Carl spoke up: "As I said, Jim, we'll take care of the problem ourselves."

"I want this problem to disappear, Carl," said the president.

The two men left the Oval Office. Director Dorman stopped, looked at Tommie and said, "Well, that sure went well. Tommie, you need to take care of this."

***

Wyatt looked up the address of Johnson's Body Shop and Automotive Painting and drove there, arriving as soon as they opened at 7:30. He kept with him the crumpled invoice he found in the defeated terrorist's van, and thankfully, the account number was still readable: 36928. He was going to talk to the owner, and he wasn't going to leave until he found out who this customer was because this customer could potentially be the key to finding the terrorist organization. FBI be dammed; he would figure this out himself.

"Hello there. How may I help you?" said the body shop clerk.

"My name is Harold Thompson, and I wanted to talk to the owner about some fleet project contracts."

"Sure, wait here, have a seat, and I'll go get him. He's in the shop."

Wyatt waited a few minutes, not sure exactly how he would get the information he needed from the owner, but his first move would be to show the FBI badge that was furnished to him when he worked for the agency and Special Ops previously. If that didn't work, he figured he'd have to go to plan B, which would most likely involve some kind of stress. Applied pressure.

"Hello, Mr. Thompson. How may I help you?" They shook hands, and the owner escorted Wyatt into his small office, which was cooled to a frigid 69 degrees by a super swamp cooler.

Wyatt pulled out his FBI badge and credentials and showed them to the owner. "I'm the FBI agent in charge of a crime that occurred here locally, and I wondered if you could help me with the investigation."

"Sure, I respect the FBI and would love to help. May I ask what the crime was?"

"I can't give many details, but it has to do with large amounts of fentanyl being smuggled into the area by drug kingpins that we've been looking for now for several years. Fentanyl is killing many of our young kids and we need to stop it."

"That's for sure, Agent Thompson. Damn drugs are killing our future generations."

Wyatt watched the man's body language, looking for clues as to whether he might be reliable or not, and so far, he seemed okay. Wyatt handed him the invoice he found in the van and asked him if he knew who the customer was.

"Can't say that I know this customer. We work on a lot of vehicles here, but doesn't look familiar."

"Are you able to look it up for me to give me the name please?"

"Sorry, sir. FBI or not, customer names aren't something we release. I can't help you without a warrant from the court."

"Really? Are you sure you want to stand by that statement? You see, because if you stand by that statement, I will be forced to make you give the information to me, one way or the other, and depending on what you decide, one option will be painless, and the other option will involve *significant* pain on your part—perhaps an extensive FBI audit of your books because you're being uncooperative and therefore a potential co-conspirator. Our forensic auditors are quite good at finding things that can bite you in the ass. Your choice, sir."

The owner glanced around his office, then out to the shop as if he was being watched, then said, "Okay, give me the account number, and I'll print out the invoice on my computer, and you can take it. Just leave me alone and don't make trouble for my business."

"36928."

After typing in the account number, the owner found the invoice, printed it out, and handed it to Wyatt. *Harry's Van and Limousine Rental and Maintenance*.

"Thanks for your help. This will help us a lot with this drug case.

CHAPTER 34

Instead of the usual two footsteps that were either behind him or off to the side, hiding in the shadows, Wyatt felt the presence and sound of four to six distinct footsteps now. They were there at the grocery store, restaurants, church services, and in the hospital. They were everywhere now and seemed, to Wyatt, to be multiplying like little robot copies. Wyatt knew they were good men, simply following orders, and they were men with whom he may have gladly served if asked to in the context of war. But it was different now. He knew they were closing in on him more aggressively, like hunters, waiting for the prey to make a mistake or fall down and sprain an ankle. He figured it had to be the van incident, and they were putting him on a tighter leash now until eventually, they would strangle him in their own way, or at least keep him permanently away from the action.

What was their goal? To keep him from acting on his own, obviously, but they didn't know about his gift. Only Gentri knew that truth, but he wasn't sure that she believed him. But at the moment, he hoped the Bureau was interrogating the van driver, that is, unless the civilians got to him first and charged him with a felony rather than an attempted act of terror. Wouldn't they be thankful for his actions that most certainly saved the lives of scores of innocent civilians? What behavior would the shadow men not allow, and if they didn't like his behavior, how aggressive would they be in trying to stop him if he chose to respond to some future event that he might see in one of these premonitions? How should he respond? Wyatt didn't trust the FBI to figure this van terrorism attempt out. He realized that they could do their investigation with forensics—DNA, fingerprints, etc.—but he would do his own investigation, whether he had visions or not.

Wyatt had no clear answers, but he understood that he needed to protect himself because he didn't know if the visions would keep appearing, and he had to save lives somehow. He wasn't going to compromise his conscience. He decided to spend more time at the hospital and volunteer for more on call-duty at night so he didn't have to go home.

Now he often slept in the hospital, and although the sleep was fitful and often interrupted by calls or emergencies, he believed it was much safer here, protected by the hospital environment, keeping busy with surgery, and doing what he was trained to do: save lives the best he could. He stopped taking his car, because he was sure it had GPS trackers all over it, and instead, began taking public transportation or riding his bike. He sometimes stayed in different hotels when he was off duty, traveling to these hotels using the recon and evasion techniques he learned in Ranger and survival school, although this survival was urban. He was always armed with his Sig Sauer, a zebra pen in his pocket, razor blades in the hem of his pants, and another razor taped to the inner-facing section of his car shoulder harness—the usual difficult-to-detect operator equipment he always carried out of habit, even though he was a civilian now, or maybe a pseudo-civilian. But he was reassured because Palmer was on his side and would protect him no matter what happened. It was good to have friends in high places.

"How is she, Kev?" said Wyatt on the crypto "red" phone.

"She gets up early, goes for her morning run, goes to work, shows clients around, and goes home. During her runs, we follow in a car or have one of our guys run close by on the other side of the street. I don't see anything out of the ordinary. No one following her or staking out her house so far, Wyatt."

"Thanks, Kevin, for protecting my lady. But I have another job for you if you don't mind."

"And what would that be this time?"

"I want you to do some surveillance for me. That's your specialty, isn't it?"

"Yes, surveillance, protection, and private detective work."

"I need you to do something very important for me. I want you to do some surveillance on this place: Harry's Limousine and Van Rental and Maintenance. Just find out who their favorite or recurring customers are, and see if there's anything suspicious about their operations. Let me know what you find out as soon as you can. It's important and may save lives, my friend."

"Will you tell me any more information on this, or once again, your lips are sealed?"

"Sorry, Kev. No can do. But I do need to ask, is Gentri dating anyone during my absence?"

"I figured you would ask that, Wyatt—just didn't know when you'd pop the awkward question. You'll be the first to know, and if she does, you can damn well know we're going to check his ass up and down until we're sure he's squeaky clean."

"That wasn't the answer I was looking for, Kev. It seems you've already put our relationship in the grave. Can't say I blame you because the whole thing is bizarre. But, no, she won't be dating anyone. At least I don't think so, but then, hell, I don't know much of anything anymore."

"Right, Wyatt. Of course. Got to go. Talk to you later, bro."

Wyatt finally lay down on his bed in the surgery on-call room and closed his eyes. And then, the visions presented themselves again while he watched a fly circle around the dome light he kept on in the bathroom so he didn't trip and fall in the dark when he was called to an emergency.

In his vision, he saw a young boy watching his father, who may have been some type of missionary or teacher, speak in front of some men. In front of this man, he heard some voices say to him in broken English, "Convert to Islam, or you, your child and wife will be killed." Then, he heard the missionary say, "Repent of your sins and believe in Jesus Christ, and you shall be saved, my brothers." Then, he saw the young boy was crying and alone, and next, he saw the growing boy in a Madrassah school, speaking with his Ma'alim reciting the verses of the Koran in the perfect

Arabic he knew. The last scene to present itself was a grown-up blond gentleman in a suit, sitting in a classroom at MIT. It wasn't clear what the connection between the child and the MIT student was; it seemed illogical and disjointed. It was such a bizarre dream or vision that he noticed sweat dripping down his forehead despite the cool, air-conditioned room. He hoped it was nothing more than a strange reverie.

He awoke, sweat dripping down his face, then paced the room. After a while, he ventured down the quiet hospital hallway to the doctor's lounge, where he poured himself a cup of coffee. It was almost 3 a.m., and he smiled because he watched the cup only shake for a few seconds during the pour, then, the shaking stopped as soon as he willed it to cease completely.

CHAPTER 35

bdul had now formulated his latest plans for attacks in the United States in the name of the FFWP. This was based on inflicting maximum casualties in large gatherings of soft targets, especially sporting events and large concerts and celebrations, destruction of police stations and military bases as well as hacking of oil refineries, power companies, and community water supplies. He allowed his Chinese Communist Party contacts to do the hacking of the IT structures of these institutions, but he demanded full control of the operations. He was proud that much of this would be accomplished by using his aerospace front company that already owned coveted government contracts that were grossly overinflated, with excess money siphoned off to create malicious drones right in the US.

He enjoyed popularity in political circles and proved to be effective as a charming party host for the rich and famous, owning a smile and a rakish walk that he used to easily gain entry into any woman's mind, no matter what inane line he used. But his secret life remained well-protected. After all, who would suspect that a tall, handsome, blond, blue-eyed businessman with a PhD in aeronautical engineering would be a ruthless embedded terrorist imbued with a fanatical desire to purify the world by killing the Muslim Shia—revisionist enemies—and then the crusaders—the classic infidels—especially in the United States.

It was all to be accomplished by UAVs (drones) that he specifically designed to be immune to ECMs that he helped design as well for the US defense department. He also designed a variant of the "Danger Drone," which was essentially a flying hacker laptop that could fly close to the target network or land next to it and then hack the system undetected. After all, this capability already existed with Chinese-manufactured drones and readily available Chinese computer chips. He could use it to get into range of a power plant's Wi-Fi network and carry out cyber-attacks, but cyber-attacks didn't have the shock power of massive bloody carnage, his preferred method of attack against innocent civilians.

His particular interest was in defeating ECMs. Clearly, UAVs could be defeated by anti-aircraft guns, but those weren't practical, due to legal and safety reasons in populated areas. He devised a system that would defeat most of the radio jammers he knew existed in the US arsenal, since he helped design some of them. He wasn't involved in all the purchasing and procurement for secret programs, but he *did* provide some technical help to the Defense Department. His techniques employed combinations of SSJ (self-screening jammers) and SOJ (stand-off jammers)—units that remained just outside the range of enemy weapons. He also employed radio frequency diversity and deception against Continuous Wave Doppler and Pulsed Doppler Deception, using spurious doppler shift technology. The key was using this technology yet keeping the UAV small and fast while carrying a small laser-guided missile that could cause significant destruction. His aircraft carried a variant of Helios, the anti-laser laser, that prevented drones from being shot down by a laser, essentially stopping the defensive laser from focusing on the target by disrupting the systems controlling the beam. His system could also defeat the AUDS defense system and the portable "Drone Defeater" ray gun, in large part because the Drone Defeater had a range of only 400 meters, and his aircraft had a 1000-meter firing range.

The small attacks he already planned to carry out in schools and via 'message' attacks on innocent individuals paled in comparison to the glory he knew he would enjoy with these new targets. The enemy had no idea what was in store; and stupid, lucky drunks wearing Cubs caps would be no match for his UAV technology. He never lost sight of his other goal either—finding and killing the cowardly infidel who killed his beloved son and heir to his operation in the US.

***

Gentri found herself propped up in her bed on two pillows with a glass of red wine on her bedside table. She knew she shouldn't be drinking wine right before bed, or in this case, *in* bed, and it would potentially cause insomnia, but these were desperate times, and to hell with sleep. The wine loosened up her neurons enough to release the words on to paper without hindrance, and certainly less of a filter, but then, sometimes she felt she wrote better completely without a filter. She finished chapter three of her novel, starting with a sentence she had rewritten several times and this time finally settled on: *He told her that he was a missionary and that was why he needed to be gone so long. But she knew by the way he walked and how he confidently handled himself in front of others that he was no damn missionary. Did she want to know the truth? What she really needed now was his lips on hers and his arms holding her close while his skilled hands searched—*

The phone rang, jolting her hands on the computer keys, creating a gibberish sentence that made her laugh. "Wyatt, darling, well that's funny, I was just thinking of you!"

"I love it when you think of me. Sends shivers down somewhere below and I'm not even there with you in bed. I sure would like to drink some of that wine with you that you have in your hand, and I'll even let you keep that wine spot on your right lip all night," said Wyatt.

"Wyatt, how did you know again, about the wine?" Once again, he'd surprised her with what appeared to be an ability to almost be in the room with her, without physically being there.

"Just a lucky guess, honey. By the way, what are you writing? I know the first sentences of a chapter are often the most difficult to get right, but once the first sentence is under your belt, the rest will come much easier."

Her mouth dropped wide open, but she didn't mention her surprise this time. He seemed to feel everything. Wasn't a woman supposed to have secrets? Not with Wyatt, it seemed. He certainly did have a sixth sense now, or some gift of vision that few owned. It was obvious, and she needed to learn how to deal with it if she still wanted a relationship with him. She gathered herself and let the butterflies stop fluttering around her stomach, then said, "Just finished chapter three. Glad you asked. It's starting to get hot and steamy now."

"That's my favorite part, honey."

"I know, Wyatt. That part is obvious, and I must say, it's good for me too."

"Well, I miss you, Gentri, and wanted to make sure you were okay."

"I'm okay but way too lonely, honey. When will this all be over, Wyatt? When will all the cloak-and-dagger hiding away be done for good?"

"I wish I knew. All I know is that I am always here for you, and we'll be together soon. Don't lose hope, Gentri, my love."

"Sweet dreams Wyatt, and they better be of you and me on a nice tropical beach, enjoying the sun and a drink or two, okay? By the way, how are your other dreams ... I mean, *nightmares*, Mr. Trout Whisperer?"

"Everything is fine, dear. No problems. The trout aren't laughing at me anymore, and I'm assuming they're happy, being fed with the best flies."

"Sweetheart, that's bullshit and you know it, but it's clever bullshit, nonetheless, so I'll give you some points for that. I'm sending you a kiss. Goodnight."

CHAPTER 36

Two men were assigned by Kevin to watch Gentri. Both of them worked twelve-hour shifts. One was assigned to watch her at work and the other to watch her at home. Of course, they never met her and stayed out of her field of vision, practicing their best surveillance techniques. observed her coming in and out of her brokerage office, and they found she usually arrived at 8 a.m., after stopping at Starbucks first. Sometimes, she left for lunch with one of her clients, and it was always at Ronnie's deli—a short walk from her office, down the block. She left for lunch at noon and returned by 12:45, although sometimes, the lunch ran later, and she would return at 1:30.

One of them followed her home. Usually, she stopped at the grocery store on Mondays before she arrived home. He noticed she used to run in the morning, but now, she stopped running alone (at Kevin's request), and instead went to the gym after work, at least three times a week, in the early evening, before darkness came. He didn't sit in the car when she was inside the gym but put on his exercise clothes and worked out near her. He saw that young men did try to start conversations with her, but she just smiled, and they walked away after a few minutes. When his shift was over, Jerry—Kevin's other employee—took over by parking across the street from her house, and he kept her house under surveillance. There were no male visitors, but occasionally she received a doorbell ring from an Amazon delivery man, and she never answered the door, as instructed. At About 9:30 every night, Jerry observed her bedroom light turned on; then, she turned it off about one hour later. She had no social life at all, and nothing seemed out of the ordinary or unsafe.

***

Tommie's other burner phone rang—the one not reserved for agency operations. He knew who it probably was, although the number was encrypted.

"Hi."

"Not a very warm greeting, considering what I did for you, but hello, nevertheless."

"Sorry, but you know, in my position, I must be careful with warm or familiar greetings."

"Of course. I have the same problem, except that I'm in private business and you're a government employee, although some spooks don't exist, I'm told. But *you* do. You're a desk operator now higher up in the organization. Did you have anything to say to me, Mr. Hop Along?"

"Hop Along? Why do you call me that?

"You know why. Everybody can see the way you walk. It's not too obvious but easily identified by a trained observer."

"Okay, I get it. It's just that no one has ever referred to me that way. Thanks for offering to take care of my problem. That's a load off my back for sure. Just make sure you protect the transaction well."

"No problem. He'll come to my secure offices, make a delivery to my hungry guys, and we'll pad his palms so he shouldn't be a problem for you anymore. I'm in Riyadh now doing some business, but when I'm back in two days, I'll arrange for you to meet me after this is taken care of for you. You know, with me, it's about business and money. For secretary Robinson, whom I'll meet later, it's political influence, power, and money. And for you, it's … well, you know, keeping you clean with free shoulders to do what you do best to protect us here in America."

"It's against my better judgment to meet at your place, but I'll do it. I've got cover."

"Of course you do," replied Erik.

**

Wyatt had been sleeping either in basic hospital on-call rooms or cheap hotels for the past several weeks after putting Kevin in charge of Gentri's security—and the other surveillance job using the info obtained from the auto paint shop owner. Kevin told him he saw no activity at Wyatt's house that he had surveilled twenty-four hours a day and thought it was probably safe to go inside and get some of his things to put in suitcases, but Wyatt didn't want to take a chance. Hospital scrubs became his usual attire when he wasn't wearing the jeans, black T-shirt, and Nike running shoes Kevin gave him. Scrubs had the advantage in that they didn't require him to launder them because he just threw them in a hamper in the surgeon's lounge and then grabbed another couple of pairs to wear; however, they were too showy in public. It was getting old. He had already rented a car, a Ford Mustang GT with 435 horsepower, a prize the rental agency saved for specific buyers who wanted to impress with speed during their short vacations in Denver. And of course, he taped the razor blades under the shoulder harness, as he always did, and kept his Glock in the glove box along with the rescue hammer and the trusty bolt bag. The Land Cruiser, he knew, had to stay in the garage at his house because it was most likely still rigged with GPS locators, likely placed by the crafty shadow men after the van incident.

Wyatt needed some sleep, that is, if he was able to sleep at all due to the recurrent headaches and nightmares, although the Minipress did decrease the frequency of the nightmares somewhat, and that was a long-overdue benefit for Wyatt. But Gentri was a huge worry for him, and her safety was of the utmost importance. She had to be protected at all costs. She was innocent and absolutely could not become a victim of this brutal terrorist plot. However, long ago, Wyatt had learned that a soldier will never receive precious sleep with worry occupying his mind, and usually those worries would be reduced via daylit preparations. The problem was that most shit happened at night.

On this night, he was lying in a creaky bed in one of the surgeon's call rooms, partially covered with abrasive hospital sheets and pressed white pillow cases that felt like sheet metal. He was thankful the call room was empty tonight, not being used by exhausted surgery residents because they had the day off, mandated now by resident working-hour regulations. These residents were kind of pussies now, it seemed to him. It seemed like they received Swedish massages and plenty of days off, unlike the good old days of brutal beatdowns of interns and residents who could barely walk from exhaustion, yet were asked to perform perfectly. He tumbled into sleep intermittently, but every ninety minutes or so, when REM shouted its muscle-paralyzing arrival, the blown-up body parts burst into his active subconscious, and the helpless cries of his dying comrades woke him up. With sweat dripping from his forehead and each time, he'd turn his blurry eyes to clock digits on his phone beside him, and sure enough, it would be approximately ninety minutes later—in coordination with the REM sleep cycle. So much for the effectiveness of Minipress.

It was 5 a.m., time to drag his legs into the surgeon's shower, even if his brain proved recalcitrant, and he hoped there were towels. He would try to have breakfast in the doctor–nurse practitioner lounge, hoping the nurse practitioners and physician's assistants would allow him in for a short time and leave a few morsels of food for him.

His first case of the day entailed the placement of a tunneled venous catheter for an oncology patient who needed to start chemotherapy. The second case was a bowel resection for a localized tumor—or at least that's what the scan and endoscopy showed. By 1 p.m., both cases were over, and he hoped he was successful in hiding his tremor from the staff by always keeping his hands busy.

Later that night, he decided to stay in a Motel Six that he hadn't been in before. He chose to take the city bus for transportation, aware that the shadow men could try to disappear him if they felt he was a danger to the mission. By this point, he'd concluded he was way past compromised. They had damn well better make it clean and think about it carefully, because he wouldn't go easily, and he knew there would be a garage full of nasty paperwork for the agency desk people to whitewash. But he figured the most likely possibility was that the terrorist organization would eventually find him first, and somehow, he needed to be ready for that eventuality.

He jumped off the bus two blocks away from the Motel Six and walked to the light, which was always on, as they said, wearing a black wig with a ponytail and mustache, weapon in his waist belt. He heard a crack, a simultaneous pop, and a rip in his side. He fell to the ground, hitting his head on the curb; then, everything went black for a few seconds, and when he regained consciousness, he had difficulty catching his breath and his right chest burned and made a sucking sound, his shirt bloody. He instinctively rolled into the bushes and out of sight. He touched the chest wound, and his fingers filled with blood.

Fucking amateur snipers can't shoot worth a damn—thankfully for me.

He ripped off a piece of his shirt and stuffed it into his sucking chest wound, then reached into his right pants pocket, pulled out the red phone, and called Kevin. "Hey bro, I've been hit. I'm on the sidewalk across from the Motel Six on Silverthorne. Come scoop me up before I'm fertilizer. But careful man, you'll have to . . .". He struggled to form the words in between painful breaths. "You'll have to snoop and poop like the swoopy dudes, Kev. There's a fucking amateur sniper on the west side of the Mile High City who's not happy with my presence here, and I'm sure he'd love to take you and your colleagues out as well. Couldn't locate the shot origin, but I'm guessing it was from the apartment complex rooftop across the street."

***

Erik called an emergency meeting of the FFWP Executive Council in his Rondell Industries secure bunker. His staff had become accustomed to these meetings and knew there would be lots of tongue-lashing and accusations if things had gone wrong. Maybe even some face-striking or blood as well. They never knew what would happen.

"Is my woman, Gentri, dating anyone?"

"We're not sure, Sahib," said Farid. "We've been told by some of our people on the ground that she's been seen with a guy they say is a doctor. We asked people about her personal life, and that's about all we have so far. We haven't had any reports of her with a man recently, however— she's always alone now it seems."

"Doctor? What kind of doctor?"

"We don't know. Apparently, she was spotted with a man at the Broadmoor in Colorado Springs and also at the Buell Theater in Denver.

"No solid descriptions?"

"Just that he was relatively tall, had a scar bisecting his left eyebrow, and carried himself well."

"What the hell does that mean? Carried himself well? That's a really dumb thing to say because it means nothing to me. How the fuck can I take action on 'carried himself well?' "

"That's all we have."

"We need to find out who this man is. I'm much better than any doctor with a scarred face. I have more money and power, and she *will* become mine—that's for sure. It'll take some time and finesse for me to win this prize, but I know she'll respond to a romantic man who gives her the attention she deserves."

CHAPTER 37

Although Kevin was a former Army Ranger, he was also trained in Army Intelligence Signet (signals intelligence) as well as HUMINT. His company proved to be highly skilled in the realm of ground surveillance with human eyes as well as electronic eavesdropping. That's why he was surprised to see that Rondell Industries was so easy to surveil. His guys were able to follow multiple Cellini's Pizza delivery vans in and out of Rondell, and when they were stopped—loading or unloading at the shop—they were able to place electronic-ink trackers that could sometimes be tattooed on skin but, in this case, on pizza boxes, and with GPS locators and transmitters with audio capability also placed in and out of the vehicles themselves. Of course, the Cellini's Pizza hats and T-shirts with Cellini's logos were easy to obtain with the correct stealth, and they hired some of Kevin's men on as delivery employees at the busy Cellini's organization. In this way, Kevin's team was able to make some solo deliveries to Rondell with electronic bugs surreptitiously placed by his men in various locations, including desk lamps in the main offices, under chairs, etc., especially in executive suites, where they were surprised that pizza deliveries were given such free reign.

Kevin placed small high-tech parabolic audio receivers outside the Rondell facility to pick up voices as well, and it was fairly easy for Kevin's guys to disguise themselves as street workers or utility workers. He knew Wyatt was into some deep shit, and the leads he gave him to investigate Harry's limousine and Van Rental led him directly to their trips in and out of Rondell, and at the same time, there seemed to be a relationship with Cellini's pizza. He didn't ask Wyatt where he got the leads. It just was none of his business.

The first recordings Kevin's team collected were in the garage on the intercom:

"Hi, Erik. I hope you're hungry. It's Giovanni. We brought you a whole lotta hot pizza, my friend."

"Excellent," said Erik. We'll let you in, and my guards will escort you to the executive suite where we can talk and do business while they eat."

Giovanni then walked into the complex, with one of Kevin's men, a new hire for Cellini, whose job was to carry multiple boxes of pizza to the executive suites.

"You ain't eating?" asked Giovanni.

"I'm not hungry when I'm working. I need to focus on business, not my mouth."

"I'm the same way," replied Giovanni.

He buzzed them in, and the guards took Giovanni and Kevin's undercover man up to the executive suites. Although there seemed to be a significant amount of extraneous noise at the receiving end for Kevin's people, it eventually settled down, and the conversation resumed with Giovanni and Erik.

"You know, this hotshot has a lot of debt we covered. He got in over his head, and you know, we don't tolerate late payments. We take care of things ourselves in these situations," said Giovanni.

"Yes, but Mr. Palmer isn't your typical guy you can wipe out, as you say. He can wipe you out too, my little pizza monger, and he serves his country with distinction. He just doesn't want his gambling activities traced."

"I don't care if he's Mother Theresa. He owes us $350k.

"I thought he told me it was $300k?"

"Interest jacked it up, Erik."

Erik showed him a money wire transfer. "Now this should take care of his debts to you, free and clear, and there's a little extra in there to keep you quiet and away from us now, and you'll make sure this never happened."

"Yes. Of course. Thank you for investing with Cellini's and purchasing stock in a great company, my friend."

***

Later in the afternoon, a BMW drove up, obviously a private vehicle. A tall, well-built man got out. He was wearing sunglasses and a golf cap from Gulf Shores Alabama. His distinct features included that slight limp and right pigeon-toed walk, and he had no right fifth digit. Kevin knew just who it was. Tommie arrived first, and they appeared to meet alone, and Secretary Johnson arrived several hours later with his entourage.

The smell of pizza invaded the whole room, and Tommie guessed what had already transpired after seeing the familiar Cellini's boxes. "Let's get down to business," said Tommie.

"Thanks for coming, Tommie. Sally brought us coffee and some bourbon."

"I don't drink. I appreciate what you've done for my financial problems, though, Erik. Now, tell me what I can do for you. Of course, it has to be within the bounds of my position, without compromising national security."

"I would never put you in that position, Tommie. But I *am* concerned about some rogue vigilantes that are scaring the Muslim community. Some of my business partners are from Muslim countries as you know, specifically the Saudis. We're all Americans, Tommie, and as you know, my company provides the best UAV technology for the Department of Defense. We do our part to protect America. Clearly, we must protect *all* Americans, and not single out people who don't look like us and label them as radical Islamic terrorists. To that end, I want to know if you can give me any information on the vigilante who disabled this devout Muslim in a van recently. He obviously has some special skills which we could find useful in our organization. And, I heard your agency may have an ex-special forces doctor and operative in town also. He might have the talents I need to work for my organization. We need some good men. Hopefully, we are not talking about one man here."

"Sorry, I can't do that, Erik."

"Are you sure, Tommie?"

"Yes, I can't compromise this person. He is a patriot for this country and certainly meant no harm to the Muslim community at all. He acted alone, and we have no explanation for how or why he did this."

"Okay. That's your choice, Tommie. You can live with your debts and the loss of your family and job, or you can live with releasing a small amount of information that won't hurt anyone. I figured you would help me because, you know, it would be sad if the government found out about your financial transactions."

There was silence, and Tommie put his head down, then took a long drink of water. "Okay, I guess you have me, Erik. But he's a good man, and so help me God, if you try to harm him, you'll have to deal with me, and you won't survive that encounter."

Erik remained stone-faced after that comment. "We won't touch this hero. We just want to talk to him and perhaps give him a job in security here."

"His name is Dr. Wyatt Barton." After that, Tommie got up and left.

After Palmer left, the third visitor to Rondell was Secretary of State John Robinson. Kevin observed that he came with a security guard and wore an immaculate black suit, smiling to all who saw him, the consummate politician who wanted to run for president. When Kevin watched him walk in and shake hands with Erik, it made his stomach quiver with disgust. He was thankful the pizza boxes remained in the executive suite, carrying the electronic ink sensors with tiny audio receivers as well as the other electronic plants his men provided as seeming Cellini's workers.

"Coffee, bourbon, or both, my friend?" asked Erik.

"I wouldn't mind a shot of bourbon, then some coffee later," said Robinson.

"Since I now sit on the board of your organization, Giving for World Peace, and with my substantial financial support, have you been able to discuss with the president my concerns about policy regarding flying restrictions to Muslim-majority nations?"

"Yes, of course. Those xenophobic restrictions have been lifted. POTUS agreed with that plan and will sign an executive order next week.

Your requests certainly seem reasonable and humane."

"Great. I appreciate you helping to eliminate inappropriate discrimination against Muslims in this country, and that includes spying on mosques. People need to worship their God without being spied upon. And one more thing: I'm going to give you a million-dollar check for your presidential run, and I'll now be your number-one supporter since you're so agreeable to meet with me and discuss important issues.

Johnson downed a shot of bourbon, then smiled. "It's a pleasure to work with such forward-thinking patriots in this country, whether Christian, Muslim, Jewish, or otherwise. We need to meet again sometime, Erik, maybe for dinner at one of my favorite Washington restaurants."

"That would certainly be an honor, my friend. Let's keep in touch."

Just as Tommie left, Kevin and his crew outside took photos of both men and vehicles and saved the audio files. Then, they packed up and left, stunned by what they had just witnessed.

Wyatt was right, thought Kevin. His friend Wyatt had stumbled on some deep shit when he found that paint and repair shop invoice, leading to the van and limousine rental service that did business with this foul-smell Rondell company.

CHAPTER 38

Kevin brought Gentri personally to Mercy Hospital in Denver to see her Wyatt. She didn't say a word to him while they drove and continued her stony silence when they entered the hospital. She stopped and bought coffee at the hospital Starbucks, one for herself and one for Kevin, who watched her hands tremble while holding the steamy cup, causing the coffee to spill a little, thankfully dropping onto the floor and not her dress. They took the elevators up to the fourth floor's east wing, the Surgical Intensive Care Unit, and they both stayed in the waiting room to talk to the thoracic surgeon, who agreed to meet them when he was finished with Wyatt.

"Hello, I'm Dr. Davis. Dr. Barton sustained a through-and-through gunshot wound to his right chest and lung, and luckily, it missed major blood vessels, and so that's why he survived and I was able to repair the lung injury."

"Thank God," said Gentri.

"He also sustained a mild concussion after the shot, when he apparently fell and hit his head. The CT shows a quite small subdural hematoma, but it may be old, suggesting a previous injury. Whatever the case, it will not require surgery, and he'll need some follow-up scans down the road. He may have some short-term memory loss with periods of confusion. He's got a few lacerations on his face and hands, but overall, he's quite lucky to be alive."

"Thanks for your work, Dr. Davis. Will he recognize me when I go in to see him?" said Gentri.

"Don't know. We'll have to see. Just go in and say hi and take his hand and see what happens."

Gentri walked into Wyatt's ICU room, followed by Kevin, who as always, was checking the surroundings—the doors, hallways, and windows. Wyatt's eyes were closed, and bandages covered his forehead and the left side of his face. Gentri took his hand and squeezed, causing him to open his eyes.

"Gentri, it's you. I'll remember that smooth skin forever." He tried to smile, but the lower edge of the bandages trapped the free movement of his mouth. "Thanks for coming. I knew Kevin would bring you to me, dear. Sorry, I look like shit. I must be a pretty ugly sight to behold." He visibly winced as he talked.

"Oh, Wyatt, why did this happen to you? Why do people shoot surgeons who save lives? I'm so thankful you're alive, and it looks like you'll be okay."

"Yeah, I'm okay, but this sure won't help my headaches any. Don't think I'll win any beauty contests either. Maybe I'll win Miss Congeniality. As far as the why, that's not clear to me either."

Kevin rolled his eyes. "Sorry to say this but you had no chance to win any beauty contests before, and certainly not Miss Congeniality." He smiled and then added, "Rangers lead the way."

"Yeah, Rangers lead the damn way, Kev. I appreciate your encouraging words, and thanks for bringing my girl."

Kevin smiled, then left the room to watch for threats who might make the mistake of trying to enter Wyatt's room.

Gentri was sitting quietly in the chair next to his bed, holding and squeezing his hand. Wyatt looked at her and said, "Gentri, have you finished your epic romance novel yet?"

"Why, no, I haven't, Wyatt. Thanks for asking. But I must say, your adventures are giving me a hell of a lot of free material to write about, bless your heart. It doesn't require me to be very creative now with my writing. It seems that your crazy scenes and adventures keep popping up, begging me to write about them, or at least change them around a little. In fact, it seems your adventures have sucked away my creativity, and now it seems I'm just using what I see you do in your life as the action in my scenes—that is, if I choose to write it. I'm just not sure right now because it's too painful for me, dear."

"You may be right. But I hope the material I'm giving you will inspire your sex scenes especially. Those are the details I care about, if I am in fact, your inspiration."

She laughed, but Wyatt just showed a half-grin because he didn't want to worsen the pain.

"The nurses said your CT scan showed a small subdural hematoma. Too small for surgery and it was probably old, from a previous injury, so they said they were going to observe you for a couple days and repeat the scan to make sure it doesn't enlarge. Clearly, you're going to need a lot of rest for healing. But was that injury from the plane crash in Zaire?"

"Well, probably, I guess. They tell you everything but not me. They must think I won't understand it. I'm just a banged-up trauma surgeon; that's all. I wonder if another head injury like this will *help* my headaches."

She looked at him after his silly remark, knowing he was simply trying to keep things light in a difficult situation for her, and she bent over and kissed him.

Kevin popped his head in the door when he heard Wyatt's last response. "Yeah, a trauma surgeon who's gotten blown up again, now for the umpteenth time. Just do what they say, Wyatt, and don't give 'em shit, okay? Be a good patient for once," said Kevin.

"Sounds like good advice, mom," said Wyatt.

The nurse pointed to her watch, indicating that visiting hours were over. Gentri saw this, then said, "Sorry we have to leave. Please rest and get better, dear. I love you."

"Love you too, Gentri, but you know, you have to be—"

"I know, honey, but we need to go so you get some rest and heal properly."

Kevin escorted Gentri to the waiting car, and had his driver take her back to her safe location, waved goodbye, and then when she was out of sight, went back to Wyatt's hospital room.

"You're back so soon. Did you miss me?"

Kevin looked at Wyatt and said, "Sorry, but I need to tell you some information now in private, about that interesting little surveillance job you gave me. I don't know, after your injury, if you're able to take this all in or not, though."

"Now or never, Kev. Let it spill."

"My crew and I have done some surveillance on this Harry's Van and Limo rental place you asked me to check out. We've followed the ingress and egress of their vehicles now for several weeks. Seems most of their rentals or repair customers are companies with fleet contracts. Sometimes churches or private schools. But there's one customer we found suspicious."

"Why suspicious?"

"The business is in the Denver Tech Center. It's called Rondell Aerospace. Apparently a defense contractor of some type in the aerospace industry. Their CEO is an aerospace engineer by the name of Erik Jorgenson. They must be pretty important, because we saw a state department car with Secretary of State Robinson in it enter the compound."

"Okay. I'm not sure how suspicious that is if they're important in the defense industry, I suppose. We do supply aircraft around the world to our allies. Whether we *should* or not is another question, as well as why a government official is hobnobbing with a private defense contractor. Anyway, is there anything else you found out?"

"Well, this Rondell corporation entertains some other interesting guests. They must love pizza, though. At least twice a week, I see a Cellini's Pizza delivery Van arrive; then, it's flagged in by security and drives straight into the secure garage complex, with simply a salute from the guard. I never saluted a pizza delivery guy before. Matter of fact, I've never seen a red-haired Italian guy before. Anyway, you don't need to know details, but we infiltrated Rondell by getting some of our guys hired as pizza delivery boys by Cellini and actually were able to get inside. Just so you know, we also were able to video the finger-tapping of the access codes to the building by their guards. I'll give you the codes if you need them for some reason. Anyway, our listening devices focused first on the guards, and they said, "Come in, Giovanni." Not sure that has anything to do with anything, but it does make me hungry now. They make a great deep-dish Sicilian. We also observed another guy come and visit Rondell, but he only did it once and he came alone, without a security team.

Did you catch this guy's name, by chance? Or your electronic surveillance didn't pick it up very well?

"No. but he was tall, maybe 6'4", and walked with a slight limp, favoring his right leg. A little pigeon-toed on the right. Oh yeah, and he's missing his pinkie finger on the right. I have some audio tapes and visual files that I'll leave for you to review, my friend. But I don't think you need me to tell you who this guy is because you know him. I'll let you decide if those documents are useful for you or not. Anyway, I hope that information helps you, my friend, but I still wonder why you send me down these rabbit holes—and what you're looking for."

"Thanks, Kevin. I appreciate your efforts. You've provided me with some interesting information. Go home now and get some rest. And by the way, I don't know if I'll ever need them, but go ahead and text me those access codes to my red phone, just in case I get hungry and want to attend a pizza party at Rondell for some reason."

***

Wyatt lay in his hospital bed and pondered that exchange. It just didn't all make sense to him with these visitors and the Cellini's pizza cravings and whether it meant anything or not in the grand scheme of things. But thinking about the guy with the limp and four fingers on the right caused him to wince from his chest wound because it rocked his soul.

Now he knew he had to review the audio and visual recordings Kevin had provided because this is what he was looking for. Then, his mind drifted to the first time the words *I love you* were spoken between him and Gentri. It felt good. Really good, actually. Suddenly, the headaches once again bulldozed themselves into the front and side of his head, and he fell asleep from the Percocet he finally allowed himself to take.

***

An hour after closing time, Wyatt had another visitor.

"I'm sorry, sir, but visiting hours were over an hour ago. We can't have you visit him tonight. You can come back tomorrow morning again after 10 a.m. to visit if you want. We have strict visiting hours here for the benefit of our patients," said the surgical ICU nurse.

"Of course. I understand. But I think you'll make an exception for me. It'll be a quick visit."

The guard hired by Kevin stopped him at the door and asked him for his ID.

Palmer opened up his fold-out badge for her to see. He chose to display the FBI badge rather than the nondescript government agency badges he carried.

"I'm just going to say a few words to him. He's an old friend."

The guard and the nurse let him go to the room but watched closely on the closed-circuit monitor at the nursing station close by.

"Wyatt, it's Palmer."

"Palmer who?" said Wyatt, pretending he'd lost his memory.

"You know, your buddy Palmer from years back. We used to—"

"Yeah, Tommie, how could I forget that silly face? Tommie my friend, why did you let this happen to me? I thought you were on my side here, brother? I thought you guys were protecting me from bad guys, not just myself."

Palmer looked up to the ceiling, searching for words as if they were painted on the ceiling for him to read out loud like a teleprompter. Then, he looked down at Wyatt. "I'm not sure you'll remember this after your injury but I'm here to protect you, my friend. You can count on that."

"Who's responsible, Tommie?"

"We don't know. But I'll personally find out. You need to know, though, that Dorman at Langley wants you out of the picture."

"What does that mean?"

"He wants you conveniently disappeared."

"How do you know?"

"He talked to me because the president has his underwear in a wad about this crazy van thing you did. He wants someone to pay for the bad publicity that the Muslim community is releasing to the media because of the stupid TV coverage suggesting possible Islamic terrorist involvement, whether correct or not. So, it appears as though you will be the one they're after to take the fall for this, my friend. I called Dorman, and he said he knows nothing about this attack on you and certainly the agency isn't involved."

"That's reassuring. Glad to know I have him as a friend and the CIA didn't shoot me on the streets of Denver. No wait, the CIA is never involved with attacking ordinary US citizens, right?"

Tommie smiled gently. "I've got your back, Wyatt."

"Tommie, I appreciate you coming here, and I know this looks bad on your watch. I know you'll help me here and figure out who did this and we'll take care of it together."

"I will take care of this shit mess, Wyatt. But notice, I didn't say *we*? You see, Wyatt, you need to lie low after you recover here, because your life is in danger, my friend. That's obvious to you, right?"

"You ain't just whistlin' Dixie, Chief," said Wyatt.

"Okay, Josey Wales, I'm going to leave you now to get your beauty rest. We've got lots of security here in the hospital to keep you safe. And remember, dying ain't much of a way to make a living, is it?"

"Hey now, there's only one Josey and you don't squint properly when you repeat his quotes." Wyatt grinned his bandage-curtailed grin. "Thanks, Tommie. Give Julie my regards, will you?"

"I would, but we've been living in separate places for several weeks now, but I'm sure it will blow over soon."

"Sorry, Tommie. I hope you can work it out. Have you stopped that stupid gambling stuff? It's going to get you in trouble if you don't stop it, my friend."

"I'm resolving that problem completely, once and for all, and you won't have to worry about me anymore. I'll see you someday, Wyatt, under better circumstances."

"Beaucoup dinky dau," said Wyatt.

Tommie walked away, then stopped at the door and turned around and looked at Wyatt. "In case you're wondering, you know that if we wanted to do it, our snipers would have taken care of the job completely. It wasn't us, Wyatt."

"Of course it wasn't, Tommie. Take care, my friend."

Wyatt watched Tommie walk away with that slight limp he'd come to know so well over the years—and the slight pigeon toe on the right and the absent pinkie on the right—and Kevin's description of the visitor at Rondell hit home brutally. It had to have been someone else, or certainly, there had to be an easy explanation. He lay there in the hard hospital bed with the sheets that felt like iron and couldn't stop thinking about all this bizarre information he just received, but he knew he needed to figure it out and take care of things. Wasn't he supposed to be recovering from his wounds rather than listening to all this craziness?

CHAPTER 39

H ello, Dr. Barton, I'm Tim Collins from the Neuropsychiatry Department. Pleased to meet you."

That introduction began ten feet away, which Wyatt thought a little unusual, but Wyatt sat up in bed and extended his right hand. Wyatt didn't like him already because of the loose way he shook hands.

"Nice to meet you, um, I presume, Dr. Collins, right?"

"Right. PhD from Harvard neuropsychology, masters in neurorehabilitation from UC Boulder. Your neurologist and neurosurgeon thought it would be best if we did some neuropsychological testing to see if you need any cognitive rehabilitation after this head injury. It happens all the time, and since you're a surgeon, well I—"

"Yeah, I know. You want to see if I can still operate. Go ahead, hit me with your best cognitive questions, Tim."

Dr. Collins pulled up a chair to the right of Wyatt's bed, but Wyatt got out of bed, held his chest tubes in his right hand so they didn't pull out, and pulled up a different chair folded up against the wall, brought it over quickly, and sat face to face with Collins. He hated the vulnerability of being in bed. *Let's get this over with*, he thought. *It's mandatory, per closed head injury policy. I'll go along with it, and hell, I might even learn something.* He was pleased there was no dizziness getting out of bed and making his way to the chair, in fact, he felt surprisingly light on his feet. He hoped his brain would be just as quick.

"Do you remember what you had for breakfast Wyatt?

"Well, sure. I had um ... let me think."

Dr. Collins stared at his notebook, flipped a few pages during the silence, and then wrote down a few words.

"I forgot, I guess. Must've been scrambled eggs and toast."

"No, the staff told me you had pancakes with syrup, bacon, sausage, and wheat toast with strawberry jelly."

"Yes, of course. Now I remember." Wyatt scratched his chin, and the realization that his mind was blank about breakfast scared him. That happened a few times before, and most recently during the mission after he woke up in the Neuro ICU at Landstuhl, but it came back fairly quickly. This time it was completely blank, at least with regard to short-term memory, he hoped.

"That's no problem, I hope you enjoyed it, sounds like a hearty breakfast."

"Do you remember what educational degrees I had and where I obtained them?"

Again, blank stare from Wyatt. "You're a PhD of course."

"Where did I obtain my degrees"?

"Stanford."

"No, PhD from Harvard and masters from UC Boulder."

Wyatt remained silent and started pulling his bandages off.

"Sir, I must ask you please to keep your bandages on. I don't think your surgeon wants them off yet. I'm going to go through a few more sets of tests; then we'll be done in about fifteen minutes if you don't mind."

He removed the bandages anyway. "These lacerations need air to heal. The bandages are just to protect your eyes from the image of my carnage."

Collins looked down at his papers and continued, unphased. "I'm going to give you five words and five numbers; then, I want you to repeat them after one minute, okay?"

"Hit me."

"Safe, peak, fire, terrier, judicial, 38, 96, 10,15, 84."

After one minute, Wyatt started the recall: safe, fire, judicial, um, 38,

19, 84 and, wait, oh hell, that's all can do."

"Who was the Prime Minister of Great Britain during World War Two and who were the other two presidents to meet him at Yalta?"

"Churchill was the PM, the other two were Roosevelt and of course, Uncle Joe Stalin."

"Good. Now tell me what was the most important news of the day when you were in first grade? Can you remember?"

"Kennedy was assassinated and I remember the black and white TV show, sitting glued in front of it with my parents and sister, watching the parade of the flag-draped casket down the parade route and everyone was crying."

"Okay."

"What was the name of your first-grade teacher"?

"Mrs. Shepherd."

"Okay. Well, I of course can't verify that at this moment, but your answer was quick. So, here is a test I want you to take. Please fill it out to the best of your ability, and I'll be back in a few hours to pick it up and review the case and make some recommendations."

"It doesn't matter, Tim, whether you can verify it or not. It's obvious that I have short-term memory loss from my subdural and closed head injury. It's not my first one, but I hope it's my last. I have a history of coming around pretty quickly. It's also obvious that my long-term memory is quite well preserved, which is also common after my injuries. Now I appreciate the time you've taken to examine me, but I've got a headache from this word scrabble fest, and believe me, you don't want to see me when my head starts to explode. Oh, and I didn't tell you, I've already been through psychotherapy for PTSD and it only works partially, but they do call me the Trout Whisperer. So, if you'll excuse me, this trout whisperer is going to lie down now, and I will wish you a good day."

After Collins left, Wyatt's headaches accelerated, but he had to struggle through them without medications because he felt that darkness was following him closely and he needed to move quickly while he still could. He had to go into hiding, and he most assuredly would be at risk to lose his job at the hospital, but he knew what he had to do, and that he was the only one who could accomplish it. It was a lonely feeling, but for some reason, he felt compelled to take it on without hesitation, as if some force was holding him up in the background. He examined his chest tube and the collection chamber for the tubes, saw that the bloody drainage had stopped with no air leak in the water-seal collection chamber, and then he used his hospital password to log in and review his own chest x-ray image. Luckily, he found no pneumothorax, and the pleural cavity was clear of blood. He then found his pocket knife, cut the chest tube sutures, took a deep breath, held it so air wouldn't go into his chest, then put a four-by-four strip of gauze over the incision and taped it with the silk tape the nurses left conveniently on the bedside table. He left the bandages and hospital gown in the room and threw the psychological tests in the trash. Then, he put on the green scrubs the nurse had left him, tied a surgical mask halfway on his neck so it rested on his chest, put on his running shoes, and walked down the corridor past the nurse's station. Thankfully, they were busy charting and didn't notice who he was in scrubs, and he slipped away into the crisp mountain air.

Face the fear head-on so the fear won't have time to consume you.

***

His first trip after his escape from the hospital was to call an Uber to his favorite Motel Six, change clothes, and then pay a visit to this famous Cellini's Pizza place. Wyatt needed to quickly tie up some loose ends. It seemed like Cellini's pizza was everywhere in this city, including Tommie's secret briefing room, which was filled with Cellini's Pizza boxes, and then, a personal delivery van driving up and inside the secure garage of Rondell Enterprises?

Why couldn't they just knock on the door or ring the doorbell and leave the pizzas at the front door for the office staff to distribute? With such a high-powered aerospace firm, wouldn't their security be wary of such a delivery van? And why is everyone so crazy about Cellini's damn pizza? Wyatt looked up pizza delivery companies on Google and found about one hundred companies in the city, and interestingly, Cellini's only had two locations in the entire metropolitan area. Wyatt thought, *It's time to do some digging.*

Wyatt sat down and ordered a personal-size deep dish pizza with standard sausage and pepperoni, extra meat, his favorite. He was famished, and he devoured the pie in about seven minutes total. But before he finished, he asked the waitress if he could meet the manager.

The waitress said, "Why the manager, honey? My service bad?"

"No, you're fine." Wyatt gave her a twenty-dollar bill before he continued, and she blushed with surprise. "Just wanted to compliment him on his delicious pizza."

"Sure thing. He's in back in his office. He loves compliments from his customers."

A red-haired man with a round face, wearing a nice sport coat, a neatly ironed white shirt, and dress slacks came up to Wyatt's table. Wyatt thought it a little strange that a pizza manager dressed so nicely while working.

"Hi, sir. How may I help you? I'm the owner and manager here. Buck stops with me."

"Mr. um—"

"I'm Giovanni Basile."

"Well, Giovanni, I would like to say that is the best deep-dish Sicilian pizza I've ever had. I'll tell my friends to come here when they want some excellent pizza."

"Thanks, bud. I appreciate that, but I need to go. I have some office work to do. So many phone calls today from people, but that's business you know."

"Okay, Giovanni, of course. I have to go to the airport now—heading to Sin City for some fun and gambling. Hope I get lucky at the tables."

Giovanni suddenly turned around and walked closer to Wyatt's table. "Mr. um—"

"Davis. Harold Davis."

"Well Mr. Davis, since you mentioned Vegas and your upcoming leisure activities there, I do know some people there who can help you gain success in the casinos. I only do this for special people that I trust, you know. But, if you want, we might be able to work something out."

"Really? Well, I'm still a novice gambler, and I can't afford to lose too much, you know."

"I can help you get started without much risk, Mr. Davis. Here's my card. Call me if you are interested and my people will work with you for a mutually beneficial business relationship."

The two men shook hands, and Giovanni left.

Wyatt thought, *Giovanni likes to personally deliver his pizza directly inside the compound of Rondell Enterprises. Interesting that he had such a secure welcome at an important US aerospace contractor's place of business. And, it seems he's quite knowledgeable about the gambling industry as well.*

Wyatt walked down the street a block away from Cellini's and decided to call his friend Ron Cavanaugh, Deputy Director of the FBI. He figured he would help him out here since he had helped Ron a lot overseas.

Colonel Stanley had given him his direct number, and he decided it was time to use it.

"Hey, Ron. It's Wyatt Barton. Been a long time!"

"Wyatt. Beaucoup dinky dau."

"Thought I was the only one who used that phrase nowadays. Congratulations on your new position. Things going okay with you, Ron?"

"We're busy as hell catching bad guys in this dangerous world, Wyatt. And you? I heard you retired and work as a civilian surgeon now, enjoying the good life, although apparently, you got some people all ruffled up about this van bomb incident. You're a hero, and we have you covered."

"No hero. I just do what I have to do so I can sleep at night."

"If it's about that case, you know we're working it up now, doing fingerprints and DNA profiles and going over that thing head to toe. But I can't discuss any more details. So, I hope this call isn't about that."

"No, of course I don't want information on that case. I leave that up to you experts. I hope you find the organization that funded this asshole. What I *do* need, though, is for you to investigate the owner of Cellini's Pizza, Mr. Giovanni Basile."

"Why do you need this information, Wyatt? I can't stand out on a limb for you unless you are in danger. Did you get into the wrong crowd, Wyatt? Is this a damn Mafia thing? You know we have our hands full with drug dealers and internet fraud, and the mafioso are not high on our radar anymore."

"Could be Mafia, I guess. He just smells bad for some reason."

"That's all you're going to give me on this?"

"Afraid so."

"I need more. But since it's you Wyatt, and we go way back, I trust you, even though trouble seems to follow you. I'll do it and get back to you. I'll tell you everything we can find out. And by the way, who do you think was funding this van bomber guy, Wyatt? Do you know something we don't?"

"Thanks, Ron for your help, but no, I don't know anything. I just wondered where he got all those explosives. But there's something more. Can you dig a little on Secretary of State Robinson? I just want to know if he's clean or not, or whether he owns a gulf stream jet that he can't afford with his income, if you know what I mean."

"Damn you're pushing it now, Wyatt. If I agree to do this, I can't dig too deep, you know—before I get State after me.

"It's important, Ron. Something nefarious is going on right under our noses. If you can't do it, I understand. I'll just do it myself, albeit with far fewer resources at my disposal."

Ron paused on the other end for five cavernous seconds. "Okay, I'll give you the information in forty-eight hours. Just promise me you'll keep your nose clean and refrain from attacking any more bearded men in vans."

"Sure thing, Ron."

CHAPTER 40

How has the training of the new asylum-seekers from overseas been going? asked Abdul. They'll make good fighters for us with the new life we provide for them."

"They're ready, Sahib. Ready to assume martyrdom for the cause of world purification," said Farid.

"No more mistakes, Farid. Your life depends on it."

"You will sleep well tonight knowing of our glorious successes, Sahib."

"I always sleep well because I know who I am and what I want to accomplish and how. All I care about is action. No more talk. I told you we must start with easy missions such as suicide bombers and truck attacks on what Americans call 'soft targets.' In fact, all of these will be soft targets so we can inflict the most damage, death, and fear within the hearts of these impure infidels. But while the well-paid so-called refugee and asylum-seeking recruits are carrying out the destruction of the American Satan, I have also planned the most awe-inspiring victory imaginable—using the technology I've designed under their noses, here at Rondell Industries.

"Yes, master. The Bronco's football stadium. They call it Sports Authority Field, but the natives still call it Mile High Stadium," replied Farid.

"It's not real football, but American football, as you know, but the key statistic is that the stadium capacity is 76,125 people, less than the 100,000 seats at ATT Stadium where the American Cowboy players play, but this is local, and the effect will be just as successful, felt everywhere around the world. Soft targets, 76,000 helpless, unarmed people, yelling for their team, only to be found yelling in pain and grief at halftime—following one hell of a show. We will finally, once and for all, bring America to its knees in fear. This will be far worse than our brothers' little attack carried out on September 11 all those years ago.

"The technology I have built right here, with their unknowing support, is designed in such a way that it can't be shot down with any technology I'm aware of, and we proved this several months ago with our first attack on two of their military leaders. The good thing for us, as well, is that Americans are weak now. It's a divided country—divided against each other: liberals against conservatives—both of them trying to destroy each other by creating fake stories and lying about each other for no lucid reason. They're not standing together, but instead want to tear the other side apart. America is strange that way. I know this because I know Washington and its feckless, utterly corrupt politicians. They're the easiest to bribe because they have no conscience. Many are blind to the danger that's present in their pretty house, waiting for the time to strike while they try to further their worthless agendas. They're weak, so we'll strike while the current president cares only about weakening his military, unlike his strong predecessor. We'll strike on opening day for the NFL, Sports Authority Field in Denver. After this is accomplished, we'll unleash the group of fake refugees in the US seeking to be martyrs, while they know their families that remain will receive money to live on as long as they wish, in comfort, in an America that will soon bow to me, waiting for the FFWP flag to fly over Washington, DC."

"I salute your leadership, Sahib. As you requested, we'll soon have four drones operational and ready, with 360-degree swivel, firing laser-guided missiles, all four attacking simultaneously from each direction of the compass at the stadium. As you know, they functioned perfectly at our Rogers Dry Lake facility. We'll launch them from the rooftop of a building close to the stadium. Our people have gained the company's trust as building maintenance and HVAC technicians for the building, installing equipment easily on the roof. Thankfully, your electronic countermeasures can't be defeated by the technology that exists—that we developed, Sahib."

"Of course. How foolish they were to allow me access to their ECM technology. That allowed me to find their weaknesses and strengthen our own UAV systems. But I thank my masters at the caliphate for their wisdom and foresight to plan my education years ago. I will make them smile with pride."

"I'm sure they're already pleased, Sahib."

"Finally, with my success, no one will think that a blond man of Swedish descent, an aeronautical firm executive, friend of crooked politicians, and lover of their luscious women, could plan the destruction of the Great Satan. They will be naïve in their inglorious deaths."

"Yes, Sahib. I will accomplish these details you have provided, with perfection."

CHAPTER 41

The two-day rest at the Motel 6 proved to be enough to start the healing process, although his chest wound did limit his motion significantly, and of course, the headaches remained. He now endured two types of headaches: a recurrent sharp frontal headache associated with an aura and temporary visual "floaters" that he'd experienced ever since the mission, and a second duller headache located on the left side of his head, not affecting his vision but enough to get his attention. Either way, there was no more time for lingering, and he had to try to get back to a somewhat normal life, whatever that was. Tylenol was all he would allow himself to take as a luxury. The only clothes he had were in a duffle bag left by Kevin, and he changed after a quick shower to be a little closer to presentable.

Wyatt parked his bike in the parking garage and started his walk to the staff entrance of Mercy Hospital, hoping they would all forget what happened and he could get back to work, no questions asked. Well, at least it was worth a try. It was the only job he had left, and he liked his work. If only his other shit would fade away, he could be a decent, well-adjusted surgeon, going to dinner parties and medical conferences, and of course, eating large volumes of food with the nurse practitioners. His phone rang before he stepped into the hospital entrance. He knew who it was and that he needed to answer it. It was Dr. Rogers.

"Hello, Wyatt. It's Paul."

"I know, I have you in my contacts under 'valuable friends.' How are you, Paul?"

"Wyatt, sorry to tell you this, but Dr. Deming will cover your patients today and do your cases. Although we haven't decided to terminate your employment here yet, we have put you on probation for two weeks while the board and Medical Executive Committee review your case, and at the end of the process, you'll be asked to respond to the committee."

"Hell's bells. I figured this was coming, Paul. And, thanks for doing it on the phone rather than in person. I appreciate the warm and gentle touch."

"Sorry Wyatt, but we actually didn't want you physically in this hospital until this case has been reviewed, and the appropriate action has been taken—whether that be longer-term probation with educational and behavioral intervention or termination, if the board thinks it's justified. It seems that trouble follows you everywhere, and we must protect our institution. We wish you the best, Wyatt, and hope you can finally get some help in your troubled life. And by the way, I hope you're not on the grounds at this moment because if I see you, I'll have security escort you out."

Wyatt thought, *Hospital security will escort me out? They better bring a whole gaggle of their best if that's their foolish plan.*

Wyatt inhaled deeply, then tried to continue with Rogers. "So, Paul, don't I get to know what the allegations or accusations are against me that provide grounds for possible termination? I mean, c'mon, this isn't the Politburo, is it? Am I not afforded an opportunity to defend myself?" After he said that, Wyatt wanted to pull the words back, but then, sometimes he just couldn't help it. They'd spewed out, and that was that.

On the other end of the phone, Wyatt heard Rogers swallow hard and imagined his Adam's apple moving up and down like the pumping action of a shotgun. "Of course, Wyatt. As I said, you'll be given the opportunity to state your case to the Medical Executive Committee and the hospital board after the review in about two weeks. And well, since you asked, I will just mention a few of our major concerns. The first was your public chastising of Dr. Turner in the OR months ago, causing some tensions in the OR and among the staff. The second is the staff noticing your trembling during cases, and they worry about you. The third was your recent brief hospital stay after you were shot and you refused complete medical care; acted rude to the psychiatry consultant; threw out his test papers, and then signed out against medical advice, removing your intravenous line and your chest tube yourself without asking for permission from your surgeon or asking for help from the nursing staff. That kind of behavior is not what we expect from one of our surgeons here at Mercy Hospital. We expect professionalism, decorum, and high-quality care for our patients. Seems you can only provide one of those three, and yes, I mean patient care."

"Is that all, Paul? I mean really. You've organized a kangaroo court here against me with what I think are bogus charges, except, I agree with you, I shouldn't have signed out against medical advice. That wasn't smart, but it's complicated and something I can't discuss with you right now. Second, Turner has been terminated for drug abuse and stealing fentanyl, so maybe I am not so bad after all, it seems. Third, what evidence has been provided that my occasional tremors, or 'trembling' as you call it, has produced adverse outcomes to patients?"

"All these are points you can discuss with the board at the review, not to me over the phone at this moment. What is done is done. I need to go, Wyatt. Take care, and I'll see you in two weeks. Try to stay out of trouble, if possible."

Wyatt clicked off the phone, and his vision blurred from the sudden anvil-like headache that threw him to the grass on the side courtyard of the hospital. He held his head as always, but this time, the pain pounded on the side of the subdural on the left, rather than the front, or was it the right side—oh, hell, he couldn't tell anymore and didn't care—and then, all went black. After three slow, deep breaths, his vision slowly returned while he saw several sets of footsteps walk by his outstretched body on the grass next to the sidewalk. Maybe they thought he was some kind of wino in scrubs he'd found in a dumpster. Certainly the kind of man who should be ignored at the noble Mercy Hospital. But finally, a set of small athletic shoes with pink laces at the end of green scrub pants stopped next to him, and a young nursing student, perhaps a fresh graduate with lots of energy and compassion in her eyes, asked Wyatt, "Sir, are you okay?"

He forced his best smile and said, "Doing great. Just enjoying the feel and smell of natural grass in the sunlight. You'd be amazed by the rejuvenating benefits of getting back to nature."

Her cute smile gave him some hope that humanity still existed. "Sir, you're funny, but I'm glad you're okay. Do you need some help up?"

"Sure, young lady."

She reached out her hand to help him up, but he could see she wouldn't have much strength, so he half-helped himself up while allowing her to take the credit. "I appreciate you stopping by to check on me." He smiled at her and waved as he walked away from the hospital grounds, now a trauma surgeon on probation, but nevertheless, he continued with a smile still on his face. There were still good people around, and a lot of them were nurses.

So much for that civilian surgery career, because he figured other hospitals or groups would think twice about hiring him now that he was a hot potato with too many brown spots to cut out. He should have never said yes to that mission. It had destroyed too much. And sure, he could fight this cabal against him in the hospital, but he wasn't sure whether the whole effort would be worth it, at this point. At least he had love now, or did he? His heart filled with desire for Gentri, and the vision of her long hair blowing freely in the wind while she smiled at him and called him sweetheart flooded him with emotion, and he felt it difficult to swallow that apple stuck in his parched throat. He must protect her and give his love unconditionally whenever she needed him. He may have failed in his quest to be a civilian surgeon, but he couldn't fail to protect her innocent and precious life, even if it meant potentially losing her to a man who didn't have a mountain of baggage on his back and a mind full of visions and nightmares.

CHAPTER 42

Wyatt called Kevin. "I need a car as soon as possible."

"Where the hell are you, Wyatt? You signed out from the hospital against medical advice, or rather, I'm sure you didn't ask for advice at all, right? And a more practical question is whether you can physically drive a car or not."

"Thanks for your support, Kev, and you're right, I'm always disgusted when patients do that to me—sign out against medical advice. I just tell them, 'Good luck. You're on your own, but you'll be back.' Oh, by the way, I'm sitting at the bus stop on Arapahoe Street. And yeah, I didn't sign out; I just walked."

Kevin didn't hesitate. "Roger that, Wyatt. I'll send one of my guys with a black Range Rover. He'll park in front of you, get out, and walk away. Just don't wreck it. I love that bloody British beast. So, what's your plan now Earp, if you're in the mood to share the goodies?"

"Not much of a plan besides staying alive, I guess. I need quick and effective transportation first, but best I not tell you too much. It's bad enough that Gentri might be harmed because of her connection with me."

"She's safe, Wyatt. We've still got her under twenty-four-hour protection, and we've transferred her to various safe houses. She does ask a lot about you, though, and asks how you're doing after the shooting. She seems to be carrying a pretty good attitude and going to work and all that, but she's getting tired of the process, I'm sure. I always tell her you're doing great, of course, but is there anything you want me to tell her since you insist on giving me only small crumbs of information to chew on?"

"Tell her I love her and I'm doing fine—and that I'll be coming for her again someday if she still wants to wait for me. And, your surveillance work for me has been top-notch. I appreciate you, Kevin.

"That's all?"

"Yep."

"Guess that's enough," said Kevin.

"I feel she's still in danger, Kevin, but there's some business that I need to take care of."

"Snoop and poop, Wyatt, but remember to try to grow some eyes in the back of your head when you get around to it."

"Yep. The Outlaw Josey Wales taught us that a man always has to look for the advantage, like the sun at his back. So, I have my advantage too."

"What's that, Wyatt?"

Wyatt smiled and said to Kevin, "Rangers lead the way. Thanks, Kevin."

***

The only way Wyatt could fasten his seat belt shoulder harness was to reach with his left hand and gingerly buckle it on the right buckle clasp, since using his right arm sent spikes of pain through his still fresh and stapled right chest surgical incision and fractured ribs. The ribs themselves made a dull crumpling noise when he moved too much or took too deep of a breath. With his left hand, he found the standard razor blade he always kept in the hem of his pants and taped it under his shoulder harness, never forgetting his operator habits. They were second nature, including the bobby pin taped on the inside of his belt which was handy for zip-tie escapes. He had a Glock 16, 9-mm, in his waist holster and a Sig on a leg belt. After placing his bolt bag under the front seat, checking his pocket kit—including cash, a red burner phone, handcuff keys, a zebra pen, and a collapsible knife, most of which he hid in various aspects of his clothing and body—he took off in the Range Rover Kevin's people left for him.

After about thirty seconds of driving, he could sense the black sub-urban following him, trying to stay far enough back to not appear suspicious, but the way the guy handled corners and cut off other cars to stay in sight of Wyatt's Rover was enough information for Wyatt to conclude that he was being followed. By using the accordion evasion technique, he traveled through as many stoplights as possible to stretch his pursuers out, however many there were. He stopped and started multiple times. First, at a hotel lobby for five minutes, then at a Starbucks for ten minutes, then a bookstore—all designed to increase the chances he could lose his pursuers, without their realizing he was losing them on purpose. It didn't work. The other car continued to follow him. He now realized his next move had to be a PIT maneuver (Precision Immobilization Technique) on his pursuer. He'd learned the PIT procedure in operator training and the CIA farm, and it was effective in immobilizing pursuers in a car, without necessarily killing them. He headed out to the southwest toward the reservoir where the traffic was significantly less, but he kept his speed at 40 to 45 miles per hour despite the mostly 35-miles-per-hour speed limit, knowing the effect this higher speed would have on the success of the PIT. The guys behind him were in a suburban, a high-center-of-gravity vehicle that was perfect for the technique. He allowed them to close in on him, knowing they wanted to come alongside his car and potentially fire at him. He made a quick but wide left turn, allowed them to pass, and just before they pulled up alongside, he tapped his brakes slowing from 50 to 40, and then he chased after the suburban that now found itself in front of him. When his front bumper was even with their rear tire, he swerved and ran into their car, smashing it at 40 miles per hour, accelerating even after impact, causing the other vehicle to flip several times, landing on its roof. Then, as he sped away, he saw the car upside-down, but not on fire. Wyatt ended up in the wrong lane, and while using mostly his left arm, he saw a car approaching, at which point he swerved sharply to avoid a collision; then, his Range Rover flipped into a deep drainage ditch on the side of the road, upside down in three feet of muddy water.

The water poured in, and he took a quick deep breath before he found himself submerged in swirling silt, and he couldn't get his shoulder harness unbuckled, so while holding his breath, he took the razor blade from underneath the harness and cut off the shoulder belt quickly while it was under tension, and with his hand submerged, he grabbed his Sig from the leg pockets above him and fired four rounds into the driver's side window. Then, with it shattered, he broke through it with the butt of his steel Sig, and extricated himself from the deathtrap.

Upon reaching dry land, he ran from the scene, wet with mud, hair matted, holding his bolt bag and thanking God he still had his Sig, but unfortunately, the Glock was gone, and there was no way he was going back.

The ambulances and fire department arrived at the scene of the upside-down suburban within several minutes, pulling out both occupants alive, but shaken up. Wyatt's disguise was gone now, submerged in the upside-down Range Rover, but he wouldn't look back—he just ran. He found a hiding spot behind a bar grease container and called Kevin. No answer.

Strange. Kevin always answers this phone

The headaches returned, and he felt the blackness cascading heavily, occupying his consciousness, and taking over. He fought to stay in the light, and he saw Gentri in his vision, and she was showing a house somewhere. She was struggling with a tall man with blonde hair who called himself Erik, but his men were addressing him as Abdul, and she was being overpowered by this devil, who Wyatt figured had to be the evil terrorist whose son he'd killed, and who was behind multiple US terror plots that he had recently visualized.

He woke up startled, put on a change of clothes from his bolt bag, including a John Deere hat and sunglasses, ran to the nearest parking lot, hoping the authorities hadn't seen him, but it was unlikely. He was on foot, and he realized he was lucky to have survived that PIT maneuver. He knew what he had to do, alone, but each breath felt like a new stab wound from his surgical incision, and although he needed to run, he could only manage somewhat of a limping jog. He found a parking lot at a Big Lots store, then slowed down to an easy walk so as to avoid attention, trying to slow his labored breathing, and he found the perfect car—a 1999 Honda, like a Toyota, which most operators knew was one of the easiest to steal. There was no time to commandeer valet keys at a local restaurant or commandeer a car at an ATM machine while someone's back was turned. He broke in easily, then broke the plastic housing on the steering column with his screwdriver attachment, proceeding to pull hard on the steering column. He then separated the lock cylinder from the lock body, inserting his screwdriver, turning the solenoid, and ignition occurred. In training, this took two minutes, but he was sure he was quicker. He was off now, no one following him that he could see, police or enemies, whoever they were—no shadow men trying to make him disappear, as they say, or terrorist assassins. It didn't matter at this time who it was anymore. He had a mission to accomplish and the hot car was a necessity, and he would dump it as soon as he could do it safely and still take care of what he had to do.

CHAPTER 43

entri agreed to meet the new client at the house she had listed at 1 p.m. As always, she published details about the house printed on a glossy foldout advertisement on the kitchen counter display stand with mint Milano cookies and bottled water for the client's enjoyment—although they rarely ate the cookies but predictably did take the bottled water. She also placed a box of shoe booties like surgeon's wear, at the front door for the clients to put on their shoes to respect the seller's floors. Over the phone, he said he was an executive visiting from out of town, and she'd been recommended by a friend.

Gentri noticed he parked at the neighbor's house, and his BMW had shaded windows, which seemed strange. If he saw the house number, why park so far away? After a few moments, she heard the knock at the door and she let him in. Her client was about 5'9", average height, but she noticed his wide, athletic shoulders and impeccably tailored black suit. But the long black beard, down to his mid-chest seemed way out of place for that outfit, and well, for this neighborhood. She felt a cold arctic wind, even in the house with closed windows.

"I'm Rahim. Nice to meet you."

"Gentri. Nice to meet you as well, Rahim."

He smiled a polite smile, and they shook hands, but the cold wind didn't let up, and in fact, it felt stronger when she noticed his dark, emotionless eyes study her hair then body, top to bottom, then back up again.

"Here's a pamphlet for you to review while I show you the house. Do you want to begin the tour, Rahim?"

"Let it be so."

She hesitated. Strange way to say yes. She fumbled uncharacteristically for her cell phone in the purse hanging over her shoulder and held the phone with speed dial to Kevin as they walked. Kevin or one of his associates was always nearby and that gave her some peace of mind.

"The house features four expansive bedrooms, three and a half baths with an elegant limestone flooring and—"

Erik suddenly opened the door and walked right up to her, but this time, he wasn't displaying that wide, self-loving grin she had seen before.

"Erik, why are you—"

"Yes, my dear Gentri. I recommended my friend to use your services since you helped me so well. I came to take over ... I mean, to help him to make the right decisions on this potential purchase."

She now realized that something bad was definitely happening here, and the hair on the back of her neck started to stand up. None of this seemed right, and she felt extremely suspicious not only of Erik's surprise visit but also of his new frosty demeanor. "Oh, okay. Great. Excuse me, you two, but I'm going to use the bathroom. Go ahead and look around. I won't be long."

She made sure she never used the bathroom in a client's house before, even if she was close to wetting her pants, but this time she was in the bathroom for a different reason. She closed the bathroom door and locked it, then grabbed her cell phone and dialed Kevin immediately, but almost simultaneously with the dialing action, she was knocked to the ground by the door being kicked in. Erik grabbed her hair, pulled her up, and led her out the door, walking on her right side with Rahim in back, his gun hidden inside the rolled-up house pamphlets.

"I advise you not to run or scream because Rahim is behind you, and although he doesn't work for me as a sniper anymore, he never misses at close range, my little flower," said Erik.

Rahim put her in the back seat of the BMW, next to Abdul, and then

Rahim did the driving. "Don't worry, Gentri. I'll have my staff send a check to the owners to pay for a new door and a little extra for any convenience we may have caused. We'll have someone come and get your car later and keep it safe, so give me your keys."

"Hell no, asshole! Oh, and by the way, what's your real name anyway? Who do you work for, the Mafia?"

"Oh, I love your spunkiness! You're right. My real name is Abdul, given to me by my adopted family in Pakistan. But, to answer your question, the Mafia is a group of kindergarteners. They're nothing compared to our organization, and we consider them lowlife thieves who sometimes help us in certain situations like black market organ harvesting when we need to make some extra money."

"You've got to be kidding. Who do you work for then?"

"I work for myself and for my God. More on all this later. But what you need to know is that you can make this whole situation pleasant by being a nice girl, or, you can make it painful by not cooperating. Which do you prefer, my sexy American slut?" He showed her a six-inch knife, then pressed gently against her side.

"You'll never get away with kidnapping me, you slimeball. Too many people will be looking for me, and they'll find you. Just where are you taking me?"

"Ha. No one will find you, dear. Even that pussy doctor Wyatt can't handle our power. That's right, we know who he is and he's the enemy. Are you surprised?"

She gave no answer and kept staring ahead, as emotionless as possible, but her stomach churned like a wringer-washer when she realized they were after her lover.

"But forget all that now, and listen to this. All the women I've taken say I am without question, a lion in bed and they prefer my manhood over any other. You will too, very soon. Believe me, my little American kitten."

"You make me want to vomit."

"Of course, but let me ask again: pain or pleasure, dear? Simple question but important for you because no matter what you choose, I'll receive plenty of pleasure."

She reached into her purse and fumbled around longer than usual because of the blindfold, then handed over her keys because she realized he meant business and she had no other choice at the moment. He clearly was a dangerous man who didn't care about innocent lives. That she was sure about. Wyatt was right, damn it; she *was* in danger, but where was Kevin? Where was Wyatt? Would they be able to find her?

Abdul secured her hands in zip ties in front of her, then kept her blindfolded until they arrived at his secure facility in the Denver Tech Center, and after they were inside, he removed Gentri's blindfold. Rahim drove up to the parking garage, punched in the secret code, nodded to the garage security guard, and drove inside, where another security guard met them at the inside entrance, bearing an AK–47. Abdul walked her inside, Rahim still following, and she noticed that the receptionist's desk was empty, even though it was only 1 p.m. in the afternoon. No other employees were in sight, but there were the usual potted plants, computers, printers, etc.—all that would be expected in a modern office. Down the corridor—adorned with photos of aircraft, drones, and Abdul shaking hands with government cabinet members and generals—there was a bank of elevators, and Abdul then told Rahim to leave. At, least she assumed that's what the command was.

Upon reaching the fourth floor, they were met by two more guards, also with weapons. There was a reception room in the middle with a TV, a bar equipped with a wide array of bottles of alcohol on the wall shelves, a refrigerator, and a microwave. On the side of the elevators to the left was a steel door, and a star and crescent was placed above the doorframe, to the right of which was a silhouette of a shapely woman in a Burka. On the far right of the elevator bank was the same star and crescent insignia, above some steel doors, but it displayed a gold-framed photo of the blond god himself, Abdul, the man she'd formerly known as Erik.

Abdul motioned for her to sit in the reception area, and he guided her down, hands tied in front of her while he motioned the guards by the elevator to leave as soon as he sat down next to Gentri.

"Gentri, I know you're uncomfortable, but that will only be temporary. I'm going to make sure you're comfortable and well-fed from here on out, and I need you to get some good sleep, so you can always be fresh and energetic for me," said Abdul.

She glared at him.

He took her by the tied hands into the room with the star and crescent and Burka woman, then removed her blindfold.

"Beautiful and romantic, isn't it, Gentri?"

She said nothing, just quickly scanned the large circular bed in the middle of the spacious room: mirrors on the ceiling—Hotel California style—Dom Perignon with two champagne glasses on the table, a massive makeup room with three sinks, a marble shower that could fit what she thought would be a small sorority, and no other doors ... all serenaded by surround sound stereo.

"This is yours, my dear, and of course mine too, when I come to consummate our marriage."

"I am *not* your dear, and you can go fuck *yourself*, pig. And by the way, all that alcohol in your reception area shows me you're not a good Muslim," said Gentri.

He slapped her hard enough that she let out a sharp cry. "You will not use filthy infidel language near me—and never talk about pigs in reference to me or any of my followers. And the alcohol, if you must know, is for my infidel Christian or Jewish guests. His frown didn't last long, and after a little hesitation, he smiled again and said, "Get some rest tonight. Breakfast is served American style at 0800, tomorrow and you will take all your meals in your room alone unless I decide to join you. You'll be pleased to find a full wardrobe in the closet for you—evening gowns, night club skirts, heels just your size, thigh-high stockings of multiple colors, panties, G-strings, and bras—everything you need to display your amazing body. Carefully picked out by me, of course. You won't need a Burka with me because you're special and an infidel. But not for long. Make yourself pretty for me, baby. I'll be patient and savor our first moment of intimacy."

"No cause could be worth this. What is your cause, whatever your name is?"

"Abdul. You'll call me Abdul-Sahib. And when we meet again tomorrow, we'll have a nice long discussion about me, my organization, and our majestic cause."

entri barely slept, but then she must have slept *some*, because she remembered dreaming about Wyatt dancing with her again at the Broadmoor, safe in his arms, and her nightmare with this terrorist was over. She quickly got out of bed, looked at the clock on the wall across from the bed with its hands inside a crescent with the star inside the clock face, and saw that it was 5 a.m. She found a pair of jeans and a frumpy sweatshirt and athletic shoes, then sat in the drawing room, looking at the walls, and prayed not only for her welfare but also for Wyatt and that of the American people who surely were at risk from this devil.

Her captor came in at about 9 a.m., an hour after her breakfast was served.

"Did you enjoy your eggs, toast, fruit, and oatmeal, my lover?

"Yes, my leech, but I'm not and will never be your lover. Would've been better if you would've served some nice crispy bacon, although I certainly would have enjoyed greasy bacon dripping with the fat of the pig, so I was disappointed. Not pleased at all." She knew the multiple references to pigs would be small revenge for what he did to her.

"Never will I serve bacon taken from a dirty pig! And remember, I am not a leech; I am Sahib, you infidel bitch!"

"You will serve me bacon in the future, nice and crisp, if I'm still here.

If you want me to be happy, then you will do this, whatever your name is."

"Enough. I'm going to get to the point, as I promised you. We're going to kill your boyfriend."

"I don't have a boyfriend, so that would be impossible."

"Right, well, I figured you wouldn't admit it. Does the name Wyatt Barton, MD, sound familiar to your pretty little ears?"

"Never heard of him. Why should I know him?"

"Suit yourself then. You've just provided us with a green light to destroy him, although we certainly didn't need your feeble permission for anything we do. And by the way, you've always found me attractive physically. I know that you had to be moist with lust when we first met. I saw it in your sultry eyes when we met that day—when I mentioned that I'd just come to town, looking for real estate to buy."

Gentri stuck her index finger in her nose, purposely trying to disgust the beast—that is, if it was possible to disgust him with an act. Then, with a juicy bugger stuck to her fingertip, she wiped it on his nicely upholstered queen Anne chair and rubbed it in with vigor.

Abdul watched, frowned at the crude action she performed, then opened up a bright and charming smile. He leaned over and touched her hair softly, and she pulled away. "You're a classy woman, dear, and you don't fool me in the slightest. You don't even know how to act dirty. But I know and *we* know you've been dating him—or *were*—and since he's our prime enemy here in the US, other than the American infidel population in general, he'll soon be dead. Unfortunately, he's a hard target to follow and knows how to take care of himself. It took us a while to figure out who he was, but our sources here in the US have been quite useful in providing pieces of information that we weren't initially privy to. You see, money nearly always makes weak American lips vomit words nonstop. The doc needs to pay for what he did, and we'll be the ones to make him pay dearly for his crimes against our organization and cause."

"What could an innocent doctor do to harm you or your sick cause?"

"We believe he killed my son. He was a fierce warrior for our cause. He must pay for this, and he'll also pay by realizing that his woman is now mine, and that will be extremely painful for the helpless piece of shit to watch."

She said nothing, trying her best to look emotionless for Abdul's searching eyes, but in reality, she wanted to retch. She didn't understand what he meant about killing, since Wyatt had told her he was on a medical mission in Africa. Maybe this asshole was referring to Wyatt's previous service in the army, but the truth is, she didn't understand *anything* about this whole chapter of her life since she met Wyatt … except she *did* understand she was being held captive by a sex maniac terrorist. She continued the tactic of picking her nose and wiping her finger on the man's fancy chairs.

"Smells like bacon in here. That's the greatest smell in the world, and I feel like you're holding out on me." She knew references to pork would continue to incense him.

"Either way, you can deny it or not, but it doesn't matter to me. I prefer you alive, and you will be my woman—my wife .. or one of my wives—and like the others, you will honor me by bearing my children for the cause, and our children will grow to be loyal fighters. After you produce for me many splendid children, you can stay alive if you join our worthy cause, or if you don't join the cause and fight with us, you will just be a pretty American dark-haired slut for me, doing my wishes whenever I want or need you, until I no longer find you attractive or worth keeping around. Then, I'll throw you in the garbage."

"I have genital herpes and it's active now."

"We'll see, but I doubt it. Nice try. I'll have our gynecologist Sahid examine you before I take you. We'll take all precautions to preserve the health of my strong, manly body."

"Tell me about your cause you keep talking about, Abdul my leech."

He got up and slapped her across the face, knocking her to the floor, then kicked her in the legs several times. "Never disrespect me, you slut! The correct word in feudal times between a superior and a vassal was *liege*. You are nothing. My seed and our cause are everything this world needs. Now get up off the floor. From now on you will call me Sahib, your master."

She slowly limped back over to her chair, in pain, but with her back board-straight and head upright and proud. She knew she dare not touch her bruised cheek as a sign of weakness to this lowlife scum.

"No cause can be worth all this. What is it that you're so dedicated to?

Providing food to the starving masses? Cleaning the oceans? Providing computers to poor children so they can have a better education?"

"You're a naïve infidel, but soon, you will change. But yes, since you're my possession now, you must know the truth. My parents were Christian missionaries, and when I was ten, they were killed in Pakistan when they wouldn't convert to the one true religion—Islam. I was raised as an orphan in Islam, taught to fight the Jihad against infidels and it turns out, I flourished under Islam, the more I learned about the religion and the teachings of the Qur'an. I was groomed early on, due to my looks, to be the leader of the Jihad in the Satan West, and due to my skills, I was sent to the US with the visa I had issued to me from my parents and educated at Stanford and then MIT, receiving my PhD in aeronautical engineering. I founded Rondell Engineering and became a consultant for the US Department of Defense, and I also secured contracts to build guidance systems and specialized UAVs for the Air Force. Oh, and along the way, I became a successful lobbyist in Washington. Now, twenty years later, I'm here, secretly embedded in this heathen country, a leader of the FFWP, or Foundation for World Purification, and my goal is to kill *many* Americans, striking fear into the hearts of all. Your leaders will come to adore me and protect Muslim extremists, who will be lumped in with all the good and peaceful little pussy Muslims, especially the Shia. Those weak, 'peaceful' Muslims we know, will not rise up against us, and our strategy will make the US afraid to appear to be 'anti-Muslim,' and by doing this, we will destroy the US from within—annihilating its institutions, schools, and teachers—and eventually establish a caliphate safely within the US. All schoolchildren will be forced to pray to our God in school, and we won't allow any other religious affiliation or pledge of allegiance to any flag other than the glorious flag of the FFWP. Does any of this scare you, my lovely flower?"

Gentri said nothing and just stared at him in disgust and disbelief.

"Okay then, your tongue is paralyzed with fear, so allow me to continue. As I said, there are many peaceful, non-violent Muslims, but they are of no use to us, and oftentimes, they are our enemies. I am proud to say that no one knows about me and our lofty plans, except the Chinese, who are helping us in this glorious quest because we both have similar goals of dominating and finally destroying your evil country. Unfortunately, it seems your ignorant boyfriend is the only one who somehow finds himself foolishly standing in our way, and frankly, I have no idea how he does it. I respect his skills but abhor his lost soul. Either way, we believe we have already killed him. Yes, it seems that he abandoned you, my dear. You are alone now, in my house. I have pledged bay'ah to the caliph and every morning along with prayers, I recite my favorite verse of the Qur'an (8:12) which I will recite perfectly for you: 'I will cast terror into the hearts of those who disbelieve. Therefore, strike off their heads and strike every fingertip of them.' Get some rest sweetheart, I want you to look good for your virile and conquering husband tomorrow, and soon you will be reading the verses of the Qur'an with me in my bed."

After his diatribe, she waited until he walked out of the room; then, she leaned forward, fell to the floor, and finally let herself sob uncontrollably because that news about Wyatt ripped at her suffering heart.

CHAPTER 45

It was $150 per night—not a bad price, as it included everything he needed: a complimentary breakfast, microwave, small refrigerator, a bed, and a quiet location. The Best Western Hotel on E. Arapahoe now had a new customer, although certainly for only one night, if that, depending on what progress he could make on finding Gentri and Abdul. He knew he had limited time. He grabbed a frozen meatloaf dinner at the convenience store nearby, zapped it in the microwave, and consumed it in two minutes. It was the first real meal he'd enjoyed in days. PayDay bars proved to be the best option in his pockets when he was on the run. But that damn parking lot was so wide open, putting the stolen Honda at high risk of being found, but he needed to take the risk for transportation.

Wyatt picked up his tier-one red phone, called Kevin, and again, got no answer. He saw a fleeting image in his vision for a few shocking seconds, of Kevin in a Range Rover, his head nearly blown off from a high-powered round. Then, his mind quickly transported itself to Gentri, and he saw her crying on the floor of a fancy bedroom with a circular bed in the center and a tall blonde man nearby. But the vision he wanted to keep—Gentri—was quickly interrupted by excruciating headaches, this time on the left side, and Wyatt fell to the bed.

All went black.

***

"Now, my American slut and doctor lover, I've decided to have you make a nice call for me to your lover to see if he is still alive, and if he is, tell him to come to the parking lot of Embassy Suites, 7525 E. Hampton Avenue where he can find you and you will tell him to pick you up there. Tell him that your protector, Kevin, is dead, and you are safe, but you need him to take you home finally so he can protect you himself, Okay? I know you'll do this because you don't want me to make your pain worse, do you, sweetie?"

"Yes of course."

"Address me properly, my woman."

"No, if you want this Wyatt guy, you will not hear those stupid words from my mouth," said Gentri.

Abdul smirked, felt the ski mogul-like dimple on his chin, and thought for a few moments. "Good point. You're smart. I usually don't care about smart women, just their hips, asses, and breasts. But you're different. You'll be special. In fact, I have laid out what you will wear for me tomorrow night: a short and tight black cocktail dress, black thigh-high stockings, a tight sweater, and a scarf around your pretty head. This will please me greatly, and my coveted seed will swim swiftly and eagerly inside you, starting tomorrow night. But tonight, I want you to rest. We'll have someone come to do your nails, work with your hair, and give you a nice massage in preparation for our passion tomorrow. I could take you now, but since you're special, I want to prolong the desire we both share together so that when it happens, it will be powerful and intense. Oh, and one more thing: tomorrow is my birthday. It will be a special day for me, and I will be honored in many glorious ways. You will be my gift that I will take for what I deserve—repeatedly. I told you where to tell him you will meet him, and then you will have effectively given him to me if he's still alive. I know he will come to wherever you tell him to go. I know this because I read about men who have a real love for their women. Apparently, it's a powerful emotion. So, you know what to do. Now do it."

***

The red phone ringing next to his head on the bed startled Wyatt awake, and he was still a little dazed. *Thank God. Seems Palmer pulled through for me and has found her. He must be having her call me now.*

"Wyatt, it's Gentri."

She sounded so cold and business-like, her voice quieter than usual. He heard no sweet words or expressions of love and excitement. She was alive, but the voice he perceived on the other end was anything but typical. He quickly perceived that she was being coerced.

"Gentri! You're alive. Where are you, my love?"

Her pause struck him as all the more ominous, and Wyatt's breath quickened. She finally said, "Kevin and the other guards are dead."

"I know ... or at least, well, I expected as much. Where are—"

"Wyatt, I want you to pick me up. The Target store on E. Hampton Avenue at 8 p.m. I'll be waiting for you like a missionary waiting to go home to Minnesota."

Abdul slapped her in the jaw and the phone flew out of her hands to the floor, and Wyatt heard a scream and then the phone went dead. "You bitch slut! You didn't follow my clear instructions."

Wyatt had to think quickly. The address seemed to be close, in the Tech Center area. *Missionary going home to Minnesota*? No Southern girl would ever go to Minnesota in her right mind, and the missionary must be a code for the dangerous operation he'd told her about. Target? Did she remember the gruesome beheading at the Navy Pier Target and she was saying she was next? She was clearly warning him not to go to this address. He cleared his mind to think and prepare himself for the flow of knowledge he prayed he would receive stat. He immediately called Palmer and told him what had happened.

"Tommie, help me find her."

"We're working on it, Wyatt. We'll keep you informed."

"You better."

"Don't worry. We'll find her and keep her safe for you. Just stay out of it. You're inactive. Trust me, my friend," said Palmer.

"I can always count on you, Tommie, but do it quick."

Although he thought he trusted Tommie, he had some questions about his behavior, and the information he received from Kevin about his friend's visit to Rondell had shaken him up. He understood that much of this he must do on his own, no matter what the cost. And now he wasn't sure he trusted anyone close to him anymore. No one understood his gift except for Gentri—or at least, she *tried* to understand—and the Almighty, who brought him back to life. He had to use his gift wisely as commanded by the warm light of love, but the clock was ticking too fast.

CHAPTER 46

Wyatt stared out the window of the Best Western, into the dark parking lot, and realized tomorrow was October 20. Why was that significant? His mind produced only blankness but he continued to take his mind back to the date, chewing on a PayDay like it was his last meal, then closing his eyes to connect and receive. He turned off all the lights and pulled down the room-darkening shades, hoping that he received a vision this time. Then, he started to pray to and meditate on the loving light that had saved him. *Yes, no killing.* He found himself floating above the Sports Authority Field, and it was the Broncos playing New England. But what the hell did that have to do with Gentri, or anything for that matter? He erased the doubts and let himself float some more, and the visions came like a movie played in fast forward. October 20, tomorrow, was a Sunday night NFL game with the Broncos and Patriots. He saw the vision of UAVs taking off from a building complex near the stadium, and the and the sign outside the building complex read, "Diamond Hill Commercial Buildings, 2460 and 2480 W. 26th." The launch activity seemed to be occurring from two building and both buildings demonstrated a clear rooftop visual of nearby Sports Authority field. He wasn't sure how the UAVs were armed, but he experienced brief flashes of visions of thousands of people at risk.

Sweat dripped down his forehead as his mind received the brutal information, but he wouldn't wipe it, leaving it to drip into his eyes, not wanting to break his receptive trance and the vision that now flowed continuously—an awful attraction—like a horror movie uninterrupted by commercials or popcorn. Yet, despite the gruesome details, Wyatt had to concentrate like never before—taking everything in. The sweat now soaked his tight black T-shirt, plastering the wet material to his skin.

He then saw Gentri, hands tied, sitting in a large room, looking frantically around for a way to escape. He couldn't tell what she was wearing, but he saw her face and her eyes as if he were in the room. Her mascara had been smudged by the flow of tears. Then, he saw a brief flash of a street sign and the address outside her building—five-something West Denver Tech Center Parkway. That seemed like a familiar address. A quiet tree-lined street briefly entered his vision, and the building didn't appear out of the ordinary, enjoying much less traffic than most Denver streets, but was this that Rondell building he was told by Kevin that was owned by Erik Jorgenson, frequented by Giovanni Basile, and visited by the Secretary of State as well as his good friend Tommie?

He jumped out of the chair and reached for his red phone once again. It was October 20, 5 a.m., and the game was scheduled to start at 8:20 p.m. There would be thousands of football fans, in a full stadium at risk of death by terrorists, and simultaneously, the woman he'd finally found—his love—might lose her life or be raped by the same terrorist mastermind.

Who should he call? Who would ever believe him about any of these events he saw? They were simply visions—the gift given to him by God the day he nearly lost his life. He had no tangible proof he could give to provide to anyone that they were real events that were definitely going to occur in the future. He knew if he called the police or local FBI, they would likely laugh at him and think he was drunk, psychotic, or on drugs and if he was wrong, his career, and probably his life would be over. It would be impossible to imagine the possibility of a sophisticated multi-pronged drone attack here in the US. His heartbeat raced rapid-fire when he realized that all these visions, when they chose to enter his mind, did actually come to pass—the beheading at Navy Pier (although this was after the fact), the church bombing, and then the van loaded with explosives.

Not one vision was incorrect. He had been able to intervene successfully in one, and *this* one ... well, this was on a whole other level in terms of potential loss of life.

CHAPTER 47

Y ou betrayed me, and once again your pretty head hurts, my little flower," said Abdul.

"Betrayal only applies if two people start with trust. We never had any trust, to begin with," said Gentri.

"You wanted me when we first met, Gentri. I saw it in your eyes. You looked at me with such sexual eagerness. We were both clearly sexually attracted, but you also trusted me enough to take me on as a client, and you made some easy money on that cash sale, I must add. So be honest with yourself, and don't fight your innate desire for me, and well. I'm very disappointed you wouldn't give your pussy boyfriend the address I told you. Instead, I had to strike you. Either way, though, you've proven that he's alive, and we'll catch him at the Target you mentioned. Now you're bruised on your sweet face—not as pretty as before—but that won't turn me off in the least. In fact, I appreciate that you're wearing the short black skirt and outfit I asked you to wear all day, before our romantic dinner tonight. But why the hell did you say that about Target? Is that the special place where you two met? Or is it a secret code between two lovers?"

"He's no pussy, unless of course, you call a lion a pussy. And yes, Target is a nice store with some good bargains, and we love to shop there."

"No question he's a pussy because he let this happen to you—put you in danger because of his actions ... or inactions. But you know if I really like you and you give me what I need, you'll be very safe for the rest of your life, assuming you follow the rules. Either way, he needs to be punished for killing my handsome young son, a great warrior. I think there's a lot you don't realize about your Wyatt, and a lot we don't know too, but we're not worried. He's become an easy target, and now, unfortunately, we know he's alive because he accepted your call like bait for a sucker fish. Either way, he'll be eliminated soon, and perhaps you will see his head with the scar on his eyebrow on the floor right in front of your sexy eyes."

"Obviously, your son wasn't a very great warrior if he was killed by a civilian trauma surgeon, a pussy as you say, and if your little boy was anything like you, he *deserved* death."

She braced herself, expecting another blow to the face, and it came, splitting her lip, which begin to stream blood down her chin from the side of her mouth. She felt dazed and dizzy but wiped the blood off with the back of her hand and sat back upright and proud. Despite the pain, Gentri wondered about the gunshot that hit Wyatt. Whether this pig terrorist was involved or whether it was someone else. She now believed it was Abdul's organization although she wasn't going to admit to this animal that she was aware of the attempted assassination and that he had gone into hiding in some unknown location. She was frightened, though, because Kevin and perhaps some of his men were killed, and Wyatt was being set up for a trap.

"Tell me, Mr. Blond Terrorist, how many times a day does your heartless soul find the putrid need to flatter itself?" More blood dripped, and he gave her a tissue to hold on the wound. She accepted it, holding it on the side of her mouth.

He didn't answer but came close to her and put his hands on her naked legs, at knee level, inching upward, slowly up her thighs, touching her gently while she squeezed her knees together tightly.

"My love, when you fight me, it turns me on immensely. It arouses my manliness. I'm really loving this prolonged tease, because each time I'll go farther with you, and the more you resist me, the more you'll be beaten, if necessary, until you actually give me what I know you want, and you'll realize at that moment, that it was destiny for us to be entwined together in my bed. And I'm sure our mating will result in many handsome warriors who will grow to be productive and respected members of American society, like me, trained to fight for the cause of FFWP. My people are all around, and they say your lover is nowhere to be found, so I'll savor the prize that your Wyatt gave to me in four hours. That's when we'll start the courtship: with dinner at 5 p.m.—before retiring to the bedroom for a night of passion.

She gathered some liquid in her mouth, which she figured was pooled blood because of the iron taste, then spit directly in his eyes.

Snarling, he hit her again, and this time, she lost consciousness briefly. As she lay on the floor bleeding, he walked away.

CHAPTER 48

Desperate to act quickly and decisively, both to prevent the deaths of thousands of civilians and to find his Gentri and take her to safety, it suddenly crossed Wyatt's mind to call his friend Colonel Stanley at Peterson AFB in Colorado Springs, remembering their conversation over beer about his secret UAV Threat Elimination Team. He would use his still-active CIA identification number and warn them of information that he had about a drone attack. He figured the Air Force, although they would be doubtful of the credibility of his claims, would be suspicious of this bizarre but troubling information, especially since there had never been an attack like this on American soil. Moreover, everyone was determined to ensure that another 9/11 never came to pass. As such, he hoped Stanley would be available to deploy the powerful Anti-UAV Force Threat Elimination Team to the stadium area to be available to neutralize the threat while protecting innocent civilians.

Wyatt immediately used his red phone to call Peterson AFB Command Center, then was successfully patched through to his friend Colonel Stanley at Peterson Air Force Base. Wyatt told him about the date and time of the attack he saw in his clairvoyant vision and the W. 26th Street location and buildings used for the launch of the armed UAVs against the nearby football stadium. He wasn't sure any of them at Peterson believed he was

236 | S. R. CARSON

anything more than a deranged prankster, but his phone was untraceable, and Stanley trusted him. At least he hoped he still did. "Do you trust me, Chuck?" asked Wyatt.

"Do I have a choice?" replied Stanley.

"Yes, but if you make the wrong decision, Chuck, many thousands could be killed, and this would make 9/11 seem like a walk in the park."

"We have never formally activated the UAV Force Threat Elimination team on US soil, and this is going to be a whopper for me to sell to General Norton at North Com. Yeah, I'll just tell him my friend is a clairvoyant. I think it's highly unlikely I'll get authorization from above my grade on this one, Wyatt, but I'm going to try to believe that you wouldn't stick your neck out like this to get it chopped off so easily, so I'm going to give it my best try for you. Hell, it will probably ruin my career, but being promoted to general officer isn't the holy grail, you know. I'll call General Norton and ask for authorization to deploy, and that's all I can do, Wyatt, but I think there's probably a snowball's chance in—"

"I know, Chuck. You need to know that all my clairvoyant visions have come true, unfortunately, after my near death. Thanks for trying. I've got to go now." Wyatt hung up without a goodbye, rushing to find another plan. After he hung up, he called the number-one man he could trust who could help him find and rescue Gentri.

***

The man Wyatt figured he could trust to help him in times of extreme danger met him quickly, as requested, at the Starbucks on E. Belleview Dr. This was the most strategic location he could find in the surrounding area. Palmer arrived ten minutes late, which was unusual for him, and Wyatt had little time to spare.

"Tommie, my friend, this is shit we both know about—Abdul. I need you to find this guy and take him down. He's a dangerous extremist—a terrorist. I know you think they were just daydreams or PTSD nightmares, but why do you think I was able to find and disable this terrorist who almost blew up a large gathering of people at a picnic right in front of the FBI's nose?"

"I don't know Wyatt. You're acting strange, though. I know *that*. The agency doesn't get officially involved in mainland terrorism, and you know as much. That's for the Bureau boys. We've got better things to do internationally, as you well know. But you're now a vigilante, my friend, and the directors want you disappeared because of that van stunt, and my ass is on the line because I told him I'm taking care of it."

"I'd expect nothing less from you," replied Wyatt.

"But yes, we're definitely aware of this scumbag, and we've been close on his tail. He uses the name Erik, but his given name, as far as we know, is Abdul Mushara. He's a pretty slick dude: a ladies' man and quite well-connected in the Beltway."

"What?"

"Yeah. Washington social life and lobbying. We hear he's close to the Secretary of State, and we believe he may be funneling money for Dirty John's campaign for president. He's specifically interested in Muslim policy in the US and also wants some political influence in other areas. Since there seems to be a connection to Muslim extremist organizations abroad, the FBI has asked us to bring in a few of our assets."

"What do you mean you're close on his tail? Do you know where to find him?"

"He's been hiding the last four or five months, staying out of daylight. Seems he's tired of the Washington life."

Wyatt looked at him with a cold stare and remembered what Kevin told him about the man without a pinky finger and a slight pigeon-toed limp. "Answer my question, Tommie. Do you know his location?"

"Yes."

"Hand it over to me, friend."

"No way."

"Why? He's got my girl, and he's hell-bent on massive destruction of soft targets here in the US."

"I seriously doubt he's kidnapped your lady friend, and we have no information to corroborate that bizarre terrorist accusation … and neither do you, I assume."

Wyatt's face flushed, and his eyebrow scar hit the danger color of blue-red. "Why the fuck haven't you taken his ass down? What are you afraid of?"

"We're not afraid of this guy, but we *are* a little leery of *you*. You see, we're monitoring the situation closely, and hoping to catch him preparing for an attack, and then we'll send a team from DEVGRU to take him out."

"Get off your ass then, and do your job, Tommie. We don't have time, and *Gentri* doesn't have time, and this *country* doesn't have time. In fact, something will happen tonight at—"

"Excuse me? What do you mean?"

"Now give me the damn address now, Tommie!"

"I told you before. No looney vigilantes here. We have a job to do, and we'll do it ourselves. Stay the hell out of this, Wyatt. You're inactive, and you're a civilian now and way out of bounds. I'm losing patience with you and may not be able to protect you from the shadow men if you keep flopping down this ugly path. We will *not* give you the physical locations he's been known to frequent."

"Suit yourself then. I'm going to take him down alone since you're obviously too afraid or incompetent to accomplish it. I am ashamed of you, and you don't seem to be the man I used to fight with," said Wyatt.

"How dare you say that to me after all these years! You can't do this alone, Superman. You'll be killed and certainly jeopardize our operation. You need to go now, Wyatt, before I tell the boys to disappear you—just like the director instructed me to do. But I held them off. They're parked across the street watching us by the way."

"I know. I waved to them when I walked in." Wyatt didn't touch his coffee. It was just a prop. But he noticed Tommie's hand tremble as he lifted the cup to his mouth. He even buried his eyes in the cup, a mistake in split-second vision obstruction that can cost your life—something Tommie never did before.

"It's quite easy for me to call your wife Julie, you know. I have her cell, and she always liked me since we were in the Rangers. But I wonder what she will think when I tell her about all that money you have been sucking away from the family account that was spent not on her but on your Vegas gambling problem?"

"You wouldn't dare. That's our little secret, Wyatt."

"I don't care about your damn little secrets anymore. We're not dating for God's sake. Give me the address."

"Not going to happen."

Wyatt looked at his phone, found Julie's name in his contact list, and punched in the numbers quickly.

"Don't, Wyatt, you son of—"

Wyatt connected. "Hi Julie, it's Wyatt. How are you these days?"

"Hello, sweetie, long time no hear, as they say. It's been way too long. How have you been?"

"Doing as well as could be expected, I guess." Tommie glared at him and motioned with his first finger at his neck to cut it off. Wyatt continued to listen to Julie and smiled.

"I know," she said. "T.P. told me you were experiencing a little trouble."

Wyatt wondered what trouble Tommie told her he was in but decided it was fruitless to ask for details. Tommie got up and walked to Wyatt, threatening to grab the phone, but Wyatt fended him off and Tommie quickly jotted something on a piece of paper and thrust it at him. Wyatt looked at it and then smiled. Address: 8500 S. Wabash Way, Denver. Suite 200.

"So, Julie, I know T.P. has a birthday in a couple weeks, so I wondered if we could arrange a little surprise party for the old grunt?"

"Great idea," said Julie. "How thoughtful of you."

"Let's keep in touch," said Wyatt. He smiled briefly because Julie's honey-dipped feminine voice reminded him briefly of Gentri, but it just wasn't as sweet—not by half.

Tommie grabbed Wyatt's shirt and didn't care who was watching while sipping their lattes and trying to look important. "You're a damn son of a bitch."

"I got what I needed, Tommie. You would've done the same thing if the role was reversed and your wife was in trouble, rather than Gentri."

"Get out of here now and stay out of our business," said Tommie. "You're in way over your head now."

"Tommie, you guys need me, and you know it. Here's where I'm staying tonight, and in fact, I'm going back there now to get some things. I reserved a room there for the next few days if you want to give me some more information." He wrote the address on a brown Starbucks Napkin and handed it to Tommie: Motel 6, South Tech Center, 9201 E. Arapahoe Rd. Greenwood Village. Room 109. "Nice price, and it's quiet."

***

An hour later, four heavily armed retired operators arrived at the Motel Six address Wyatt gave Tommie and broke down the door.

Wyatt was nowhere to be found. The note they found on the neatly made bed with crisp corners said, "Sorry, guys, but if you had only asked nicely, I would've given you the keys and left you a cooler of ice-cold beer for your troubles. Rangers lead the way."

CHAPTER 49

Wyatt's thoughts raced to the next option, and he knew he couldn't depend on Stanley, no matter how hard his friend tried to sell this "hunch" mission to his superiors at North Com. It was clear that he couldn't depend on this best military option to eliminate the destructive UAV threat. Wyatt knew that if these authorities couldn't or wouldn't prepare to abort the attack, he would have to make the brutal decision that would haunt him the rest of his life: to personally stop the attack preparations at the Tech Center address and kill who he had to against the direct warnings of the light that provided his gift ... or go directly to save Gentri at the other address he saw in his visions at Denver Tech Center, knowing thousands would die while he saved only one woman—the one he loved. He knew it would be impossible to accomplish both at the same time, and he didn't want to make such an intestine-ripping decision. Yet, maybe there was one last option to consider.

He figured his last option now was to call in a bogus bomb threat to Sports Authority Field, creating some details and locations so the FBI would think it was a credible threat, set to happen at halftime. If the authorities took it seriously and evacuated the stadium so it was empty, he hoped the horrible strike would be called off due to the lack of targets perceived by the terrorists, or if not, at least it would minimize casualties drastically. But he thought there was a decent chance it would work or simply create delay, so more defensive measures to be deployed against the attack drones themselves on the buildings on 26th. Maybe the attack would be diverted somewhere else, like Fiddler's Green outdoor music theater, a much smaller venue, and without the potential for massive loss of life, but the best hope he had was that these animals would call the attack off when they saw their target was less attractive due to less potential loss of life.

He decided he needed help to make the bomb threat hoax to the stadium credible, so he called his friend Ron Cavanaugh, the FBI Deputy Director in Washington. It would be his second call for help, but it was a chance he had to take. Like Stanley, the two men trusted Wyatt no matter what because they'd served together in Special Ops, so he avoided the local FBI and called Deputy Director Cavanaugh in Washington.

"Hi, Ron. It's Wyatt. Yeah, I know. A second call for a favor that may be difficult for you to accept, my friend. I know this is going to be hard to believe, but trust me: There's an imbedded terrorist organization in Denver, and they've assembled attack drones near the Sports Authority Field to attack thousands of people tonight. I'm calling in a bomb threat now, to you my friend, so you can get that place evacuated while I talk to Chuck Stanley at Peterson to send in the anti-UAV team quickly.

"Wyatt, it's damn hard to believe that could be happening here in the US. Are you out of your fucking mind? Where did you get this information? Is it remotely credible?"

"I knew you would ask that, Ron. I can't tell you right now how I obtained the information, but yes, it is credible and I will stake my life and career on it. We simply do not have the time now to meditate about this and investigate, because it will happen tonight at approximately 8 p.m. if we don't act now to protect innocent lives first and foremost, then destroy the drones.

"Is that all, Wyatt? You want me to simply pull some strings and get the Sports Authority Field evacuated before the game tonight from this measly non-corroborated information you have given me and a fake bomb threat?

"You got it, Ron."

"You know if this is bogus, I *will* lose my job and I *will* personally come after you."

"I know. But it isn't bogus. Remember back on the missions. We were a team that stuck together. Do you trust me, Ron?"

"Yeah, I trust you like family. I'll cover your bomb threat hoax, my friend, although this is a huge risk for me. And by the way. I have some information on those two guys you asked me to check on for some reason. I don't know why you asked, but here it is for whatever it's worth: Secretary of State Robinson doesn't own a Gulfstream, but he does have a Learjet for personal use and a yacht in Florida. We know his income as a lawyer in a Washington firm was only $350k, and he can't afford such a lavish lifestyle, so yes, we're looking at him for possible payoffs from somewhere, but we have no idea who they're from, so there's nothing we can do. He's on the board of directors of some benevolent front organization, which we think is dirty. This diplomat has a smell to him, and will do anything to successfully run for president. But we don't have enough on him, and he's too connected for the Department of Justice to go after him without consequences from the deep state. As far as the Giovanni guy, he's a Vegas bookie and runs a Mafia gambling shake-down loan operation. Cellini's Pizza is his front organization to show he's a 'clean' businessman, but it seems he has some very influential clients."

"Thanks, Ron. Could one of his clients be Tommie Palmer, by chance?"

"Yes, Wyatt, unfortunately. It seems Tommie just let his gambling addiction get out of control, so now he has financial debt to Giovanni. We'd been hoping that Tommie could resolve this on his own before he stepped over the line and *we* have to step *in*. After all, he's a good man and our friend—and a patriot, as you know."

"Yes. This all seems to fit now, Ron. Thanks for your information, and yes, Tommie is a friend and a patriot who needs some help."

"God speed to you Wyatt … whatever shit you've got yourself into this time."

"Thanks, buddy"

CHAPTER 50

H ey, Chuck. Good to hear from you. How are things there at Peterson Field in the Springs?" said General Norton, commander of North Com.

"Well, the base operations are fine, but I have a little problem I need to fix, and I need your authorization," replied Colonel Stanley.

"Okay, I'm all ears. What can I do for you out there?"

"Well, it seems we may have a major terrorist threat in Denver, tonight, with drones attacking the stadium during the Broncos game—or at least when the stadium is full."

"What? That's not possible. What information do you have on this?

"Well, General Norton, I have nothing solid. Just a hunch I guess, from a friend of mine, Dr. Wyatt Barton. He seems to have visions, and saw—"

"Who the fuck is this Dr. Barton, and why is he involving the Air Force?"

"He served with me in Special Forces, and he's an ex-CIA operator, and I trust him. I don't know why exactly, but I do. He has requested me to mobilize our UAV Threat Elimination Team to the stadium tonight, before the start of the game, to find and knock out these potential threats."

"Are you out of your mind, Chuck? The Air Force doesn't deploy our secret teams on American soil, simply to defend against a hunch from some looney crystal ball watcher who has seen too much war, and I bet his head buzzes with PTSD, right? Is he on psyche meds?"

Stanley was silent, and the phone was slowly slipping off his ear as he cringed at the general's loud voice. "I had to try, General."

"The answer is no, Colonel Stanley. No authorization for this deployment to Denver. In fact, if you keep up these crazy requests, I'll personally see to it that you never get to Brigadier General. Now go get to work on some real Air Force Missions." With that, the General hung up.

***

It was October 20 and four hours before the start of the Broncos–Patriots game. The stadium was closed, and no fans were being let in—the game delayed until the bomb threat called in by Wyatt, then corroborated by Cavanaugh at the FBI, was cleared. The bomb threat was apparently leaked to the news media, and the Sports Authority Field communications team assured the public that the game would be resumed once the threat was removed. Cavanaugh made sure the local authorities took Wyatt's desperate false bomb threat seriously, and the bomb squad, equipped with multiple remote-controlled robots and bomb-sniffing German Shepherds searched the stadium completely, starting in the restroom stalls as Wyatt had mentioned. After four hours of extensive searching, the FBI and the Denver Police bomb Squad cleared the stadium of any threat, and the game was unfortunately allowed to start, allowing the fans to enter the stadium safely now, only an hour before kick-off. The only advantage of the whole bomb threat was that the stadium would be slightly less full if and when the attack started.

Wyatt briefly watched the announcement on TV. The chief of the Denver Police department was making an announcement. "The stadium is cleared of any threat, and our security is strong. There was no bomb, and this was clearly a hoax by some deranged individual. We have delayed the start of the game to 8:30 p.m. and urge the public to be calm and enjoy the game."

A reporter asked, "Are you able to get any leads on the person who did this?"

"No comment. Our chief concern is the protection of our citizens, and of course, the perpetrator will be found and prosecuted to the fullest extent of the law."

Yeah, Wyatt thought. *I'm a deranged psychotic who needs to be boxed up and sent away forever.* Obviously, his first attempt to thwart the attack by scaring the attackers didn't seem to be working because the stadium was now slowly filling up, but the game was at least delayed. His only hope now was that Colonel Stanley had taken his "crazy" friend seriously and help was on its way, but that was very doubtful. There was, unfortunately, nothing more he could do to help the innocent football fans, except to race to the launch site and take on the terrorists himself, which would likely be a suicide mission. So, he made his fateful decision. His focus now narrowed completely on Gentri, because unfortunately, it seemed there was nothing more he could do to save the lives of innocent civilians he knew were in terrible danger of a massive and fiery death, brought on them by an unknown evil who placed no value on human life, including children with their parents and friends, coming to enjoy an NFL game. He had to take care of one more thing, quickly, if he could, before he ran after Gentri.

CHAPTER 51

Anxious to spend some time with his Julie and put this bizarre situation behind him, Palmer hurried out of his office, relieved now that his boys would keep pesky Wyatt quiet now, so he could finally do the job that the government paid him to do, free of any financial weight on his shoulders. With Wyatt out of the picture, there would no longer be a threat to compromise their important mission. He closed the back door, then turned around instinctively and noticed the plain-clothed guard was gone. Looking right then left, he quickly bolted back into the room, but someone slammed the door quickly behind him, and two vise-like hands clamped on Tommie's hands behind his back and quickly zip-tied them before Tommie had any time to react. And then he saw him.

"What the hell do you think you're doing, Wyatt? Where are my men?"

"First, those are fine men, retired operators who have chosen to become civilian contractors—not official government employees—and they aren't employed directly by you. They're not your men. Second, I did something similar to them that I did to you—rendered them temporarily ineffective, and they are, in fact, now taking some well-deserved power naps."

"I'll have you arrested and sent to Leavenworth for the rest of your life for treasonous acts against the United States Government."

"You will, huh? Well, Tommie my friend, you're now confronted with two choices. One is easy, and one is not-so-easy … and somewhat final. But before you answer, remember that I'm over-the-top psychotic, as you know. Talk to me and tell me everything I need to know, or die. Which do you prefer?"

"Damn it, Wyatt, I'm your friend. Remember all those times we—"

"Spare me the maudlin history lesson shit. I don't have time, and frankly, you have even less time than I do."

"It's okay, Wyatt, I'll take you to find Gentri. I'll even let you join our mission as an observer, but you cannot engage at all. Just get those ties off of me, and we'll go."

"Right, well, the only problem, Tommie, is you lied to me and set me up. That was the wrong address you gave me, and you sent your men to my room to disappear me. It was a trap."

"Never would I—and what makes you so sure it's the wrong address?"

"I just know."

"You won't kill me, Wyatt. I'm your war buddy, and I think your multiple head injuries over the years, including this last mission, have made you unstable. You'll be caught, Wyatt, and charged, and you'll go to prison."

"Maybe you're right, Tommie. Maybe I've lost my mind after all this, or maybe I know *exactly* what I'm doing, but that's why the choice you make will be the most important of your life, bar none. Is Wyatt crazy or is he shit-hot truthful? Beaucoup dinky dau." Wyatt pushed Tommie to the ground, face down, hands tied behind his back, and kneeled on his legs.

"No question, you've lost that once-bright mind, Wyatt." Tommie's words were still intelligible when he turned his face to the side to talk, saliva pooling in the corners of his mouth.

"I'm going to have to hurt you, Tommie, if you don't cooperate and give me the information I need. I'm a complete nutjob now, Tommie, so you best make the right decision quickly."

"I have nothing to tell you, Wyatt. I'm not sure what you're talking about."

"Tommie. You have been seen going in and out of Rondell Enterprises at the Denver Tech Center to meet Jorgenson. And also, I know about your gambling debts to Giovanni, of Cellini's Pizza, and both of you seem to be enjoying time together at Rondell.

"What? I have no idea what you are talking about, you loon."

"Really now, Tommie. I think you now have one minute to tell me the truth about Jorgenson and how he paid off your gambling debts, and what did he ask for you to do for him in return? I don't think he gives anyone money without a substantial return on investment."

"You're insane, Wyatt."

"Do you want to see your precious kids graduate from college, get married, and allow you to be a grandpa with a nice rolling beer belly?"

"Of course, Wyatt, but—"

"How much did he pay you to erase your nasty gambling debt at the cost of selling your country out, not to mention your ex-best friend? Ultimately, money was the only variable that seemed of value to you, and it makes sense now. You thought no one could figure it out, Tommie, since you had a stellar reputation—that is, until now."

"Wyatt, my f-friend, I would never—"

"Tell me now. I'm not fucking waiting anymore."

"I didn't do those things you accuse me of, and you don't have any proof anyway, Wyatt, so you're wasting your breath on this shit."

Wyatt chuckled. "You were surprisingly careless, and I have video and audio-files from a private investigator. And of course, I made multiple copies to provide to various authorities, when needed." Wyatt then carefully applied choke pressure on Tommie and at the same time, broke his right thumb, leaving it at an obtuse angle.

Tommie yelled, but the voice was muffled, air barely exiting his mouth, causing him to slap the floor with his still-functioning left hand, indicating surrender.

Wyatt reached into his pocket and pulled out a syringe filled with midazolam—a drug he had used for conscious sedation for bronchoscopies and colonoscopies at the hospital. At the right dose, patients would often sing out their secrets and laugh about it gleefully as the words flowed out of their slightly sedated, filter-free mouths. He calculated four milligrams as a good starting dose, due to Tommie's size.

After the injection, Wyatt released the hold on Tommie when he saw him loosen up from the midazolam. Then, when it was clear that Tommie's breathing remained okay for a minute, he continued for the information he needed.

"How much did Jorgenson pay you for your gambling debts and for information about me?" asked Wyatt.

"Three hundred"

"Three hundred grand?"

Tommie mumbled more than a little from the midazolam that Wyatt had injected into him, but his speech still remained intelligible. "Yes, Wyatt, I needed the money to save my marriage and my family. They w-wired it to a secret account in the Caymans. Yeah, Jorgenson took care of my debt to Giovanni, Wyatt. It was a mistake, but I still love my country. I wasn't going to let anyone hurt you. You know that about me."

"Bullshit. Now shut up. You're nothing but a Chindi."

"Ch-Chindi?"

"Yeah, one of my agency buddies was a grandson of a Navajo code talker from WWII. He taught me some Navajo, an unwritten language, and some words come in handy to the few in the know. Chindi means devil, or evil one but then, you're not going to remember any of this Tommie. I'm wasting my breath."

Wyatt clicked off the voice recording he made of Tommie's confession, kept him tied, made sure he was breathing fine, demonstrated a good pulse, and then Tommie burst out laughing and singing and intermittently crying from the midazolam coursing through his veins. He continued off-key, stuttering refrains of the old marching song: "I wanna be an airborne Ranger, live a life of sex and danger, Airborne Range-uh, sex and dange-uh, Giovanni's gone far away . . ."

Wyatt dragged him into a closet and shimmed the door in so he couldn't escape, knowing his newly minted ex-friend was safe, at least until he woke up and had to relieve himself—then, he would be uncomfortable—but Wyatt cared only about one person, and the image of her face branded an imprint on his mind. He sprinted out of the house, filled with the strength of a desperate man who had little time … if any.

Damn ex-friend is a Chindi.

CHAPTER 52

Abdul had built his laser-equipped UAVs, or at least assembled them from parts brought in from various production sites belonging to Rondell Aerospace across the country at his 5750 DTC Parkway facility. He had no time or place to test fly them in Denver and not be detected, so he had to trust in the technology since they had flown spectacularly at Rondell test grounds at Rogers Dry Lake. The night before the attack, on the 19th, four A-236 Striker UAVs were flown at midnight, 11.4 miles at tree-top level to avoid DIA radar detection, to the tops of Buildings B and C, using the empty rooftops of 2480 and 2460 W. 26th Ave, Diamond Hill Commercial Buildings. These were Jorgensen's UAVs, extensively tested at Rogers Dry Lake in the California desert and ready for launch and weapons loading on the buildings. Clearly, this was the ideal location to launch an attack since it was secluded, away from busy Speer Blvd, and only slightly more than a half mile by air to the stadium itself. The technicians waited all night, on the rooftops with the UAVs waiting for the next day's launch signal from Abdul.

Under Colonel Stanley's command, the US Air Force Space Command at Peterson Air Force Base, Colorado Springs, punched in the coordinates of the building that Stanley's possibly now crazy, ex-Special Ops colleague told him would be the launch site. The colonel gave the order for focused satellite reconnaissance of the buildings on 26th street, despite the bizarre departure from standard military protocol. Most notably, it was a non-confirmed target that could be a hoax, especially in light of the bomb threat hoax, and it was a target in a US-mainland location in a non-combatant location filled with civilians, and this was a prohibited use of military assets. Stanley paced the circumference of his command center multiple times, rubbing his chin, agonizing over what to do. He knew if he engaged his UAV threat elimination team, took it to Sports Authority field, and coordinated the mission with law enforcement, no matter what happened, good or bad, he would be court-martialed, and his career would end dishonorably for disobeying the command of General Norton. Colonel Charles Stanley decided he couldn't live with himself if his friend Wyatt was right, though, and he didn't respond with his team to save thousands of lives. If nothing else, it would be a good practice mission for his team—the last practice mission before he was relieved of command. So, he made his decision that he would engage, at least starting with focused satellite reconnaissance. He told his hesitant staff, "It's my ass. Follow my orders. I trust the source of this information, and we need to save lives if we can. If it's a false alarm … well, then no harm done and it's a training mission. He knew this endeavor was risky, especially if he had to launch the Anti-UAV Force Threat Elimination Team.

He had to try to see if there was a threat with reconnaissance, and he knew his officers and enlisted men wouldn't take this up the chain of command for several reasons, but mostly because they respected Stanley and this was an easy mission—at least the first part. The second part would be tricky.

The satellite images did, indeed, show unusual activity on the rooftops at the Diamond Hill location. Multiple men were found working with equipment near four main objects, two on each roof, while the analysts considered that they could possibly be HVAC workers, doing repairs on a Sunday evening, but the objects they were working on had rotary wings and front propellers that could be seen rotating. Stanley studied the monitors, listened to the analysts, and responded, "Shit! These are UAVs … and *big* ones. These are *not* civilian UAVs, and they're armed! Wyatt was right. Deploy the UAV Threat Elimination Team. It's time to save some lives!"

Colonel Stanley made the fateful decision to deploy the US Air Force Anti-UAV Force Threat Elimination Team, for the first time ever, on US Soil. It was equipped with directed energy weapons designed to destroy weaponized drones. It included HELWS (High Energy Laser Weapons Systems) mounted on Polaris MRZR all-terrain vehicles and also the PHASER microwave energy weapon, which could produce a microwave "cannon" that emitted radio frequencies in a conical beam to disrupt the enemy drone's circuits with a burst of overwhelming energy. The threat team notified Denver Police to blockade all entrances and exits to the buildings on 26th Avenue. The team drove under police escort up I-25 from a secret location with helicopter assets deployed in the area around the stadium.

The Denver police asked Stanley whether they should evacuate now after Stanley shared with the chief of police that he had informed the FBI field office that they now had detailed satellite images of drones on the buildings near the stadium. Stanley said it would be best to evacuate again and cancel the game, then assured them his team would destroy the threat immediately at launch, thus avoiding any loss of life and hopefully avoiding any widespread panic as well, as long as the police were able to keep people far from the perimeter of the buildings. Thankfully, on a Sunday night football game, no one wants to be around dark office buildings. It was a risk, but Stanley had a great deal of confidence in his team.

The Denver police chief asked Colonel Stanley, "And how do you propose to accomplish this?"

"We've studied this many times, and we're prepared for all threats. That is all."

Stanley's orders were to disable and destroy all aircraft prior to launch if possible, or at the moment of launch, and then the Denver police would apprehend the terrorists on foot with FBI teams as well.

The team arrived within easy striking distance at the same time the blockade occurred. The four rotary and fixed-wing VTOL aircraft were launched from Buildings B and C but achieved an altitude of only twenty feet before Stanley's team jammed their electronics and disabled the guidance systems, and as a consequence, the terrorist UAVs crashed down to the rooftops and parking lot below, killing some of Abdul's technicians.

The terror was aborted, and yet, Wyatt had no idea this had occurred because he was on a desperate sprint to find Gentri.

CHAPTER 53

Abdul watched the scene from his command post infrared videos at Rondell headquarters and couldn't believe his eyes. His greatest mission of terrorism had failed miserably, and how? It had all been planned so perfectly, and he was destined to be successful in destroying the Great Satan, without anyone even realizing he'd been involved. He took out his rage on the man closest to him, his security commander and right-hand man.

"You failed me one final time, Farid. The mission I planned for was destroyed. Now you must take this sacred knife and kill yourself as you said you would if you failed, or I will decapitate you myself." He handed Farid a ten-inch knife and said, "You have thirty seconds to make a decision."

Farid said, "Praise be to Allah." Then, he plunged the knife into the carotid artery in his neck, and the arterial blood spurted across the room, pumping initially with vigor with each heartbeat, but then, after twenty seconds of pumping, the spurting slowed to a trickle, then stopped. Abdul picked up the bloody knife, kissed the handle, and said, "Your will be done."

Now, I must take her many times and make her mine. She will give this Satan Wyatt to her new master and lord once she's been filled with my glorious seed.

CHAPTER 54

After ditching the Honda several blocks from the 5750 DTC location that he saw clearly in his vision, not Tommie's fake address, he ran between buildings, using his Ranger urban-evasion techniques. The front of the building was exactly as he'd envisioned it. The Rondell Industries sign displayed glossy black letters against a sky-blue background with small cirrus clouds scattered across it. At the far-right bottom corner of the sign was a *Supporting Our Brave Troops with Aerospace Technology* message placed in bold gold lettering. *How disgusting*, Wyatt thought.

Wyatt observed four security guards patrolling each side of the building, seemingly in charge of each side of the square building footprint, not interfering with each other, always pacing away from each other's corner in opposite directions, saying nothing. He calculated it would take him about twenty seconds to surprise and neutralize each guard quietly, which he did, taping their mouths shut and tying their hands and feet. Then, concealed by the dense bushes, he stripped the first guard of his black slacks and T-shirt, adorned with the Rondell Industries insignia on the upper-left side, as well as the security badge equipped with an RFI reader chip. With each guard subdued, he methodically shot out each corner security camera with his Glock—one shot in the glass bulb and a second shot in the electronics box. At one of the side entrances, he scanned the guard's RFI chip on the security badge, the green light lit, thus allowing him to type in LKG319Z1?32—the code given to him by Kevin and his surveillance pizza delivery team, and easily entered the previously secure building.

After one step into this building of hate, his skin felt the frigid, prickly presence of evil, and at the same time, he felt Gentri's loving presence, giving him some warmth. He felt her struggle inside his soul. At the first-floor elevator banks, he saw a listing of the departments and their locations in the building. There, he took note of the executive suites on the fourth floor, realizing that was the most likely place "Erik" would be. Abdul employed a nice middle-aged lady—currently wearing a blue scarf and matching earrings—as the lone receptionist, to provide a calm, normal appearance to the business, and her nametag said Sally. Does anyone name a daughter Sally anymore? Sally's mouth dropped wide open upon seeing Wyatt, and he swiftly tied and taped her mouth gently as well, leaving her under the desk, out of sight.

Sprinting to the elevator banks, he eyed the stairwell to the right with exit signage. He pressed the elevator button; held the car; and pressed floors two, three, and four; then ran out and sprinted up the nearby stairs, taking two to three stairs at a time. He hoped each delay with false elevator door openings on floors two and three would give him enough time to arrive behind the stairway door on the fourth floor, preparing for the inevitable confrontation with armed guards at the executive suit level, the devil's lair, no doubt. And of course, no legitimate businesses would have armed guards with AK-47s, so he had to act fast because this was no standard business office.

He arrived at the fourth-floor stairway door, waiting for the ring of the elevator, preparing to burst the door open or shoot the lock off, if necessary, but it turned out that all it required was his stolen RFI badge for access without violence. The firehose flow of adrenaline from the action and anticipation of finding his lover erased the constant pain from his fractured ribs. He heard the elevator car coming to the floor, and exactly at the point that he calculated its arrival ring, he opened the door with his badge. Upon doing so, he saw the guard with his AK-47 aimed directly at the elevator door, hoping to shoot the nonexistent occupants, thus giving Wyatt ample time to sprint and dropkick the guard down, causing his automatic weapon to crash to the floor. When the man made the mistake of reaching for it, Wyatt cocked his right elbow and fractured the bearded man's jaw, knocking him unconscious in the process. Quickly scanning the hallway and executive reception area, he heard nothing, so he dragged the unconscious guard to the corner and zip-tied his arms—and the duct tape again provided excellent benefit in the oral suppression area. He threw the guard down the stairway, careful that he landed on his sorry ass and not his head, and checked that he was still breathing, as he promised the light back then: *Nothing matters but love, Wyatt. Go into the world, and do great things with your blessings. Protect those who need protection, and help those who need help. But you must not kill anymore, and if you obey these words, then you will receive a special gift from the light of love.*

Now that the guard was subdued, Wyatt took advantage of a luxurious twenty seconds to scan the executive floor and plan his attack on the fly. The reception desk seemed out of place—expansive as a Mojave plateau, situated opposite the double elevator banks, and curiously cherry wood, rather than modern techno art. No receptionist today. Perhaps there wasn't one at all. Behind the cherry wood plateau desk was again, some matching cherry wood shelving adorned with an odd combination of multiple bottles of Bordeaux, used as odd bookends to clusters of books that seemed to be scientific—physics, aeronautical texts, and some piles of articles. Not the usual type of reception desk, but then, this wasn't the usual type of American business anyway. There were two doors on each side of the bookshelves—a wood-paneled door to the left that displayed a star and crescent above the doorframe with a dagger in between and a gold-plated photo of Abdul above it, and to the right was a wooden door with the same insignia above the doorframe, along with the silhouette of a woman wearing a Burka. He chose the door with the Burka silhouette and then heard Gentri's unmistakable Southern accent: "You lowlife shit, your body reminds me of the slobbering filth of swine."

At that point, Wyatt kicked the door down with all his force and flew to the center of the room—surprising Erik who was naked, gripping his erect penis, straddling Gentri's naked and tied body, but his pants were pulled down, encircling his thighs tightly—a distinct disadvantage that constricted his movement. What's more, Gentri's wad of spit hit Abdul in the eyes the same moment that Wyatt's fist crashed into his face when he turned in surprise to the intruder, knocking Abdul to the floor with his pants constricting his legs like a prisoner in shackles, causing him to hit the floor with a dull thud. Wyatt briefly connected with those blue eyes of hers that he'd missed for so long, felt the joy of finding her alive, and at the same time, immediately took out his knife and cut her dainty hands free. He jumped on Erik's slowly rising, unsteady body and raised his fist to release the glorious lethal blow to the devil's larynx, but his clenched fist hesitated directly in mid-air, and Wyatt said, "No, death would be too easy for you—you shit bag. We need you alive."

He remembered his promise to the light of love and took his fist down to a non-lethal position. Instead, he just decided to cause the devil some pain, so he dislocated Erik's right shoulder by slamming his acromion with the flesh of his fist while simultaneously twisting the man's right arm back and out with his left hand, pulling Erik's humerus out of its socket, causing him to scream like a panicked coyote. Then, he broke both of Erik's manicured thumbs. Not much you can do without working thumbs. Erik fell back to the floor, writhing in pain, unable to move his right arm. Then, he too received a strip of the duct tape that Wyatt carried in his handy bolt bag on his back. He knew he was violent, but this man wasn't just a Chindi but a Chindi *leader*, and Wyatt didn't believe you should treat the devil with kindness. But, as promised to the light, he let him live.

Wyatt said, "And oh yes, your son—he was easy to take care of—just like his pig of an old man." Wyatt purposely used references to pigs and swine, adding insult to injury, similar to Gentri. "One more thing, you filthy swine," said Wyatt. "You'll live ... but behind bars for the rest of your life, or maybe you'll be executed. I don't know. That's for someone else with a higher pay grade than myself to decide, but it won't be the court, because you're an enemy combatant. But now, without opposable thumbs and no use of your right arm, you'll be completely useless and helpless."

Wyatt went on, releasing all his bottled-up emotion for what this evil man had done to his life, to his lover, and to the brave men and women he worked with. He couldn't stop the gush of words that flew out of his vocal cords. "Your extremist views have no role in civilized society, and you give the good people who practice your faith a bad rap. But with you gone, the Devil has lost his right-hand man. It's a pity though, in a certain small way. You seem to have some good skills and you proved a worthy opponent. Unfortunately, you are on the wrong side of history—not to mention the good–evil paradigm—and you can bet we're going to figure out who's financing you and training you, and they will be defeated as well. The best thing I can say now is that you're an overeducated toilet bowl who will never again see the light of day."

With Abdul or Erik secured, Wyatt checked to make sure his Glock remained constantly aimed at the door, grabbed a robe from the closet, put it around Gentri's shivering body, then kissed her as passionately as he could in the tense situation and said, "I love you my sweet Southern rose."

She hugged him desperately. "You always said you would come back, Wyatt, and I knew for a fact that you would, sweetheart. I love you too."

Erik lay on the floor, twisting back and forth in pain. Wyatt had tied the man's partially working hand to a support post at the other end of the room.

Now Wyatt decided to bypass the CIA, considering recent unfortunate events and his less-than-welcome status at the agency, especially since he was apparently supposed to have been "disappeared" by Tommie and the shadow men. But now, he held two high-valued prisoners: Tommie Palmer, the CIA deputy director of clandestine operations, now turned traitor, a man who sold out Wyatt and even worse, his country, for money, and a ruthless and handsome Washington socialite aerospace executive who without Wyatt's work, would have likely killed many innocent civilians, and was responsible for the isolated beheadings in the US as well as the thwarted Van bomb attack of a hospital picnic. He called Deputy Director Cavanaugh at FBI headquarters in Washington, out of Erik's hearing range, and notified him of the traitor Tommie Palmer's location in a closet—tied up, safe, and probably with wet pants. Then, he told them his location and that they should send a group of agents to pick up Erik Sorenson, a.k.a. "Abdul," a terrorist they likely had minimal information on because Tommie was in charge of the operation and had kept it from the FBI, so as to help himself—a terrorist so secretive and respected in Washington that Wyatt was the only one who had managed to pinpoint him.

Wyatt kept a close eye on the Chindi, who lay motionless on the ground, occasionally moaning in pain, while he took a warm washcloth and patted Gentri's cut lip, then kissed her gently and hugged her again, then asked, "Do you want to put on something different—a little less revealing—and freshen up before the feds come?"

"Yeah. There are some clothes in the closet—some jeans and a sweat-shirt—but I won't set foot in this creep's shower. Just take me home, sweetheart, my knight in shining armor—a man who has suffered so much to save me. But how were you able to find this place?"

Wyatt glanced at the man who called himself Abdul lying in the corner, tied to a post. "First of all, my pain is nothing, because I was the one who caused all the trouble for you, Gentri. Your kidnapping was because of me and the people who chose to try to destroy me. Second, as far as find-ing you, I have received many blessings that we can discuss later, but it doesn't matter now, dear."

Erik attempted to say something, and Wyatt looked over at him, wor-ried that he might say something offensive to his Gentri, and worried that his hands might not be so gentle next time. He knew the light was watch-ing him from above, but he was curious, so he ripped off the duct tape, causing Abdul's lip to bleed, as a swath of mustache hairs was torn off as well.

"So, what did you want to say, now that your terrorist life is over?" said Wyatt.

"Mr., I mean Dr. Barton, you may be a surgeon, they say, but you're certainly not a pussy. You killed my son, didn't you?"

"Yes. But you knew that."

"What did he look like … you know, at the end?"

"Filled with fear like a cowering little girl."

Both men stared at each other, sizing each other up. Wyatt felt an ex-plosion of nausea when he thought of this evil man's Devil-owned soul.

"Did you stop my van driver at the park picnic too?"

"Well, you'll have to guess on that one. I heard it didn't work out too well for your plan on that either, did it?"

"Why won't you answer me?"

"Because I want to keep you guessing, in your prison cell for the rest of your life. However short that life may be. Either way, I really don't give a damn what you think about me."

"Tell me, who the hell are you, Barton? Or maybe a better question is, *what* are you?"

With that question, Gentri gazed with curiosity at Wyatt as well, and their eyes locked for a few moments. Wyatt could tell she was full of questions also. She had no idea about either attempted attack and that Wyatt was involved in anything. He was simply a general surgeon with a military past, probably some PTSD and head injuries after a crash on a missionary trip in Africa. Wyatt saw the questions in her gentle eyes, then turned back to Erik and answered, "I'm just a man. A man who believes in the Almighty God first, my country second, and the basic rights of human beings to live in peace and freedom from tyranny. I still believe in these things, even more strongly now than before, and I've been blessed by God with certain abilities. And now I have a beautiful woman with whom I need to spend a whole lot more time now. That is, if she wants the same with me."

Gentri smiled, and the color rushed back into the high cheekbones that set her apart from most women. She was waiting for Wyatt to get her into the conversation, so she jumped at it. "Yes, Wyatt, I want to spend time with you, my darling! I've missed you so much, and there's much we must talk about and share, and well, love." She continued to look at the two men—the battered conqueror, suffering from headaches, PTSD, a gunshot wound, and rib fractures, and the vanquished, and she saw a similarity: they both had extreme strength of body and mind, steadfast determination, and strength of convictions. Both would die for their convictions and cause. But the overwhelming strength of good overcame the false conviction of evil.

She looked back at Abdul, the evil one, and her face changed to a dark red, each time he looked at her and began to talk. Such a handsome and educated man who could've destroyed so many innocent lives.

"So, tell me, Barton, where did you get these skills?" asked Abdul.

"I'm blessed by God."

"Okay. So be it. But in case you didn't know, my greatest mission, the killing of thousands of American football fans at Sports Authority Field was thwarted by the US Air Force. How the hell is that possible? Did you know about *that* too, Barton?"

Wyatt smiled as wide as he had in a long time, then kissed and hugged Gentri again, now realizing his friend, Colonel Stanley had come through against all odds, sacrificing his career for Wyatt's desperate request. "Nothing can stop the US Air Force! Off we go, into the wild blue yonder, climbing high into the sun. Down we dive . . ." He looked back at his lady, and the tears were now streaming down her face.

"So, it was you, all along, wasn't it, Wyatt?"

At that moment, ten FBI agents with automatic weapons drawn, burst into the king's room and took over, removing the moaning Abdul. Wyatt held Gentri's hand, sitting on the bed, and said to the federal agents, "Could you boys please take us home? We're exhausted."

yatt asked Gentri, before they entered the government cars, whether she needed to go to the hospital for treatment or not, and she said no. She hadn't been violated by that devil, thankfully. She had a few cuts and bruises, and Wyatt could take care of those while not making a scene in the hospital from which he'd been quasi-fired. Wyatt told the agents in the front seat to drive them to Gentri's place because he had no idea what shape his own house would be in … or whether it was booby-trapped or not.

As soon as they entered Gentri's house, they both commenced kissing as if there was no need to breathe at all. "Oh, Wyatt, I needed that so much—it's been so long!"

Wyatt said, "I need more and more until our lips become sore."

They stopped for a while, caught their breath, and then Gentri went to the kitchen liquor cabinet and brought out a bottle of Pinot Noir and two glasses.

"Pinot is great, love," Wyatt said, "but I thought scotch would've been a better choice after all this. What the heck, though; we need to practice good heart health, right?"

Gentri responded, "Our hearts have both survived one hell of a stress test, so I think they're functioning quite well. So, you're right, It's whiskey time. She went back to the Liquor cabinet and brought back a bottle of Glenlivit 12 single malt scotch and poured each of them a shot. "Now shut up and drink, you big hunk."

"Yes ma'am." They both downed the soothing shots simultaneously, heads tilted back at the optimal angle for quick and satisfying gulps.

"It sure as hell wasn't a medical mission in Africa was it, Wyatt? Probably wasn't even on the continent of Africa, was it?"

"Well, not in the usual sense of medical mission, no."

"There's no way you can hide it anymore, Wyatt. I knew you were never a true medical missionary, or at least there were some pretty obvious clues. It became obvious to me when I looked for details of the crash in the news and electronic media, because it certainly would've been newsworthy. I was also suspicious at the end of our date at the Broadmoor. I figured that although you were a surgeon, you certainly displayed a secretive, confident air, and when you took that emergency call, even though you weren't officially 'on-call,' I knew something was out of the ordinary with you. But I must admit, I was fascinated by you for some reason—I sensed that you were involved in danger somehow. Then, when you said, "Be safe, sweet Gentri. I'll bring you back here again,' I sensed a bleak finality."

"You are quite perceptive. I couldn't fool you, could I?"

She didn't respond but instead, wanted to continue her thoughts. "Although I *am* curious about the horrible things you must've gone through on that trip—I mean, mission, so to speak—I guess I don't want to know about the details, sweetheart, and I know you won't give them to me anyway. I've already written a scene in my new novel about a handsome medical missionary who comes home hungry to ravish his woman who's been waiting patiently for his return. The bottom line is that I don't want to mess up a good scene with other details that might complicate things too much for my loyal readers."

"Ah yes," said Wyatt. I don't want to ruin your novel scene with boring details, but it's highly likely that I'll mess up your hair in a few moments."

"Are you going to wait all day to mess it up?" said Gentri.

Wyatt kissed her neck on the right first, and then gave equal attention to the left, while he carefully listened to her breath rate quicken, gauging his effect on her. She attempted to talk, but he put his finger on her full lips gently to prevent the words from coming, then whispered in her ear, "The medical missionary is home and hungry—no, famished—and he wonders if his sexy novelist is ready to be devoured the way she writes about her hungry missionaries, only better, much more intensely?"

She giggled, said nothing, put her hands on his ass, pulled all of him tight and close as melted chocolate on ice cream, then took one hand away and placed it on the back of his head for an attempt at control while they kissed passionately again, allowing her other hand to leave his ass and explore his excitement in front. Then, she whispered in his ear, "Devour me now, Dr. Stud."

He picked her up, carried her to the bed, laid her down on her back, and slowly took her tight jeans off while exploring her quivering body with his sensitive mouth and tongue, always looking up to see her mouth open with moaning pleasure while he took what was finally his—again and again. The creaking of the bed springs continued, building to a crescendo, then slowed for a while, only to mount once again, causing Gentri's Labrador to howl with each love noise. Wyatt made love to her as if it was the first and possibly the last time they would feel the paradise they had yearned for for so long.

CHAPTER 56

Wyatt knew that any CIA upper management employee who committed a treasonous act while working for the agency would theoretically be investigated by the FBI first; then, the proper protocol was to report him to the Department of Justice. But the CIA most certainly wouldn't want a public trial, and as of yet, there was no solid evidence against Tommie, except for the taped confession that Wyatt obtained, and that could theoretically be thrown out by a good attorney working with a federal judge, claiming it was obtained under duress—and there was plenty of duress. So, the CIA office of the OIG would become involved, avoiding the Congressional Intelligence Committee, instead reporting to the CIA director to keep the matter internal. Tommie would receive counsel; that much was for sure. But, most likely, the agency would keep things quiet for security reasons and to avoid significant public embarrassment.

Although Wyatt was devastated by his long-time friend's selling him out for money, at the risk of jeopardizing innocent lives, no lives had been lost beyond the tragic Chicago beheading and the North Carolina church bombing, and theoretically, no national security issues had been significantly compromised, as far as he knew—mostly because Wyatt had been able to intervene and prevent further loss of life. The only damage done by Tommie's betrayal was to Tommie himself—along with his family and

Wyatt's friendship. Yet, it was impossible to say who knew what exactly. What did Secretary of State Robinson know? Most likely Tommie wasn't aware of the extent of Erik's plans for mass terrorism. Maybe his desperation for money had blinded him. Either way, it was up to the CIA to decide what to do with him. Maybe they would 'disappear' him or place him in permanent limbo, giving him a job he couldn't refuse but no one would voluntarily take—somewhere far away from the pleasures of life he once knew and the family he loved.

As far as Abdul, Wyatt hoped the FBI would consider him what he was: an enemy combatant—a terrorist and not a criminal, thus avoiding the expensive court system filled with ACLU-loving lawyers to defend the slime. He hoped Abdul would be handed over to the CIA for interrogation, without Miranda Rights, and that the agency would extract as much information as possible about his organization, then send him to some black site for permanent incarceration, protected from pardons by any future president who might be pushed by political factions and the sultry lure of ill-informed voters to do the wrong thing.

It wasn't long before Wyatt finally found himself in the CIA director's office. He felt a chill, almost making the three-day-old whiskers on his chin stand up straight when he entered the man's office in Langley. Wyatt thought it a bit of a strange office for a man in his position. It was in an aircraft motif with a shiny silver metal desk with tapered edges like the leading edges of a jet aircraft, similar in appearance to the bookshelves behind his desk. Strange. He hadn't realized that the director had any aviation experience, though he was aware that the man had originally come up through the ranks as an operative.

"Hello, Wyatt," said Director Dorman. "You've been through hell and we're glad you've made it—and that you're all in one piece."

"Thanks, Carl." Wyatt didn't have much patience at this point and wasn't in the mood for small talk, so he dove right to the point. "You know, I found for you, myself, without the help of your man, Palmer, the most dangerous embedded terrorist on US soil, despite the fact that I know you wanted me gone due to certain events you didn't understand at the time, shaded by pressure from your well-heeled political friends."

Dorman played with his chin briefly, then said, "You're an aggressive and confident man, Dr. Barton, and you did a great service for your country, but you're not aware of all the facts. Of course, we were following your footsteps the entire way, and if you faltered, we would have stepped in if we thought we were going to lose this guy."

"Bullshit. You had no idea what was going on, who he was for real, and what his plans were. Hell, you probably even went to Washington parties when he was there lobbying for his cause—a quiet yet radical Muslim and Chinese takeover of our American values, sponsoring radical Congressmen to fill the capital with their ilk, protected by feel-good political correctness. No, you didn't have a clue, but you will, of course, take the credit. That's fine. I don't care. I also know that Tommie was probably charged by you to get rid of me, under threat by you, so I wouldn't embarrass the CIA or the Muslim community that Washington took pains to court and pacify. Either way, Tommie was my long-time friend. Not sure what he is now, besides a traitor, but I hope he's still a good man, deep down, somewhere in what's left of his troubled heart. He lost his way due to his gambling debts and found himself salivating about easy cash. Before that, he served his country well, until the end, and his service shouldn't be forgotten and thrown into the dark cave of infinity."

"You're leveling quite a few accusations there for a recently fired civilian surgeon. But I will tell you that we're keeping the matter in-house Wyatt."

"Thought you would."

"Tommie betrayed his country and you, but we'll figure out something for him that might work for us, using his skills, and he'll always have a shackle to deal with of some type. We'll bypass the Department of Justice. He'll never really be free anymore, unfortunately. Retiring to a cottage on the lake and fishing for prized bass isn't going to be an option for him."

"Got it. Right now, I don't want to think about him too much. What's your involvement with Abdul right now?"

"Wyatt, I just want to thank you for all—"

"You are welcome, Carl. You already thanked me. I do what's right and you know it, and you do your best in your job as well. Now, don't stall on my question now. I've got to get back to my life somehow."

Director Dorman stared back, contemplating his response to Wyatt's salvo of piercing words. "Wyatt, the FBI is investigating him thoroughly right now. He hasn't been charged with any crimes yet, and there's no court date yet."

"*Court*? No, I want him sent to a black site, then Guantanamo—that is, unless it's been shuttered already with peace and love signs put up after prisoners are released to kill us again. He sure as hell isn't any garden-variety criminal. Bank robbers and child molesters are smiling babies compared to this animal. He's an evil terrorist and, thus, an enemy combatant. And I'm being generous to him."

"Wyatt, we can't intervene because—"

"You *will* intervene with the Bureau. You know why? Because maybe you and tricky John, the Sec State, are martini-drinking buddies socially. My guess is you're not aware of the contributions John was receiving from Rondell Industries in order to attempt to influence national policy."

Dorman chuckled. "Unfortunately, you've suffered too many head injuries, Wyatt, and you're quite delusional. I have no idea what you're talking about regarding the Secretary of State. Not only that, we looked at your records. You're lucky to be alive, and yet, you're a hero with a screw loose, it seems. Obviously, I didn't know of any payments from Rondell to the Secretary."

"Right, of course. Sorry to bring it up. I'm not accusing you of anything."

"Be careful, Barton. I know you've been fired from Mercy Hospital and you want your job back. We're a powerful organization and—"

"Don't mess with me, Director. It will not serve you well at all, as you have seen. Black site then Guantanamo. At the same time, I request that you guys stay away from me and let me live my life, because if I find you snooping around me, I might get pissed again and I'm sure you guys don't want that," said Wyatt.

"You're one man. We're a large organization with multiple, long-range tentacles, and you know you can't tell us what to do."

"Your choice, Carl. I'm going now. I'm sure you'll think long and hard about what I said, because after all, I know you love your country as well as your job, right?

"Okay, Wyatt. You're a hero. We won't stand in your way. But we still haven't figured out whether you're an amazing asset or a pain in the ass. You've got your wish, but I just want you out of our hair too, and we can all live happily ever after, finally, in our beautiful little fairy tale world of peace and love."

"Roger that. Beaucoup dinky dau."

CHAPTER 57

I t was their first Christmas together and he knew he had to take her back to the Broadmoor Penrose Room and finish the date that had been interrupted by that fateful call a year ago. They both deserved it, having gone through some horrific experiences in a short time period, never realizing the hell that would be unleashed on them after that phone call.

Wyatt picked up Gentri at her home, kissed her, and took her to the Penrose Room. Their car was met by two uniformed valets with brimmed, almost military-parade-type hats, one opening Gentry's door and the other opening Wyatt's. The couple walked up to the entry, and Wyatt took her arm gently and smiled as the guards stared at his stunning date. She wore a long flowing black dress, tightly fitted to her delicate waist, with a slit on the sides, to show her fit and tanned legs, forcing the eyes to then admire her pumps, red on the bottom, accenting her calf muscles, which were partially showing through the side slits. She was a divine symphony of feminine perfection, and Wyatt felt lucky to be allowed to conduct that symphony, not having known if this day would ever happen as he planned. They rode the elevator up to the Penrose Room, and he took the opportunity to kiss her passionately but gently against the elevator wall, not caring when others stared at them when the door opened. He took her hand and led her to the Penrose Room Bar to relax a little before dinner with a glass of wine and enjoy the hotel ambiance hotel: the Victorian-style drapery at the elegant bar, adorning the windows overlooking the lake; the Queen Anne Chairs arranged around the bar sitting room; and the famous paintings hung over the fireplace. They admired the Winchester 45-70 rifle, enclosed in a case to the left of the bar—once the property of Spencer Penrose, the original owner of the restaurant. His initials were carved into the wood stock.

Wyatt bought her a glass of wine, and then they reviewed the paintings. First was a piece from 1887, *Death of Minnehaha* by William Dodge, but they found it somewhat foreboding. Next, they moved on to the 1875 painting by John Mix Stanley, *The Courtship on the Plains,* showing a plains cowboy and his girl on a horse during a courtship. They found that much more romantic and suitable for the start of the evening.

Eventually, the maître d called them to their table in the main dining room, and they passed the U-shaped booth they'd sat in the first time, with the Bisttram paintings decorating the wall behind it and the 16-foot chandelier, which looked like a shiny umbrella over that elevated dance floor.

Wyatt looked around and felt relieved that the shadow men were nowhere to be seen, and he felt the freedom to enjoy life without the stress of constant eyes on him. Now the roving eyes were just from other couples, admiring the dashing couple. Unlike before, Wyatt now allowed them to sit far from the exits. It wasn't as strategic as before, but he wanted to sit by the window, overlooking the lighted trees surrounding the sparkling lake below, glittering in the gentle wind. He ordered Gentri's favorite wine, which he remembered from before: Chateau Beausejour Saint Emilion Grand Cru, 2001. She smiled, and they toasted. Then, Wyatt kissed her again, in front of everyone, tasting a combination of elegant French wine and red lipstick.

They enjoyed their six-course meal, which was perfectly timed for maximum enjoyment and flavor. Then, Wyatt took Gentri by the hand back through the private chef's dining area, and they went out into the crisp mountain air and watched each other's breath form clouds in the air. He held her tightly as they both gazed out over the lake that reflected the soft light of the full moon. Wyatt found himself transported to that same light he felt during his near death on the mission far away, the light of warmth and love that brought him back to life, and love. A soothing energy enveloped him once again, giving him the sensation of floating, and he was instantaneously closer to the source of knowledge, surrounded by the amazing non-earthly colors he remembered from before. But the light didn't beckon him higher, and he felt the power of His presence once again, and the communication that was provided to him via telepathy was: *I am proud of you. Your faith has been demonstrated as a solid rock. You have used your gift well and heeded the warning. You will remain, because you have much more to accomplish if you simply continue to believe, with love.*

Wyatt looked at Gentri, who like him, was staring out at the lake, and he was pleased that Gentri didn't notice his soul's brief absence, because it seemed again, that the light of love provided infinite knowledge without relation to time. He embraced her and held her body close to him, kissing her long this time, in privacy, on the chef's deck, enjoying the softness of her lips and curves of her waist and those merciless hips. They stopped, took some breaths, and Gentri finally said, "Wyatt, my hungry missionary, I love you."

Wyatt smiled and said, "My sexy romance novelist, I love you too. Let's dance."

So, they went back inside and made their way to the dance floor. He took her right hand in his, then her left hand in his right, and they danced alone on the floor while others at the tables surrounding each side of the dance floor watched. He smelled the elegant seduction of her Boucheron once again, kissing her neck so he could taste it as well, and at this time, they realized they weren't dancing alone. They were joined by the woman in a Bordeaux dress and the man in a dark suit dancing in the old mural painted behind them, set off by mystic moonlight. Love and romance spanned the ages, remaining embedded within the human spirit—truly timeless.

THE END

www.ingramcontent.com/pod-product-compliance
Lightning Source LLC
Chambersburg PA
CBHW011341010726
47493CB00009B/2913